10/10

a novel

KATHI ORAM PETERSON

Covenant Communications, Inc.

Cover image: Portrait of ninja holding sword, photography by PNC © Getty Images.

Published by Covenant Communications, Inc.
American Fork, Utah

Printed in Canada
First Printing: January 2009

16 15 14 13 12 11 10 09 10 9 8 7 6 5 4 3 2 1

ISBN 13: 978-1-59811-551-2
ISBN 10: 1-59811-551-0

For my mother, who taught me to have faith in God

DISCLAIMER

Please bear in mind that although I have cast well-known people from the Book of Mormon as the main characters in this book, this is a work of fiction. For the sake of the story, I have invented certain details, changed timelines, and created various characters.

My hope is that after finishing this novel, readers will compare it to the Book of Mormon to learn the details of what actually happened.

ACKNOWLEDGMENTS

A heartfelt thank you to the critical and professional abilities of the members of my writers' group, the Wasatch Mountain Fiction Writers, and especially to my dear friends who listened to me read week after week: Dorothy Canada, Kerri Leroy, Charlene Raddon, Alice Trego, Roseann Woodward, and Peggy Ramsay. I would like to express special appreciation to Brenda Bensch and Kathleen Dougherty, whose talents in both the technical and creative aspects of writing kept me on course.

A big thank you goes to my friend and fellow writer Elizabeth Lane, who through the years has been a great inspiration and mentor.

I am grateful for my supportive family: my husband, Bruce, who has always believed in me; my son-in-law, Greg, who set up my Web site; my daughter, Kristina, who encouraged me to keep writing; my grandson, William, who has a most extraordinary imagination; my daughter, Patricia, who listened to many "what if" scenarios; and my son, Benjamin, who suggested I write a story about the stripling warriors. With a black belt in karate to his credit, Ben knows a great deal about the martial arts and helped me write the fight scenes of this book.

I used many resources for my research, but the late Hugh Nibley's book *Teachings of the Book of Mormon: Part 3* opened up the world of Helaman and his stripling warriors. They became living, breathing people with shortcomings, passions, and an ever-abiding love for their Heavenly Father.

Thank you, Mr. Nibley.

CHAPTER 1

So Great a Courage

The promised land, near the city of Judea
66 B.C. The twenty and sixth year of the Nephite/Lamanite war

My feet pounded the ground as I ran; my heart thumped against my ribs. I did not know where my strength came from, for I had been running with my army of brothers for two days. I tightened my grip on the hilt of the double-edged sword and held up my shield, which was emblazoned with the noble crest of my heritage, as I charged toward battle.

No more would we run and hide.

No more would we look over our shoulders and wonder when they would attack.

I did not fear death.

God would deliver me.

God would deliver us.

ǂǂǂ

Salt Lake City, Utah
A.D. 2010

"What did I do?" Uncertainty vibrated in Colin Staker's voice as he followed close on my heels, acting like he cared. I, Sydney Morgan, a girl who should have known better than to let what a guy said get under her skin, was not stopping for an argument. Not now. Not when his words had cut so deep. I'd already stayed too late after school looking for him. I didn't have time to argue. I had to go home.

"Was it something I said?" He grabbed my arm, preventing my escape.

"Take your hand off me," I said quietly. The frosty October air made the words come out in visible puffs. I looked up at his tall frame and into his usually sincere green eyes. He stared at me with the pretense of caring.

"You walk me home from school every day," I said. "You were late today, so I went searching for you." The more I thought about the situation, the angrier I became. "You know that I watch Gracie right after school every Wednesday." The scene of him laughing with his football buddies flashed in my mind's eye. "You were with your doofus football friends." A small crowd had gathered around us by this time. As I glanced sideways at the students surrounding us, I desperately wished I could click my heels and be transported somewhere else, anywhere other than the school lawn, where the entire student body of Suncrest High now watched my emotions bleed out onto the grass.

I determined that if Colin didn't let go, I was going to give him a snap punch to the stomach. You might not think that a sixteen-year-old girl who is only five foot five would be much of a threat to a football player. But Colin knew better. He knew I had a black belt in karate—and that I could flatten him faster than he could flinch. I glared at him as if I could melt him into a puddle.

"You heard?" His face paled. "Look, Syd, the guys and I were just kidding around. Come on, you know how guys are."

I stared at his flustered face. I'd always thought he was cute in a scruffy sort of way. And I'd always felt comfortable with Colin. After all, we'd been friends since the second grade. How could I have been so wrong all these years? I guess that's what I got for letting my emotions rule my mind.

"Colin, let go of me," I said in a low, monotone voice.

"If I do, you have to promise to stay put until we can work this out." His forehead was wrinkled, his mouth curled in that *come-on-let's-be-friends* smile that would ordinarily make me stop and rethink. But this time was different.

I pretended to relent and relaxed my stance just a bit.

He lifted a hand to pat my cheek and then reached up to tousle my short hair, which he said made me look like a boy. My anger bubbled over at the condescending gesture. I dropped my books, grabbed his wrist with my right hand, and jabbed his elbow with my left hand. Off balance, he flipped to the ground. Keeping hold of his arm, I twisted it just a little—not enough to hurt, but enough to make my point—and glared down at him.

"Don't follow me, don't call me, and don't try to pretend you didn't say what you said." I glowered at him for a moment, making sure he understood. The small crowd around us had grown very large. I heard someone say that Principal Jefferson was coming our way. Quickly, I let Colin go, snatched up my books, and ran.

As I walked into Mom's karate studio, I glanced around the front foyer looking for Gracie. No sign of her.

"I intend to develop myself . . ." The small class of yellow-belt hopefuls repeated their creed from the front dojo. I peered through the observation window. Mirrors banked the walls of the large exercise room.

Mom stood at the head of the class. She was decked out in her red *gi* and seventh-degree black belt. She taught on Mondays, Wednesdays, and Fridays, and I taught on Tuesdays and Thursdays. I loved to watch my mother at work. I was proud of her. For a woman of fifty-two, she was strong yet beautiful, with short black hair and sparkling brown eyes that reflected her Shoshone heritage. She noticed me, smiled, and pointed in the direction of the office.

I understood. That was where I'd find Gracie.

As soon as I walked through the office doorway, Gracie glanced up, looking at me in the mirrored wall. "Syd, I s'ayed on the chair like Mummy said, didn' I?" Her halting speech could not hide the excitement and pride in her voice.

I gazed at my ten-year-old sister, whom I loved more than life. Her long, honey-blond hair framed her pale face, which was sprinkled with brown freckles. How could Colin have told his friends that my Gracie was a *retard?* The way he'd said it was maddening. Just *retard,* like she was a castoff. Gracie was far from being a castoff. Colin, on the other hand, fit the bill perfectly. I mentally grouped him with the person I considered the ultimate castoff in my life—my father, Logan Morgan, who had walked out of our lives ten years earlier.

"You did exactly as you were told!" I said enthusiastically as I patted Gracie's back. "Guess what I found on my way home from school?" I set my books on the desk. Gracie's eyes grew wide. She shrugged, knowing full well what I'd say next.

"A tickle bug!" I yelled and chased her around the small office cluttered with sparring gear. She squealed gleefully.

"Wait!" Gracie froze, staring up at me. A smile curved her lips. "I see a 'ickle bug." Then Gracie chased me. This was our ritual, our *hi-how-was-your-day* routine.

Finally collapsing in the chairs across from the desk, I looked at the mirrored wall and gazed at our reflections. Gracie had inherited our father's Caucasian traits: sandy blonde hair, pale skin, and blue eyes. I had inherited Mom's half-Shoshone traits: black hair, honey-colored skin, and brown eyes.

By just looking at Gracie, you wouldn't suspect at first that she was mentally challenged. Her handicap was only evident in her speech and thought patterns. A childlike innocence radiated from her smiling face, which could brighten a room. And by just looking at me, you wouldn't suspect that I had an IQ of 140. This was only evident in my straight A's. I didn't have Gracie's glow. For reasons that even I didn't understand, a darkness followed me. We were two very different sisters, but that was okay. We were family—just Mom, Gracie, and me.

"Let's make dinner," I said. I knew Gracie loved to help. Her special ed teacher had encouraged us to include her in almost everything we did. At times this was trying, but mostly it was fun.

She immediately headed for the stairs that led to our apartment. I quickly retrieved my books, waved good-bye to Mom as I passed the observation window, and followed Gracie.

Poached salmon was on the menu, along with steamed rice and romaine lettuce topped with bacon bits, chopped boiled eggs, golden raisins, and slivered almonds. I loved to cook. Mom had taught me to enjoy cooking, and I had never looked at it as a chore.

Gracie was in charge of the salad, and she set about her task with gusto. As I reached above the kitchen island to snag a pan from the pot rail, I noticed a light blinking on the phone's message machine.

I pushed PLAY.

"You have three messages. Tuesday, October 15." I smiled. Today was Wednesday, not Tuesday. And it was the sixteenth, not the fifteenth. But the month was right at least. Our machine had a severe case of dementia.

"Message one.

"Syd—" It was Colin's voice. I pressed the DELETE button.

"Message two.

"This is Principal Jefferson. Mrs. Morgan, please call me as soon as possible. We need to talk about Sydney."

Again, I pressed DELETE. I'd talk with the principal in the morning. No need to drag Mom into this.

"Message three."

At this point the machine decided that enough was enough. "Garble, garble . . . hospital . . . preregister . . . Call 555- . . ."

We really needed a new answering machine. I didn't catch the rest of the number. But I wasn't worried about it. From what I had heard, it sounded like a wrong number.

Gracie spilled the almonds on the floor and began to cry.

"It's okay. Just pick them up," I told her. I smiled as I placed the pan on the stovetop. We had learned not to make a big fuss when Gracie became upset. Gracie wiped her eyes and began carefully picking up the slivered almonds one by one. At this rate I'd have the rice and salmon ready before the almonds were recovered and rinsed off.

As I watched my sister dutifully rescuing the almonds, I wondered if perhaps the hospital had called about Gracie. But Mom hadn't mentioned anything, and we always talked about Gracie's treatments. Mom always said that our family was a team and that we would work out family problems together. But maybe something had happened I didn't know about.

Gracie had finished picking up the almonds and was now retrieving eggs from the fridge. She dropped one on the floor and began crying again. I quit wondering about the call and knelt to help her clean up the floor.

✠✠✠

"Read abou' Helaman's swipling warriors." Gracie was forever dropping her t's. She snuggled down in bed, ready for her story before falling asleep. I pulled out the worn Book of Mormon. The pages were tattered and torn, a true sign of love. The story of Helaman's stripling warriors was Gracie's favorite.

Sitting on the bed beside Gracie, I paraphrased the story in words she'd understand. "Do you remember how the people of Ammon promised God they would never fight again?"

"Yeah . . ." Gracie anxiously waited for her favorite part.

"Well, when the Nephites were attacked, the people of Ammon wanted to break their promise and help fight. But what did Helaman say?"

"Keep da promise." Gracie's eyes began to droop.

"Did they?"

"Uh-huh." She yawned.

"The Ammonites' sons hadn't made the promise, though. Two thousand of them wanted to help fight for freedom." I quickly checked to see if Gracie were still awake.

Her bright blue eyes blinked opened. I briefly thought of the pile of homework waiting for me. It was getting late, but Gracie needed my attention right now.

Clearing my throat, I continued. "Helaman led his two thousand young warriors into battle. Although they had never fought, they were not afraid. Their mothers had taught them to have faith in God."

"Like Mummy, huh?" Gracie waited for me to answer.

"Yes." I tucked the covers around her. "No more talking."

She nodded.

"Close your eyes," I chided gently. She clamped her eyes shut.

"Helaman and his army fought bravely and helped drive away the enemy. After the battle, Helaman found his sons had been hurt, but not one had been killed. It was a miracle." I quickly glanced at my little sister. At last she had fallen asleep.

Laying the book on Gracie's nightstand, I looked at the picture on her wall—Helaman riding on his white stallion, surrounded by the boys he called his sons. Gracie had said their mothers were like ours. And I knew that she was right. Mom had taught us to believe in God. And I did believe in Heavenly Father and Jesus Christ. I had a testimony. But sometimes the Book of Mormon stories felt like just that—stories—about people who lived a very long time ago and lived in a very different world. It just didn't feel like they applied to me sometimes. To think about young men with faith so strong they weren't killed . . . it was hard to understand faith like that. And I couldn't help but think that out of all two thousand of those guys, there had to have been one who was rebellious . . . or one who was forgotten. I gave a sigh. Sitting there staring at the picture was not getting my homework done.

I turned out the light and gently closed the door to Gracie's bedroom. Glancing at the hallway clock, I saw it was now nine o'clock. Mom would be coming up soon. As usual, when Gracie and I had finished dinner, I had wrapped Mom's dinner in plastic wrap and put it in the fridge for her.

Even though Mom would be tired, she'd still ask why I had been late coming home from school. I didn't want to tell her I had fought with Colin. And I certainly didn't want to tell her what he'd said about Gracie. Mom didn't need another man to be disappointed in. My father had been disappointment enough.

The funny thing was, Mom never really talked about my father. It used to make me angry that she never got riled up about his leaving. Instead of being bitter, she had focused her energy on establishing a thriving karate studio. I knew she thought that one day I'd become her partner. But while I loved karate, I had other ideas.

More than anything, I had always wanted to become a police officer, a detective really. I wanted to help people. The only problem I could foresee was my height . . . and maybe the tiny issue of my quick temper. I hoped that the department would overlook my height and temper in favor of my skills as a black belt.

I heard Mom's steps on the stairs. Hurrying to the kitchen, I pulled her plate from the fridge, loosened the plastic wrap, and placed it in the microwave. I hoped that if I was extra helpful, maybe she'd forget I was late. As I pushed the START button, Mom walked into the room.

"Hi, sweetie." She plopped down on a chair. "How was your day?"

"Great, fine. How was yours?" I grabbed a water bottle, snapped off the top, and handed it to her.

"I've had better." She took the bottle. "You were late."

"Yeah, well . . ." I had never been able to hide anything from my mother, but I could distract her. "You won't believe it, but Gracie's asleep."

"Really? You have the magic touch." She took a drink of water and rubbed her temples. "Is that my dinner heating up?"

"Salmon, your favorite."

"You're too good to me." Mom leaned her elbows on the table and studied my face. Then she said, "You've fixed dinner and Gracie's even asleep. But despite all your good deeds, I still want to know why you were late coming home from school."

"Time just got away from me." I hoped she wouldn't press for more. The microwave beeped. I pulled out her dinner and set it in front of her. As I watched her examine her food, then look up at me with a smile, I realized she was a little pale and looked tired. And she wasn't eating. I hoped she wasn't upset.

Wanting to make her laugh, I said, "Hey, we really need a new answering machine. You should hear the remains of the message some hospital left."

"Syd . . ." She pushed her plate aside. "We need to talk." There was a strange tone in her voice. Why wouldn't she just let it go? I was late; it didn't happen often.

"About the hospital, I . . ."

"It's Gracie, isn't it?" Little prickles skittered up my arms. I sat down on the chair beside her.

"No, no. Gracie is fine." Mom nervously combed her fingers through her short hair. "In fact, her teacher said she's been doing much better."

Now I was confused. "Well, if it's not Gracie . . ."

The doorbell rang. We hardly ever used the front door; we always entered our apartment through the studio. The only other person who used the front door was Colin. I groaned inwardly.

"That's the bishop." Mom immediately stood.

"The bishop? Bishop Staker? Why's he here?" Bishop Staker was Colin's father. Had Colin used his father to get to me? Now I really was concerned. Not only about the hospital business but about Mom learning of the argument Colin and I had after school. It would hurt her to hear what he'd said about Gracie.

"I called the bishop this afternoon." Mom bit her bottom lip a moment, then said, "He's here to give me a blessing." She took hold of both my shoulders, staring me square in the eyes. "Syd, I don't have time to do this right, and I'm sorry, but I went to the doctor today. He said I have cancer."

CHAPTER 2
A Terrible Battle

Fire soared through the sky on flaming arrows, landing at my feet. I would show no fear. My warrior brothers looked to me for guidance. Ignoring danger and riding a wave of fearlessness I had never known before, I charged ahead, yelling with all my might, praying silently that the Almighty would be with us. Strangely, in this frenzied moment, the face of my younger brother flashed before me. His brow had been furrowed with worry as I left for battle. Would I ever see him again? Would I ever be able to tell Lib how much I loved him?

And then we were amongst them.

Amongst the enemy.

Black shining eyes stared out from red-painted faces. The foul, bitter aura of hate swam around us. Their muscles, drenched with sweat, flexed to battle-ready. An eerie quiet held both armies captive for an instant, and then we collided with blood-curdling yells, the clang of metal meeting metal, and the desperate gasp of lives being taken.

Boy against man.

Man against boy.

Numb to pain, I moved instinctively, dodging a blade and swinging my sword at my attackers. Smoke stole the air. Breathing became an effort.

Time ceased to be.

Reason ceased to be.

And then the battle grew worse.

⁂

The next morning, Bishop Staker and Colin picked Gracie and me up. The bishop's wife had offered to look after Gracie for a few days while Mom was in the hospital. I felt my resolve to be angry with Colin melt a little as I watched the kind way he helped Gracie into the car. I could tell he really was sorry for calling her a retard; he'd apologized over and over and promised to get my homework from the classes I'd miss. I began to feel a little remorseful about having pulled the karate on him. A little. After dropping Colin off at the school and Gracie at the bishop's home, Bishop Staker drove me to the hospital. By now I was late.

I pushed through the hospital doors. Mom would be in the operating room. I walked as fast as possible without running down the corridor, which was lined with windows on both sides. At the end of the hall I saw the elevator doors about to close. I sprinted forward and slipped inside. A janitor, broom in hand, stood beside a large plastic garbage can on wheels. There was a peaceful aura about him. Intrigued by the light that seemed to emanate from his kind eyes, I blinked, suddenly feeling calmer, and punched the button for Mom's floor. The elevator started to move.

The janitor looked right at me. The serene light was still in his gaze, and his smile was warm and friendly. The longer he stared at me the more I wondered whether he thought he knew me. For a millisecond, I thought I knew him. Then reason took charge. I had no clue who this man was. But I smiled back. He was attractive, with short, curly blond hair and a muscular build. He was probably in his late twenties or early thirties.

The elevator gave a lunge and stopped.

We were stuck!

Panic washed over me, replacing the calm I had felt. This couldn't be happening. Mom needed me. I punched all the buttons.

The janitor shook his head, calmly picked up the elevator phone, and called someone. When he hung up, he turned to me. His eyes were empathetic. "Should take them a few minutes to fix."

"Great," I sighed.

"So, who are you visiting?" He looked like he really wanted to know.

"My mother." The words slipped out before I could stop them.

"What brings her here?" he asked as he leaned his broom against the wall.

"Breast cancer." Why had I said that?

"Well, it may take some time for her to recover, but it's a good thing she has you, Sydney. You'll help her pull through."

I froze. Then I slowly asked, "How did you know my name?"

The janitor pointed to the gold ID bracelet on my wrist, the one Mom had given me.

I relaxed a little but then wondered why he was so sure that my mother would be all right. "How do you know Mom will recover?"

"I just do."

He looked at my confused expression and smiled.

"Let's just say that I have an in with the man upstairs." He shook my hand. "My name's Steve Smith."

"Nice to meet you, I guess." The last two words slipped out of my mouth before I could stop them. I hoped I hadn't hurt his feelings.

We heard a clank from above. Someone was trying to get us out.

"Will your father be coming to visit as well?" Steve Smith stared at me with those kind, penetrating eyes that seemed to see into my soul.

"Nope." Without thinking, I continued. "He left us ten years ago. We haven't heard from or seen him since." What was the matter with me, telling a stranger such personal details?

"Oh." He clicked his tongue. "So . . . now you've taken on the role of bitter teenager?"

"You don't know what it was like." How dare this man judge me? "My father was a drunk, and when he learned my little sister was mentally challenged, he left." I really didn't know for sure whether my father had left us because of Gracie, but odds were good that I was right. The man had left and never looked back. He didn't care about me, my sister, or my mother. There was no excuse for what he'd done, and I wasn't going to defend him—certainly not to a stranger.

"I'm sorry." Steve reached up to rub his jaw and then asked, "Why do you suppose he did that?"

"I've asked myself that question thousands of times. The only answer I can come up with is that he's . . . he's a coward." I'd thought my father was a coward since the day he left, but I had never actually said so out loud. Taking a deep breath, I let the air out slowly. I looked at the man next to me. Why in the world had I told this stranger my innermost thoughts? Was he playing some mind game? "Do you talk to everyone like this?" I asked.

"Like what?"

"Frisk them verbally about who they're going to see and find out all their family secrets." I was interested to hear his reply.

The elevator gave a lunge and began to move.

"Nope." He grabbed his broom. "Just the ones who need me."

"Well, thanks, but I don't need help." The elevator doors opened. I rushed out, anxious to see my mother and to end the conversation.

"Sydney," he called after me. I stopped, but I couldn't bring myself to look at the man whose eyes seemed to see everything.

"There are things you need to learn about your father. When you're ready to talk, come see me. I'm in housekeeping. Just ask for Steve."

What in the . . . this guy was weird. He had gone to the great beyond and back. Who did he think he was? I turned around to ask him.

But he was gone.

Vanished.

Garbage can and all.

✢✢✢

When they wheeled Mom into her room after surgery, she was pretty much out of it. A short, pudgy nurse—who reminded me of one of the good fairies in Disney's *Sleeping Beauty,* the one who liked the color blue—gave me a nod while she and another nurse moved Mom from the gurney to the bed. With Mom settled, the good-fairy nurse came over to talk. "You must be her daughter?"

"Yes."

"She'll sleep another couple of hours." She patted my shoulder. "Doctor Foster will see you soon." With those words, she left. I gazed at my sleeping mother. Tape and the tailings of a bulky gauze bandage peeked from beneath the thin fabric of Mom's hospital gown. I brushed aside the sinking feeling in my chest and pulled my chair to her bedside.

Taking Mom's hand in mine, I studied her long, thin fingers. She had the prettiest hands. I had not inherited them. My fingers were short and stubby, like the rest of me.

An hour later the doctor walked in. He was a brick of a man; his white coat hung at crisp right angles over his blocky shoulders. Worry showed on his face, the grave *I-don't-know-what-to-do* type of worry that could reduce a patient's will to tapioca pudding. His look changed to a professional mask when his eyes met mine.

"You're Sydney?" He shook my hand.

Mom stirred but kept sleeping.

"The operation went well. She should sleep the rest of the day." He gazed down at Mom, and I sensed that he wasn't telling me everything. "Will you be here in the morning?" he asked.

I nodded. I wasn't leaving until Mom told me to. "Is she going to be all right?"

"If I have anything to say about it, she will be." He smiled, and a forced cheeriness claimed his face. "I'll tell you more when your mother is fully awake. If you notice a change in her condition, page the nurse, and she'll call me." He patted my shoulder. "Don't worry." With those final words, he turned and left.

I knew from watching TV that whenever a doctor said, "Don't worry," that was the time to pray real hard. I should have demanded he tell me everything then, but I didn't . . . couldn't. I wanted to chase him down the hall and beg him for more information. Fear blocked my way. And I couldn't bring myself to leave Mom's side. I pulled my seat so close to the bed that the metal of the bedrail clinked against the wooden armrest on my chair. If Mom so much as flinched during the night, I'd know it. With a prayer on my lips, I settled in.

-†††-

The night was long and miserable. Every few hours Mom would wake up just long enough for the nurse to give her a pain pill, and then she would fall back to sleep. I slept fitfully, shifting endlessly in the hard, wooden chair. There was a recliner in the room; I could have slept on it, but I would have been too far away from Mom. I stayed in the chair, holding her hand and resting my head beside her on the bed.

Doctor Foster woke both of us as he entered the room to do his morning rounds. "Are you two awake?" He gave Mom a tender smile, and in that moment I knew he was a man who cared a lot about his patients. I rubbed my sleep-deprived eyes and quickly looked at Mom.

She was awake. "How did it go?" Mom asked with a scratchy voice I barely recognized.

"Not like we had hoped." Doctor Foster's face turned serious.

Mom put her hand up to stop him from talking. "Syd . . ." She cleared her throat and continued. "Would you call the Stakers and check on Gracie?"

I reached for the phone.

"Not here." Mom tried to sit up, but she sank back into her pillows. "Use the pay phone in the hall."

I knew what she was doing. "You're not getting rid of me, Mom."

"Please, sweetie."

Doctor Foster took my side. "You need her," he said. I knew I liked him.

I grabbed Mom's hand again. Together we could get through this.

Doctor Foster began. "As you probably suspected, we had to do a mastectomy instead of a lumpectomy. We discovered in surgery that, unfortunately, the mass had spread. I want to start chemotherapy as soon as you're strong enough."

Mom squeezed my hand and looked at me. Then she turned to the doctor. "If chemo doesn't work, then what?"

"We're not at that point yet." Doctor Foster took Mom's hand from me, feeling her pulse. "We have to be positive here. An important part of recovery has to do with your outlook. Helen, you're a fighter."

Mom smiled at me and then looked at the doctor. "You bet I am. But I want to be realistic here."

"I understand." Doctor Foster let go of her hand, unwrapped the stethoscope from around his neck, and said, "Let's give chemo a chance to work. If we don't see the results we want, then we'll talk about what to do next. Let me take a listen to your heart." He gently slid the small disk beneath her gown beside the massive bandage covering her chest.

"Well, you're heart's beating; that's always a good sign." The doctor winked and flipped the stethoscope around his neck. "I want you to rest now. I'll check on you tonight." He gave Mom's hand a squeeze, tucked her chart under his arm, and left as suddenly as he'd appeared.

"Well, that's that," Mom said. Tears welled up in her eyes, and she quickly wiped them away. I couldn't believe this was happening to my mother . . . to us.

"Syd, get my purse from the closet." She nodded toward a door. I hustled over and located the small shoulder-strap purse she'd had since I was in the sixth grade. I handed it to her.

Raising herself up a little, she opened the flap and dug through the contents, catching her breath every so often. I'd never seen my mother so weak.

"Here, let me." Taking the purse from her, I asked, "What are you looking for?"

"A letter." She inhaled deeply, clutching her side. She whispered, "Might be in the side pocket."

I dug through the side pouch, pulling out a small bottle of lotion, a checkbook, a roll of antacids. Finally, I found it.

The paper was old and yellowed. The return address was within the city. Strange. Why would someone mail a letter instead of calling or just stopping by?

"Who is it from?" I asked, handing the letter to her.

She studied the envelope and quietly said, "Your father."

The word drained the air from the room, and for a moment I couldn't breathe. Finally catching my breath, I said, "My father . . . but I thought he never contacted you."

"It's an old letter." Mom closed her eyes, a pained expression on her face.

"Are you all right?"

She opened her eyes and placed the letter in my hand. "Yes. Sweetie, I need you to do something for me."

"Anything."

She bit her chapped lips, then said, "Find your father. I need to see him."

CHAPTER 3
ENEMY MINE

I cut through acrid smoke, which threatened to cloak the battle field, stabbing at the enemy until he moved no more. The next assailant attacked from behind without warning. As he jabbed his spear at my middle, I dodged the obsidian tip and thrust my blade into his chest. He fell at my feet. I sucked in as if I were a winded horse, and glanced around.

Fire burned about us, and I knew I was in hell.

It was wrong to kill.

Yet here we were, my warrior brothers and me, fighting beside our captain, killing those determined to kill us first. I wanted to yell. I wanted to cry. And I did with each thrust of my blade. When I felt I could go no further, my mother's words came to me: "Your faith in the lord will make you strong; it will shield you and keep you alive." Her words were emblazoned upon my mind.

I mourned for what I was forced to do. Our enemies, who had once been our brethren, would not talk peace. We had enticed them away from Judea. They had followed for a time. But then they turned about and attacked our allies.

Now, I could do nothing except fight.

Fight for the city . . .

And fight for the life we once knew.

‡‡‡

I rode the bus into downtown Salt Lake City. Mom had insisted I take her purse. It held her cell phone, money—if I needed it—and the letter. All the way to Salt Lake, I was tempted to read the letter my father had sent so many years ago, but I couldn't bring myself to open the yellowed envelope. No excuse justified leaving a wife and two children.

I hopped off the bus when it stopped at First South and Main. I could walk the rest of the way. Ten minutes later I stopped, confused, and double-checked the address. The address was correct, but I couldn't believe I was at the right place.

I stood in front of a condominium. A big, expensive-looking condominium. The building was five stories tall and had mirrored windows. A moving van was parked near the doors, which were propped open to allow the movers to bring in furniture.

I had never pictured my father here, of all places. When I thought of him—and I tried not to—I always pictured him drunk and homeless. Not here.

I shrugged the thoughts away and followed the movers inside, passing by the guard stationed at the front doors. He was busy keeping track of the movers and didn't pay me the slightest bit of attention.

Plush carpeting spread down a long hallway leading to elevators. I glanced around looking for a directory and found *L. Morgan* at the top. I decided to try the fifth floor first.

Riding the elevator, I tried to think of what I'd say. Would he recognize me? Would he be glad to see me? I decided I really didn't care. I was only here because of Mom.

The elevator stopped. The doors opened. A man and woman stepped in. They were deep in conversation and didn't give me a second glance. The woman seemed to be a socialite of some type; she wore a designer suit and had a Gucci bag and shoes to match. I glanced at the man. And then it hit me like a sudden attack of the flu.

The man was my father!

My heart beat against my ribs. I felt light-headed and sick to my stomach. He stood only three feet away. I was amazed that I had recognized him after all this time. I had been only six when he left us. He was listening to the woman at his side.

"I really think you need to give this deal a chance," said the woman. "You don't have a lot of options." Her cell phone rang. She had been holding it in her hand like she'd been expecting the call. She began talking as if she were hard of hearing. Though her words rained over me, I turned her voice off. My attention was focused on my father.

He stood about six foot two, and his sandy blond hair was now highlighted with white. He stared at the elevator buttons, acting as if he were trying to ignore the woman. His tanned, leathery face showed signs of age as well, crow's feet peeking out at the corners of his eyes. A mustache covered his upper lip, and a small strip of beard ran down the middle of his chin. He looked tired, worn out—I wondered what gave him the right to feel that way. How dare he be tired when my mother was dying?

He hadn't even noticed me standing there—hadn't even look at me. Anger flushed through my veins. I wanted him to see me, darn it. I wanted him to look at me.

I cleared my throat.

He didn't turn around. Subtlety was out; I'd have to demand attention. No problem.

"Excuse me," I said in as flat a voice as I could.

He glanced at me, shrugged, and turned back again as if he hadn't heard.

And then he did an about-face.

His eyes grew as large as Krispy Kreme doughnuts. His face paled. "Sydney, is that you?" His worried expression made him look like Scrooge had when he'd seen the Ghost of Christmas Past.

I nodded.

The woman, though still on the phone, turned to see what had drawn my father's attention. She frowned, looking at me as if I were a vagrant, and kept talking into her phone.

The elevator stopped on the ground floor. The woman stepped out. But my father didn't move.

"Logan?" The woman looked at him, then at me.

"You go ahead. I'll catch up." My father's eyes never left mine. The woman shrugged and walked away, still yammering on the phone.

"Let's go somewhere private. My place?" he quietly asked.

I nodded, still unsure how I was going to tell him about Mom, about her cancer, and about how much I hated him.

But this wasn't about me. I was here for Mom. And only Mom. I had to keep that front and center.

The elevator stopped on the fifth floor. I followed my father to his door. He quickly unlocked it and motioned me inside.

The condo was immaculate. Neat, orderly, no chaos, no empty liquor bottles strewn all over the floor like I'd imagined so many times. Large paintings hung on the walls. I followed him into the living room and sat on an overstuffed brown suede chair that matched the suede couch. Shiny end tables of mahogany banked the sofa. He obviously had money.

"It's so nice to see you." A smile gentled his worn face, which reminded me of the face of an old western actor. He looked right at me. "I've wondered so many times how you would turn out."

"Really? I'm surprised you gave me a second thought."

"Syd, you're my little girl. Of course I've wondered about you." He reached toward me as if to take my hand. I moved away.

"What about Gracie? Have you ever wondered about her? She's your daughter, too." I wanted to watch him fumble for some excuse, some half-baked reason why he hadn't mentioned her.

"Gracie?"

"Yes, Gracie. My mentally challenged sister, the other reason you left besides your drinking." Now I had him.

His face blanched. His hand visibly shook as he reached to wipe his brow. "I left because I had to. I left for you and your mother."

"Right." Now was my chance to make him understand the pain I'd lived—the pain we'd lived with every day. "You left for *me?*" I laughed. "Baloney! You left because you loved alcohol more than your family. You left because you couldn't handle having a . . ." I wasn't sure I could say the word, but I had to put this in terms he'd understand. ". . . 'retarded' daughter. You left because you're a coward."

He walked to a large window overlooking the city, keeping his back to me. He stood there for a long time. A clock ticked somewhere down the hall, marking the seconds. I was not going to say anything. The ball was in his court, and I was ready for his serve.

Turning to face me, he stayed by the window. "I suffered from blackouts during that time in my life. All I know is that I have one daughter, and she is not retarded."

Blackouts? Give me a break, I thought. "Don't lie to me! I was there." I couldn't believe he was pulling the *I-didn't-know* routine.

"You were six when I left. And I *was* drunk." He clenched his teeth and continued looking at me. Finally he asked, "Does your mother know you're here?"

"She sent me. Did you think I would look you up on my own? To me, you died ten years ago." I didn't realize the cruelty of my words until they'd left my lips.

He winced slightly. A strange uneasiness prickled my skin. I'd dreamt of this moment so many times, but I'd never imagined that my words would actually hurt him. And I had also never imagined that instead of making excuses and acting tough, he wouldn't say anything. He looked as though what I'd said had truly hurt him—which was what I wanted. Yet . . . somehow instead of feeling vindicated, I felt bad. The whole scene wasn't at all what I had thought it would be.

"This doesn't make sense. Why would your mother send you?" He walked over and sat beside me.

It was time to tell him about Mom. I pictured her lying in the hospital bed—small, fragile—and asking me to do this horrible thing. I stared at the floor and said, "Mom wants to see you."

"Why didn't she come herself?"

"She couldn't." Fresh courage fell upon me. I looked directly at him. "Mom has cancer. She thinks she's dying, and she wants to see you. For the life of me, I don't know why."

Again his complexion paled. Placing his elbows on his knees, he buried his face in his burly hands. My words had been harsh, but he deserved a lot worse than what I had said. Finally, he looked up, his blue, Gracie-like eyes full of sympathy. "What hospital is she in?"

"Mercy." I stood and started for the door. I'd carried out the task Mom had given me, and I wasn't going to hang around any longer.

"Sit down, young lady." His voice was firm. I whirled around to face him.

"What gives you the right to tell *me* what do to?"

"Sit!"

Surprised by his parental command, I sat. I immediately regretted my automatic response. Just who did he think he was?

"I need to call my agent and tell her I'm going to miss a meeting. And then you're taking me to your mother."

"What?" I couldn't believe his gall. Mom might want to see him, but I was not about to deliver him to her.

"Syd, your mother asked to see me," he said quietly. "And you're going to take me to see her."

I was about to protest again but caught myself. As much as I didn't want to admit it, he was right. Mom wanted this deadbeat back in our lives. What could she be thinking? Gracie and I could take care of her. We didn't need him.

"Give me a second." He rushed out of the room.

I went to the door to wait. A painting on the wall showed a Native American woman dressed in ceremonial leathers, a child by her side. As I studied the artwork more closely, I realized that the woman had my mother's eyes.

I quickly turned away and looked over my father's bookcase, which was filled with how-to books: *How to Plant a Garden*, *How to Install Stairs*, and *How to Fix Anything and Everything*. They were all written by someone named Edward Branson. Apparently my father liked to do everything himself. Everything, it seemed, but be a father.

Suddenly I didn't want to know more about him, what he read, or what paintings he had in his fancy condo. He wasn't supposed to be well-off or living in the city where we lived, and he wasn't supposed to be concerned about my mother. He was supposed to be a drunk, a tramp—someone who thought only of himself.

"Let's go." He came back into the room and passed me on his way to the door.

-‡‡‡-

We didn't speak on the ride to the hospital. I stared out the window; I didn't want to look at him. I was surprised to learn that he drove an old Jeep Cherokee; the man lived in an elegant condo but drove a beat-up Jeep. He reached over to turn off the country music station that filled the void between us. He didn't press me to talk. The conversation we'd had in the condo replayed in my mind.

"I have one daughter, and she's not retarded." Why had he said that? He had looked shocked when I'd mentioned Gracie. How could he be so evil to claim that he didn't know about his other daughter? Maybe he was simply so filled with guilt from leaving us that he'd erased her from his mind. No. A man like my father would not feel guilt.

Guilt would have made him contact us.

Guilt would have made him send money.

Guilt would have made him stay . . .

He pulled into the parking plaza and found a space right away. I followed him into the hospital. He followed me to the elevators. I pushed the UP button.

When the doors finally opened, a swarm of people pushed their way out, and we stepped on. Surprisingly, we were the only two people going up. Since we were alone, I decided to make sure he knew what the boundaries were for this visit. "Mom's weak, so I don't want you picking a fight with her, I don't want you denying you know Gracie, and I don't want you making excuses."

He studied me, not saying a word.

The elevator stopped. He followed me to Mom's room. I paused a moment. "Let me go in and tell her you're here."

He nodded.

When I entered the room, I found she was asleep. Sitting in the chair beside her bed, I took her soft hand in mine. "Mom?"

Her eyes blinked open. She looked startled at first, but then a smile crossed her face. "You're back so soon. You couldn't find him? He's moved?"

"No. He was home." I released my hold and grabbed a glass of water for her.

"Really." She took the glass, drank a sip, and handed it back to me.

"He's in the hallway. He wants to see you."

Her eyes grew wide. Then she swiped a hand across her face, sighed, and looked at me. "Thank you, sweetie."

She pushed the button on her bedrail to raise the head of the bed. As she finger combed her hair, she said, "I must look awful, but I don't care. Would you mind asking him to come in? And then would you call Gracie to see how she's doing? I'm a little worried about her. You know how she doesn't like being away from home."

"You're doing it again," I said.

"Doing what again?" She looked so innocent.

"You're trying to send me away when you need me the most. Gracie is fine with the bishop's family. I'm not going anywhere, Mom." I went to the door. I needed to be here for this. I'd seen my father walk out of her life; I deserved to see him walk back in.

Cracking open the door, I found him standing in the doorway. He looked at me and said, "Your mother wants you to call someone." Then he stood there, expecting me to leave.

"No. *I've* never left her, and I'm not about to now," I said, turning my back on him and walking to Mom's side. Slowly, he followed.

"Helen." His chiseled, guilty face softened as he looked at my mom. "I'm glad you sent for me."

"Thanks for coming." Mom smiled as if she were meeting a long lost friend. How could she be nice?

"You knew I'd come." He sat on the chair beside the bed, the one that had been mine, ignoring me completely.

Mom turned her attention to me. "Sydney, I believe you have a class to teach?"

I'd totally forgotten that I would be teaching Mom's karate class. I glanced at my watch. Four o'clock. The class started at four-thirty. I'd called all my students the day before; I should have just cancelled classes for the whole week. I would barely have time to hop on a bus and get home if I left right then.

"Honey, go." Mom was earnest in her appeal.

"But . . ." I looked at my father.

"You teach karate, too?" He leaned back in the chair.

"What about it?" I waited to see if he would do the parent thing by saying, "You're just like your mother."

He shrugged, not taking my bait.

"I'll come back after my last class, Mom."

"No." She grabbed my hand. "I'd rather you visit Gracie."

"Yeah, but . . ." It tore me apart to leave Mom here alone with *him.* I studied her eyes, asking with my look whether she'd be all right and if she knew what she was doing.

Mom smiled, and in that moment my dogged determination to stay evaporated. Who did I think I was? After all, it was *her* husband that had rejected her ten years ago and left her with two kids and no income. Mom needed her time alone with him. I'd already had mine.

I leaned over, gave Mom a kiss on the forehead, then turned and walked out. I didn't look at him, but I felt his eyes follow me to the door.

✠✠✠

After my last class ended, I hurried to the bus. It was a good thing Mom had insisted I take her purse; she had the exact amount of change I would need to take me first to the hospital and then to the Stakers' to check on Gracie.

When I reached the hospital, I impatiently waited for the elevator and then ran to Mom's room. I slowed down as I approached; I could hear voices. I crept to the partially closed door.

"I'd better go." It was my father's voice. "But I'll be back tomorrow."

"Logan . . ." Mom sounded tired. "Please forgive me for not telling you before now." What was she talking about?

"We both have healing to do." I heard him move to the door. "Sleep well." He was coming!

My eyes darted around the sterile hospital hallway. There was nowhere to hide. But the last thing in the world I wanted to do was speak with him. I was about to duck behind a med cart, but stopped short as he stepped smack-dab in front of me.

"Syd? I thought you were supposed to be visiting your sister."

"So, now you acknowledge I have one?"

"Walk with me?" he asked. He motioned to the stairs at the end of the hallway. The stairs led to an outside exit not far from the parking plaza. I wanted to walk with him like I wanted to eat a plate of beets, but I was suddenly curious to hear what he would say. I also wanted to set him straight. He wasn't supposed to forgive my mother—my mother was supposed to forgive him—*if* she wanted to.

As we stepped onto the exit stairs, he said, "You wear a black *gi.* It looks good on you."

"Since when do you care about what looks good on me?" I wasn't about to be won over by phony compliments. And I didn't want to chit-chat about my *gi.* "What were you and Mom talking about?"

He started down the stairs. "A lot of things." He didn't elaborate.

"Such as?" I scrambled to keep up with him. Mom's purse flopped against my side.

"Her health."

"That was a no-brainer. What else?"

He didn't reply but kept descending the stairs. I followed. As we exited the building, he said, "We talked about you and Gracie."

"So you remembered her name," I taunted.

He started for the parking plaza but stopped. "Syd, I know I hurt you by leaving. I was not myself at that time in my life."

"Spare me the sob story." I didn't want to hear that he "hadn't been himself" or that life had not been fair to him. But there was something I did want to know. "How do you live with yourself knowing you turned your back on Gracie?"

"Look . . ." He rubbed his chin, and sucked air between his teeth, giving me time to add fuel to my fire.

"You're just a coward, aren't you?" I spat out.

He started to walk away, ignoring my question. But I wasn't going to let him get away that easily. I leaped ahead of him, planting myself in his path. "Answer me!"

He tried to step aside. Hot anger spurred me forward, and I reached up to grab his shoulder with my right hand as I tried to kick the back of his left leg. Unexpectedly, he stepped back, grabbed my arm, and threw me onto the grass. Shocked that he'd stopped my attack, I looked up at him in a daze.

"Who do you suppose taught your mother karate?" he said, leaning over me. "Ten years ago, your mother told me that Gracie had died because of my drunkenness. And because of my blackouts, I believed her. That's why I left." Then he walked away, leaving me lying on the ground.

I lay there and tried to comprehend his words. *Mom had told him Gracie was dead?* It had to be a lie. Mom never would have told him such a thing. Yet . . . I had heard Mom ask him to forgive her.

No, there had to be something more. Information was missing. I sat up, pulled Mom's purse to my side, and gathered my knees up to my chin. I let myself speculate on this new information. Could it be that all these years my father did love me? Why hadn't he tried to contact me, then? All these years he'd lived right here in the same city; all these years he'd stayed away.

A tear rolled down my cheek. I brushed it away angrily. No sense crying about it. Nothing had really changed. He was still the same person. I felt a pang of regret. A person I'd said some horrible things to. I'd called him a coward. Another tear threatened to escape. I wiped my eyes. And then I realized with a jolt that, for the first time in ten years, I'd seen him, talked with him. I'd been with my *father*. I tried half-heartedly to squelch the tingle of happiness that this thought brought about.

I looked up at the hospital and remembered why I was sitting there in the first place. My mother had cancer. The past twenty-four hours of worry, anger, and grief collided in me. I buried my face in my hands and cried. Not dainty little tears, but big, slobbery sobs. Through my tears, I prayed to Heavenly Father for Mom, Gracie . . . and my father. I also prayed for myself, asking that somehow everything would work out, that somehow I'd understand why all this was happening.

Suddenly I sensed someone watching me. Glancing out of the corner of my eye, I glimpsed what I at first thought was a white angel hovering close to my shoulder. I had prayed for help, but I never expected this. Then the shape moved closer. A large, wet nose nudged my cheek.

I didn't know what exactly was standing beside me, but it was no angel. Fear charged through me, and I lunged to get away. A huge shape blocked my attempt to flee—a massive black-and-white shape. It licked my cheek with unabashed friendliness. I looked up to find a black and white Great Dane standing over me.

CHAPTER 4

DELIVERED UP

The battle raged on and on.

And then, with a whimper and a cry, it ended.

The enemy laid down their swords and spears as we surrounded them. We had slain many. The battlefield was strewn with bodies.

As we walked amongst the dead, gathering our wounded, we found that many of our allied forces had perished in the fight. Fearing that my warrior brothers had been slain, I helped Captain Helaman number those who still drew breath. Death's stillness filled the air. I watched grown men weep and wail, mourning their tremendous losses.

But a miracle occurred amongst the hopelessness. Not one of my brothers had been lost. It was true that all of us had been wounded, some worse than others, but we had made it safely through the bitter torment of battle.

Great comfort filled my heart. I thought of my father, whom I had left in Jershon. He had given me a blessing before I had set out with the captain and our troops. My father was a man of indomitable faith who held his covenants sacred. He had promised God that he would never again bear arms against our enemies, and he would not break his promise. His faith was much like Captain Helaman's. Both men were committed to Father in Heaven. For that I was most grateful. Someday I hoped I would be like my father and have unwavering faith. Someday I hoped I would be like my captain and lead troops that were protected by the hand of God. I knew that my warrior brothers and I had been protected by the Almighty; and I knew that it had been through the faith our parents had taught us in our youth.

And we had conquered the enemy . . . for now.

ǂǂǂ

The dog's warm, brown eyes seemed to understand the tornado of emotions churning inside me. His large pink tongue licked my face in a gesture of sympathy. I'd always had a soft spot for dogs, especially big dogs. Before I knew it, I'd wrapped my arms around the animal's neck, wiping my tears on his fur.

I watched the Great Dane's long, thin tail wag back and forth. I realized that its master must be close by. I hated crying and wasn't about to let a stranger catch me doing so. Gaining control of my emotions, I glanced about and saw two men walking toward me. Slipping the thin strap of Mom's purse over my shoulder, I crawled to my feet. I wiped my nose, then stroked the animal's back.

"Is this your dog?" I asked as they approached.

One of the men smiled, and a dimple appeared in his right cheek. "Ximon isn't ours. He belongs to a friend we've come to visit." He reached his hand out. "My name is John, and this is Bob."

I knew better than to shake a stranger's hand, especially here in the dark. To divert the man's attention, I asked, *"Zimon?* Don't you mean *Simon?"*

"No. *Ximon,* pronounced like a *Z* and spelled with an *X.* It's Hebrew," John said.

I really didn't care. I needed to check on Mom, not stand there talking with strangers about odd dog names. Wanting to end our conversation on a friendly note, I said, "Hope your friend enjoys your visit," and started away.

"We're not visiting a patient," said Bob. I stopped, caught off guard by his patronizing tone. He made it sound like I was supposed to know something I didn't. Ximon nudged my hand, insisting on getting some attention. I didn't have time for these two guys or their dog.

"Well, see you." I started away.

"We're waiting for Steve." Bob stepped in front of me and looked down his long, sharp nose. "He works in housekeeping. He wanted us to bring him this." Bob held out a backpack.

Steve from housekeeping? It couldn't be. "Is your friend's name Steve Smith?"

"You know him?" asked John, all pleasant-like. I was starting to get suspicious of these two strange men. I had no idea what they were up to, but if they were friends of Steve, I wanted nothing to do with them.

"Not really." I glanced up at the fifth floor windows, feeling the pressing need to be there. "I've only spoken with him once. Excuse me, I have to go."

Starting away without looking, I tripped over Ximon and tumbled to the ground. The dog stood over me, licking my cheeks. I scrambled to my feet. Feeling more embarrassed than I cared to admit, I said, "He's awfully friendly, isn't he?"

"Ximon or Steve?" asked Bob.

"Steve—I mean, Ximon." I was flustered and tired of this man's questions and superior attitude. "It doesn't matter. I'm leaving now."

"Hey, wait a minute." John started after me.

I hesitated for just a second and glanced backward. John added, "Since you know Steve . . ." He smiled and took the backpack from Bob's hands. Then he focused on me. "Would you mind taking this to him?" John tried to hand me the backpack.

"I thought you two were waiting for him." I did not want to be drawn in to this.

"We have been waiting a very long time. Ximon can't go inside the building, and we need to meet with our own charges. Since you know Steve, perhaps you could take it to him?"

What did he mean by *charges?* I started backing away. "I would, but I need to visit someone."

"She'll understand." Again, John held the backpack out to me. "Your mother isn't expecting you, so what would it hurt?"

"How . . . just who . . . ?" As I tried to figure out how he knew that Mom wasn't expecting me—or even that I was here to visit my mother—he slung the pack on my arm next to Mom's purse.

"It's after visiting hours; no one's expecting visitors." He smiled, and I relaxed a little. I sighed. It really wouldn't hurt me any to help them. And besides, by agreeing to do this I could get away.

"Okay." I started for the main entrance.

"Wait." Bob stopped me. "You can enter through the back. It's only one staircase down to housekeeping that way."

"Great." I rolled my eyes and headed for the back entrance, hoping this was the last I'd see of them.

"Thanks, you really saved us." John's gentle voice made me feel less put out. I waved good-bye and hurried to the rear of the building. I'd already wasted too much time crying over my father and then talking with those two.

As I pushed through the door, Ximon dashed past me. I didn't even realize he had followed. I opened the door and peered out into the darkness, trying to catch a glimpse of the men he'd come with.

There was no sign of them.

"Come on, Ximon. You're not supposed to be in here," I coaxed.

The black-and-white speckled Great Dane sat down. He cocked his head as if trying to understand.

"Oh, nunchakus!" I exclaimed, exasperated. I'd taken to using *nunchakus* for slang. It helped me to not swear, and since nunchakus were a karate weapon, I thought it appropriate to use when I became frustrated or scared. I tried to balance the backpack and Mom's purse, grab hold of Ximon's collar, and keep the door open at the same time. I tugged on the beast's collar, but he refused to budge an inch. He was as heavy as a bag of sparring gear.

I gave up on the door. I let it close and concentrated all my attention on the four-legged creature in front of me. I noticed that on Ximon's chest, above his front legs, there were white markings that stretched like wings over his hide . . . the angel I had seen by my shoulder. *Oh brother,* I thought. My angelic visitor—and what I assumed was an answer to my prayer—was this dog. With both hands, I pulled on the animal's collar.

He wouldn't budge. He just looked at me and yawned.

I heard a noise from down the hallway. Then a door opened and out stepped Steve Smith. Ximon leaped to his feet, spinning me around. As I struggled to keep my footing, something fell out of the backpack. It hit the floor with a thud and started to roll.

I quickly bent to retrieve the object and discovered that it was some type of crystal, about the size of a baseball. It looked almost like quartz, but very clear. The edges had been smoothed, but it was apparent that the rock had once been part of a bigger piece. I snatched it off the linoleum.

"I see John and Bob asked you to deliver my backpack," Steve said as he patted Ximon's head. The dog licked Steve's hand.

"Yeah, I'm sorry I dropped this." As I held out the stone, I felt heat coming from it.

"Actually . . ." Steve squatted at eye level with Ximon and rubbed the back of the dog's ears, leaning in close, as if to speak to him. Then Steve stood. "It's all worked out for the best."

"What do you mean?" I asked. The stone grew warmer and warmer in my hand.

"I told them to bring me the rock so I that could give it to you. And now you have it." He smiled, and his deep brown eyes seemed to see through me. He was creeping me out.

"Why would you want me to have this?" I glanced at the stone in my hand. A light now glowed from within it. I couldn't pull my gaze from the brilliant, hypnotic light that had become brighter than white.

"What's happening?" Panic skittered over my skin like a spider seeking cover.

The light of the orb encompassed my hand. Its radiance grew with every passing second. I wanted to drop it, but I couldn't. Dazzling, mind-numbing light swallowed my arm. Terrified, I looked up at Steve. He mouthed, "Forgive me." Ximon lunged toward me at the same time a flash enveloped me completely.

Then I saw nothing at all.

⸸⸸⸸

The night was drenched with blood and tears. I cradled and carried one of my younger warrior brothers, quickening my step as I heard him moan.

Chief Captain Helaman instructed me to lay him in a glade along with the others who were seriously wounded. I looked at my captain, whom we sometimes called father. Worry for this wounded boy was evident in the droop of Father's shoulders and the empathy in his eyes. How fortunate I was to know, work for, and serve with such a man. I wanted to be like him in every way. My own father was a righteous and goodly man, and I loved him dearly. But I did not aspire to his *way of life. Raising corn, contending with leaf-eating insects, and pulling weeds was not what I yearned to do with my days.*

I dreamed of being a soldier in the royal Nephite army. This aspiration I kept close to my heart, never daring to voice it aloud, especially in front of my mother. She had enough worries.

"I will get help," Father Helaman said, not looking at me but staring at his sons, whose bodies had been clubbed, stabbed, and bruised. "Stay with them."

Then he left. I watched as he walked quickly up the hill. I felt my heart swell with gratitude. My warrior brothers and I, and our parents, believed in this man—loved him. And because of the love and faith he felt from us, Father Helaman would walk through hellfire for our safety.

⸸⸸⸸

Complete darkness surrounded me. The air was muggy and hot. I could still feel the warmth of the stone in my hand. Had the light burned out or was I blind?

Panic rising in my chest, I shouted, "Steve!"

Something bumped me, knocking me to my knees. I nearly dropped the stone. Feeling the ground, I found . . . dirt. Not linoleum flooring, but bare dirt. I could smell mint and cinnamon and other odors in the air. As my eyes became more accustomed to the darkness, I could see I was in a very large tent about the size of Mom's front dojo, where over thirty people could spar.

What was going on?

Something licked my face, and I realized that Ximon had been my tackler. But where was Steve? Why was I kneeling on dirt? And why was I in a dark tent?

I blindly fumbled with the backpack and Mom's purse, trying to disentangle the two so I could put the stone away and free up my hand. As I wrestled the stone into the pack, I heard footsteps and murmuring voices. Through the thin wall of the tent, I could see a faint glow coming toward me.

"My little sons fought well." The voice was male, deep, mellow, and tired.

"Not one was slain?" A woman's voice. "How could this be, when Antipus and his men were killed?"

They were coming into the tent. I could see shadows on the tent wall now. As my vision sharpened, I saw that I was surrounded by large baskets and barrels—some filled with plants, some with rags.

My mind raced with questions. Where in the world was I? How did I get here? Was the hospital just outside this tent? I moved toward the front of the structure. Just as I reached the tent flap, the man and woman walked in.

The woman carried a lantern shaped like Aladdin's lamp, only made of clay. Her head was covered with a brown shawl that she allowed to slip to her back as she entered. Long, brown curly hair bounced about her shoulders. She looked like she was in her late twenties and appeared to be very poor, for she wore a plain, tattered dress and apron, which hung to her knees. Crude sandals were on her feet.

"My little warriors have faith, Mariah." The man said as he followed her in. My eyes were immediately drawn to his dark red hair and full beard. His skin looked tough as granite. He towered over the woman beside him. A shield was strapped to his back over his tunic. He turned in my direction, and the lamp's light shone on the breast plate covering his chest. Under his arm, he held a helmet trimmed in gold. He wore a dark brown skirt. His legs were pure muscle, like a kung-fu fighter, and shin guards protected his lower legs. On his feet were leather-type boots.

His rust-colored eyes looked right at me, as if seeing through me. I thought he would speak to me, but he said nothing. My confusion grew when he turned away.

The woman set the lamp on a crate; then she and the man got to work, anxiously gathering herbs and rags from the baskets and wooden barrels. They were obviously in a hurry.

"Hey, could you two tell me what's going on?" I asked, impatient to find some answers.

They continued to ignore me. This was just plain rude. I glanced down at Ximon. The dog looked up at me as if to say, "I heard you." I cleared my throat and said, "Hey, I asked you two a question; maybe I'm not supposed to be here, but I have no idea where I am, and it's more than a little upsetting that you're ignoring me."

They continued on as if I'd said nothing.

"So you believe Antipus and his men did not have faith, and that is why they are dead?" the woman asked, sounding angry as she worked feverishly to gather supplies.

I took a breath. Maybe I was the one being rude. They were in the middle of their own conversation. I could wait patiently if I had to. I pressed the backpack and Mom's purse to me and stepped closer to Ximon, who seemed to be as perplexed by our situation as I was.

"You misunderstand." The man stopped what he was doing and took hold of her shoulders, looking deep into her eyes. "Antipus was a man of great faith. Together we planned to win the battle. My sons had never fought before, and Antipus believed that because of their youth, they would be the perfect decoys to draw Ammoron's troops from the city. We succeeded."

He continued. "Ammoron gave chase. Antipus's troops attacked Ammoron's troops from behind. The battle was fierce." The man sighed deeply, as if overcome by what he had just said.

I felt a prickling sensation on the back of my neck. The names the man spoke—Ammoron, Antipus—were strange, but they were familiar to me.

The Book of Mormon.

I tried to put the pieces together. I had seen Renaissance reenactors; maybe these were Book of Mormon reenactors. The theory didn't explain how I had ended up in the middle of their tent, but it did explain why no one would acknowledge me. The reenactors I had seen would often ignore people who weren't dressed appropriately to the era they chose. Relief settled on me.

"Antipus and his men were battle weary when my sons and I returned to help," said the man, who had now grown quiet with reflection. "I don't know why his men were killed and my sons were spared. I only know that my sons—boys who had never known the ugliness of war or the brutality of men—were emboldened by their faith. And that alone is why they are alive."

"I do not understand such faith." The woman he called Mariah stared at him in disbelief, as if ready to defy him. Then suddenly, her face gentled. "But . . . I am grateful for your help. Judea would be captive if not for you." She placed the plants she'd gathered in a basket filled with rags. Then she stood. The man did as well. He towered over her. She said, "Antipus was a *great* leader."

"Yes." The man nodded. "I grieve his loss and the loss of the others. Many of the chief captains who were not slain were taken as prisoners."

"Forgive my sharp tongue." Mariah said softly. "The war goes on and on. I miss my family. How was my sister when last you saw her?"

I decided that this was my chance to butt in. Maybe they would acknowledge me now that they were talking about the present. I cleared my throat. "Speaking of families. I need to go see my mother, so if you would please tell me where I am . . ." And then it dawned on me. I could just step outside and see where I was. I didn't need these guys. I reached for the flap but couldn't grasp hold. I tried again and still could not touch the material.

I realized then that I was dreaming. I'd had dreams like this before—the kind where I try to talk and no one listens, where I try to touch something and can't. All I had to do was wait this out and I'd wake up.

"My wife is not well." The man said, and I turned back around. His face was somber.

He was answering Mariah's question about her sister.

"The disease claiming her has taken many from our village." His eyes reddened with concern as he stared at the woman who was apparently his sister-in-law. "I did not want to leave her," he said.

"Many men must leave their wives to battle in this war." Mariah patted his arm. "My husband fights as well. No man can step aside and not fight for his people, for his country, for his loved ones. Besides, I may have the cure for her. These healing plants—" she picked up some of the greens she'd placed in the basket she held "—cause the clotting of blood and will heal the wounds of your warriors, but not my sister."

She then whirled around, searching the different baskets, and grabbed another handful of weeds. "These, when brewed, will make you happy and content where sorrow once resided. They might help, but they are not what I am looking for." She dropped them quickly, scanning over her medicine baskets and barrels until she spied what she wanted.

Weaving her way among the containers, she finally grabbed something. "This root may cure my sister." The long tuber was not the white color of roots I'd seen before, but a light green with thin red veins.

"I will send this root with you to take to your homeland." Mariah tried to hand the plant to the man. He wouldn't take it.

"I know not when I shall return home. Even though we have won the battle for Judea, we must march on to the city of Antiparah. Ammoron and his followers have gone there. He holds that city and the cities of Cumeni, Manti, and Zeezrom. Our work is far from over." The man smoothed his thick, reddish beard with his burley hand. "Keep the root safe until I can take it to her."

Mariah tucked the root into the band of her apron, then fetched the basket she'd packed, settling it on her hip.

The two walked past me. They seemed so real—not dreamlike at all. The man opened the tent flap for her to step out. At that moment, someone else entered the tent. He was Native American and about my age. There was a large gash across his cheek. He wore a skirt of some type; his bare chest was smeared with blood.

"Father," he addressed the man. "My brothers need you."

The burly, redheaded Caucasian standing before him was clearly not his father.

"Tarik, you have done enough. I will see to them." The man he called father looked at the intruder with concern. "You must rest."

"I *must* do something. So many are wounded." The boy was not giving in.

"Very well. Come, Mariah will tell us what needs to be done." The man placed his arm around the young man's shoulders and all three of them left, taking the light with them.

I slipped off the backpack and placed both it and my mother's purse on the ground. Glancing around the darkened enclosure, I shook my head. Could this really be a dream? I determined to try leaving the tent again.

Just as I reached to try and grasp the door flap, it jerked open.

In the moon's glow, standing in front of me, was the warrior Tarik. Ximon sprinted out of the tent without a second glance at the warrior, chasing after something. Tarik didn't seem to notice Ximon either; he was staring straight at me.

He could see me!

Maybe he could hear me as well.

Before I could think of what to say or do, he grabbed my arm and wrenched it in back of me, placing a dagger to my throat.

This was no dream! His grasp was hard, painful, and the sharp dagger threatened to cut my skin.

"I saw you hiding," he hissed in my ear. "Dirty Ammoron spy. I will kill you before you can harm my father."

CHAPTER 5
AND NOW BEHOLD

Holding the spy against my chest, my first thought was to kill him immediately. He would not have hesitated to kill me. He would not have cared about taking another's life.

But father had taught us differently. For that reason alone I held off.

The spy smelled clean, not of battle. His clothes were not blood smeared. He had hidden in the safety of the tent while his people were killed and others did his fighting. This one was a coward. He deserved to die.

I pressed my dagger against his neck.

One thrust and his life would be over.

Why wait?

Why add to Father's burden?

If I killed him now, Father would not know of the spy who had watched him in his tent. Yet Father Helaman had taught us to respect our enemies and to give them the chance to surrender. Once they became our prisoners, our duty was to keep them alive.

The spy was my prisoner.

Only he and I knew. If given a chance, he would fight again, kill again. Now was the time to show my strength, to show my dedication to protecting my captain, my father.

‡‡‡

Panic singed my skin like fire. I was way beyond the dream theory. Now what threw me for a loop the most was the fact that this guy had the drop on *me!* I struggled to free myself, confusion and panic coursing through my veins. Maybe this *was* a dream; if I were conscious, he'd never best me.

It's time to wake up. Wake up!

Nothing. In desperation, I decided that maybe saying this out loud would help. Craning my neck away from the blade, I said as loudly as I could, "Wake up!"

The young man actually growled, jerked my arm farther up my back, while pressing his knife under my jaw.

Hot pain shot from my shoulder down my back. True fight-or-flight fear coursed through my veins. His breath fanned the side of my face. I tried to swallow but couldn't. He smelled as though he'd been in a hard-fought football game.

I had to figure out what was going on, and fast.

"Look," I said through clenched teeth, afraid that if I moved my jaw the dagger would cut me. "I'm not a spy. I don't even know who your father is." The dagger's point left my skin, yet the young man still maintained a tight hold on my arm. I tried to squirm around to look at him. He would have none of it. If I could keep talking and distract him, I stood a better chance of escaping.

"Only a Lamanite spy would babble with devil-speak," he hissed in my ear as he tightened his grip.

Lamanite spy?

Devil-speak?

Babble?

How dare he say I babble? "Look, Tonto . . ." I began.

He moved the dagger down my throat near my jugular, and I felt moisture roll down my skin. Was it perspiration or blood? He nudged me with his knee, forcing me to walk.

The knife's blade jabbed me, making it difficult to breathe. I stumbled out of my flip-flops. If I didn't keep up, I was going to die.

"Father!" my captor yelled to the man and woman ahead of us, stopping them just before they reached the crest of the hill.

As we approached, he said, "Look who I found in the supply tent."

The man from the tent, who stood at least six-foot-three, glowered down at me. He could see me now. Why now and not before? What was the deal?

Enough was enough. I reached up to my captor's right hand, where he held the knife, grabbed the pressure point beneath his thumb, and gave a hard jerk, freeing my neck from his blade. Startled, he dropped the dagger. I turned away from him, twisting my arm within his hold and latching onto his wrist. With all the strength I could muster, I snap-kicked him in the groin. He doubled over. I dropped his arms, grabbed his head, and jabbed my knee to his forehead. He collapsed in front of me.

Before I could turn around to face the man and woman, a muscular arm clamped about my neck in a chokehold. A hand pressed my head down so I couldn't see. Pain seared through my throat. I couldn't breathe. And then everything went black.

⸸⸸⸸

When I came to, my throat was throbbing. As my eyes opened, I looked at the ground. Still grass and dirt. I took a deep breath. I was lucky to be alive. My neck could have been easily broken.

Fearful my attacker might still be about, I glanced around. The large muscular man and the woman he had called Mariah were bent over the boy I'd taken down. The man had to be the one who'd dropped me. I realized I hadn't been unconscious long.

What was going on?

Why was I here?

Where was *here?*

A thought struck me. I'd read stories about people stepping into different dimensions of time. Could that be what had happened? But how did someone just step into another dimension? I thought of the stories I had read and remembered there was always a catalyst that sent the person to the other time.

What was my catalyst?

Steve Smith's stone! Of course. Everything had changed when the light began to glow and the flash knocked me out. But why hadn't the man and Mariah see me when we were in the tent? I had been standing in plain sight with Ximon by my side.

I suddenly remembered the dog. Ximon had been with me. Where in the world was the mutt? Maybe he had returned to the tent.

That's where I'd left the backpack with the crystal stone. I had to get back there. I knew I needed that stone if I was ever going to find any answers.

As I began to sneak away, the woman noticed my movement.

"Helaman! The spy!" She pointed at me.

The man spun around and latched onto my arm. His steely fingers tightened their grip, letting me know he'd tolerate no fighting.

Helaman? There was only one person I'd ever heard of named Helaman.

I swallowed hard and said, "You're Helaman . . . of the Nephites?" My brain had a hard time wrapping around the absurd possibility that I was standing near the real man.

"Yes." His deep growling voice held but a thin line of patience. "Perhaps you expected your hero, Ammoron?" His thin line of patience was fast disappearing.

I was in full meltdown and had gone over the edge.

This was bonkers!

Maybe finding out that my mother had cancer and confronting my father after years of hatred had been too much. I was obviously delusional. There were no dimensions in time.

"Speak up, spy!" Helaman shook me.

Gooseflesh crawled over my skin. I opened my mouth to speak, but no words came out. Just what did one say to an apparition whose touch felt so totally real?

"How were you able to escape from Tarik, my most valiant warrior?" He dragged me over to the young man, who had begun to regain consciousness. As we moved, I wondered briefly if I were actually in a padded room and some doctor was watching me act out this imaginary scene.

Tarik gained his bearings and grabbed his dagger while scrambling to his feet. "Forgive me, Father. I shall see to this Ammoron traitor."

"No crime has been committed." Helaman studied me as if looking for some hidden message on my person. "For one so small, this 'traitor' is a good fighter."

Tarik glared at me, and, even in the darkness, I could feel hatred in his stare.

Mariah spoke up. "Turn the traitor or spy or whoever he is over to the guards. We need to see to those poor boys." She hefted her basket onto her hip while holding the lamp in her other hand.

Did Mariah think I was a boy? That ruled out the hallucination theory. I was pretty sure my own brain would know I was a girl.

"But there may be more spies like him," Tarik warned.

They *all* thought I was a boy! I touched my short hair a little self-consciously. I knew I wasn't exactly girly, but I had never been mistaken for the wrong gender.

"With the battle over, there are bound to be Ammoron followers hiding in Judea." Helaman looked down on me as if I were yet another problem. "With the help of this spy, we will find them. All of them."

"I can find the hiding rats without this one." Tarik gazed up at his leader. "I shall take him to the stockade."

"Wait." Helaman took the lamplight from Mariah and lifted my chin to have a better look at my face. He stared for quite a while, then said, "This one is different."

He gripped my arm, and I felt strangely humbled to have him touch me. I determined that I would not shrink from his stare. I wanted to cry, but I wouldn't. Not while he stared at me, not while my mind was spinning with crazy possibilities. I had to be strong.

"He must be possessed of evil spirits to have escaped me," Tarik defended himself. "It shall not happen again."

Helaman turned to his devoted soldier, and his grip on my arm loosened. As I looked at the pride and determination written across Tarik's face, I realized I could be in a lot of trouble here.

As I assessed the situation, I again puzzled over the fact that they still thought I was a boy. I glanced down at myself. I still wore my black *gi.* I'll admit that sometimes a woman's shape was hidden by a *gi* top—and especially mine since I was not exactly full-figured—but come on; couldn't they tell just a little bit?

"Bring him with us." Mariah started for the top of the hill once more. "When he sees what his people have done to our warriors, he will understand that we will kill him if he fights."

Helaman pulled me with him as he trudged toward the top. Without my flip-flops, my bare feet came into contact with all sorts of small rocks and stickers. I had to ignore the pain to keep up. As we reached the crest of the hill, Tarik clamped onto my other arm, almost lifting me off the ground.

The moon shone its silvery glow over a field dotted with torch lights and littered with young men . . . boys really. Some lay on the ground, some barely stood by themselves, and others leaned on their shields for support. Each guarded crudely-made spears, swords, and bows and arrows. The entire crew appeared worn and battle weary. Every one of them looked as if he were wounded in some way. Some gazed at me expectantly. I didn't know what to do.

As I continued to look out across the field, a new thought entered my mind. If I was in Book of Mormon times, how was I going to return home? What would happen to Mom? What would happen to Gracie? Panic sliced through me like a samurai's sword.

"You thought your army could kill us," Tarik spoke into my ear. He stepped back and said, "Behold, the sons of Helaman live. We are strong. We are warriors!"

CHAPTER 6
Believe Me Not

I couldn't deny it any longer. I truly was in Book of Mormon times. This realization stirred my very soul. If the young men I was looking at were the stripling warriors, then the strongly built man holding my arm in a death grip, the man Tarik called Father, really was Helaman!

Before me was Gracie's hero.

Before me was a mighty soldier.

Before me was a prophet of God!

Oh, how I wished Gracie were here. I'd just read to her the story of Helaman and the warriors he called his "little sons." I didn't know what to make of the coincidence. Something very unusual was happening, and since I just happened to have a prophet at my arm, a guy who had direct insight from God, I figured he'd be the perfect person to help me figure things out.

"Mr. Helaman, sir." I didn't know quite how to address him. By his confused expression, I knew I didn't have the title quite right. Then I realized how strange it was that we could communicate at all. I knew they didn't speak English in Book of Mormon times. I'd read in seminary that Moroni had written and abridged the gold plates using some form of Egyptian that had been altered by the Nephites. But I also remembered reading that if the plates had been larger they would have been written in Hebrew. Whatever the language was, I surely didn't speak it. And none of this was particularly relevant, because for some reason I understood them and they understood me. The gift of tongues? Maybe. I glanced up at Helaman. He patiently waited for me to speak. "I mean, Brother Helaman . . ." That didn't sound right either. Then I remembered how we addressed the prophet. "President Helaman."

"Spy, what are you trying to say?" Helaman seemed curious and yet cautious.

"I need to speak with you alone, sir." I nervously glanced at Mariah and Tarik, then back at Helaman. "Just you and me."

"Father, let me take care of him. I shall teach him a lesson." Tarik gripped my arm hard.

Suddenly Helaman let go, and for a frightening moment I thought he was handing me over to the eager Tarik. Instead, he said, "Release him."

"Captain . . ." Tarik's fingernails dug into my skin.

Helaman watched Tarik until he freed my arm.

"We need to see to those poor boys down there." Mariah started down the hill. "Tarik, come and show me who needs tending first."

Tarik didn't move.

"Do as she asks," Helaman ordered.

Tarik paused a moment. I could tell he earnestly wanted to protest, but then he gave in and followed the woman. This left me alone with Helaman.

⁜

I followed Mariah down the small hill, all the while thinking about the spy who had somehow tricked my father into talking with him alone. Even small vermin like him could cause harm to my father, and he had looked especially devious.

"Helaman knows how to deal with the enemy," Mariah said as a troop of commanders walked toward us.

"Perhaps he is too trusting," I told her as the first commander, who was carrying a torch, reached us. I took the torch.

"Do not concern yourself." Mariah looked at me. "The lord guides him."

I led Mariah to the youngest warriors with the most serious wounds. The first boy was only ten and three years. Helaman and I had wrapped the wound in his side the best we could, but he was still losing blood. Despite his pain, he gave me a slight smile.

"How are you feeling, Jacob?" I asked the boy, smoothing blood-matted hair away from his forehead as I knelt by his side. Mariah *quickly set to work, removing the makeshift bandage and placing her healing plants over the wound before wrapping it with clean dressing. When she finished, she gave the boy a tender kiss on the head, then we both stood.*

Mariah leaned close to me, so the boy could not hear. "Jacob's wound is too deep. I cannot give him the care he needs here. The nursemaids who were tending to Antipus's men have taken the most seriously wounded to the city's tabernacle, where I can better see to their needs. Have your men take Jacob there."

I signaled a few commanders and told them what needed to be done. Although they were tired, they quickly saw to it.

Mariah moved on to the next boy. We fell into a routine; I would introduce Mariah, and then she would tenderly nurse the fallen warrior's wounds. For the more seriously injured warriors, she would gesture for my men to take them to the tabernacle. I stayed by her side, holding the torch so she could see each boy clearly. We were far from finished when Mariah ran out of her plants. She asked me to fetch more from the medicine tent. Seeing this as an opportunity to find out what was happening with the spy, I handed the torch to another warrior brother and picked up the empty basket. Mariah surely knew my intent, but she said nothing as I turned and started up the hill.

‡‡‡

"Can we go back to the supply tent?" I asked, hoping Helaman would agree. Even though he held a lamp, the surrounding blackness of the night made me feel claustrophobic. And the stars above us shone so bright and close that they made me even more keenly aware that I was in a different time and place.

Helaman motioned for me to lead the way. Wanting to appear strong, I stepped forward and again had to ignore the rocks and thorns which found their way into the soles of my bare feet. Near the tent, I spied my flip-flops and quickly slipped them on my feet. I glanced up at Helaman. He studied my shoes; then he took stock of my *gi* as if seeing it for the first time.

This was good. I wanted him to notice that I didn't quite fit the bill of an Ammoron spy.

I ducked inside the supply tent. The scent of what I thought might be mint and sage mingled with other fragrant herbal aromas that I couldn't put my finger on. Helaman followed me into the tent. I motioned for him to sit on a crate. He set the lamp there instead.

"I know who you are," I said. The flickering lamplight only emphasized his look of *no-duh.*

"I mean . . ." Just how did one explain dimensions in time? Then I thought of something. "I know why none of the stripling warriors were killed."

"You heard me talking with Mariah, so of course you know." His face was stern, and he looked at me as if to say, "You have to do better."

"I know their mothers taught them to have faith in God; that faith was the reason they weren't killed." I stared up at Helaman. He didn't move; his copper-colored eyes hardly blinked.

"I know they used to be called Anti-Nephi-Lehies but now call themselves Ammonites; their fathers pledged to God that they would never fight again. I also know that those young men out there believe in you so much they call you Father." Surely, he couldn't still think that I was a spy. Still, Helaman maintained his skeptical stare.

"I know you will take back the city of Antiparah without a fight and that afterward some troops and provisions will arrive from Zarahemla. But there won't be enough." Now I had his attention. His eyes became more attentive; he shifted his stance.

"Because of your military skill, you'll be able to retake Cumeni, and with the help of your captains, Gid and Teomner, you'll be able to take back the city of Manti, too. But having all your troops so widespread will leave you vulnerable."

"Stop!" Helaman commanded. "I listen to the *Lord's* revelations about my people. I do not have time to listen to the babble of an augur." Helaman started toward the tent's flap.

Augur? I had no idea what he was talking about. I had to switch gears here, think of something that had already happened, something no one else in this time knew except him. "I know that Chief Judge Nephihah didn't allow your father to take possession of the records—he gave them to you instead."

Helaman stopped and turned around. He looked more than a little intrigued.

"I know that mighty Captain Moroni, whom you follow, will die young, that you will be a great prophet." I paused. "And I know that the Savior will visit this continent." Now Helaman sat down on the crate beside the lamp.

"Want to know how I know this?"

He slowly nodded.

I took a breath. "I know this because I've read a book about you and your people. The book tells about Nephi and Lehi and how they escaped from Jerusalem. It tells about Abinadi and how King Noah killed him. It tells how in the end the Lamanites will exterminate the Nephites."

He stared at me. I was into it now. I had to keep going. "The book is called the Book of Mormon. A latter-day prophet named Joseph Smith was guided to the record, which was buried in a hillside by the angel Moroni."

Helaman's gaze was calm. And I realized at that moment he probably already knew about Joseph Smith. Helaman was a prophet and seer; he knew far more about this world than what I could ever tell him. However, what he did not seem to know was who I was. I was confused on this point. He was a prophet; why didn't he just say, "Hey, I know you're from a different time; I'll help you go home"?

"Where is this book you speak of?" Helaman folded his arms. His wrist guards clanged as they met.

What was I supposed to say? I tried to think. I could see where this was going. I was going to have to tell him I had been thrown back in time, but I wanted to ease into the subject. Sucking in courage, I finally answered him. "At home."

"Home? Where is home?" He stared at me, waiting.

"Now, here's the thing." I had to make him understand. "I'm not quite sure how to get there."

"You are lost?"

"Oh, yeah. You could say that." I glanced up at him, trying to appear earnest and sincere, hoping he'd let down his guard and make everything all right. But he didn't. I would have to spell it out. "See, I live in the future—another dimension; it depends on how you look at it." I bit my bottom lip, hoping against all odds he'd understand.

Helaman's bushy eyebrows drew together into one line. He frowned at me with skepticism. I had to convince him. My life might well depend on it.

"I live in a time when there are automobiles and airplanes, and even ships that travel through space."

Helaman stroked his rust-colored beard, never taking his eyes off of me. I kept talking.

"The deal is . . ." I took a deep breath, and the smell of herbs from the baskets around us reminded me this was a medical tent.

Medicine.

Hospital.

Mom!

A dam of emotions burst inside me, and I could not hold back the words that tumbled from me. "I was going to see my mother in the hospital, and these men asked me to take this backpack . . ." I rushed over and held up the pack, ". . . to a friend of theirs. See, my mom has cancer, and I'm afraid she's not going to make it. She made me find my father, who had been AWOL from our lives for at least ten years, and I went and got him and he came to see her." I was babbling, talking way too fast, giving too much information, but I couldn't stop.

"Back to this backpack business. These men wanted me to take this to their friend, and, well, you see, I went to give it to him, and this stupid dog named Ximon, he followed me into the building. And you know, dogs can't be in the hospital—germs and all. Anyway, I tried to get the dog to leave, and he wouldn't, and when I picked up the pack, this stone . . ." I unclasped the pack and pulled out the smooth, quartz-like rock so Helaman could see, ". . . rolled out onto the floor. I picked it up, and the thing started glowing and glowing, and then I kind of blacked out. And that's when you and Mariah showed up. I tried to talk to you, but you couldn't seem to see me or the dog—I think we must have still been in time limbo or something. See, I think this thing sent me here to you." I took a deep breath and slowly held out the stone.

Helaman was quiet for a very long time. He looked thoughtfully from the stone in my hand to me. "May I see it?"

"Sure." I handed it to him, knowing I'd told the truth and hoping he'd believe everything I'd said, especially now that he held the object that had caused all the trouble.

He carefully studied the stone. Then he placed it into the pack and clumsily clasped it. In a low voice that was filled with anger, he said, "You are the most devious spy yet. Only a true follower of evil would steal one of the brother of Jared's priceless stones." Gripping me firmly by the arm, he dragged me out of the tent into the dark night.

"I didn't steal it," I cried, trying to break from his hold. He hoisted me over his shoulder, knocking the wind right out of me. My head banged on the shield strapped to his back, bloodying my nose. The taste of copper came to my mouth. Gasping for breath and feeling tears prick my eyes, I angrily pushed them back.

Once I caught a good breath, I said, "Please, you have to listen to me." Blood pumped to my head, pounding in my brain. Why wasn't he listening? "You're a prophet! You're supposed to know I'm telling the truth!"

He abruptly stopped and placed me solidly on my feet. I looked up at his tall frame and could only make out the shadows of his face. He said, "I have just come from battle where I was forced to kill many of my Lamanite brethren. My heart sorrows for what has happened. And you—a thief who has somehow stolen a sacred vessel of God—truly believe that I am supposed to recognize your babble as truth?"

"Yes." The word slid slowly from my mouth.

We stood silently in the dark, humid night. The tension that boiled around us was unbearable. I was tempted to plead again, but knew I'd already said too much.

He gave a heavy sigh, and then in a quiet voice he said, "I am far removed from my other calling. Too much removed from my Lord. I need time." He rubbed his bearded chin and looked at the backpack he held in his hand.

At that moment, someone appeared over the hill. By the purposeful walk, I knew the person was Tarik.

"Is all well?" he asked Helaman as he stopped. Mariah's empty herb basket was in his hands.

Helaman slowly nodded. "Why have you returned?"

"Mariah needs more herbs," Tarik said.

Helaman appeared even more tired than before, as if the weight of his war-weary world had caught up to him. I imagined I was the last thing he wanted to deal with. Taking the basket from Tarik, he said, "I want you to escort this one to the stockade. Have the guard stay with him."

"No! You're making a mistake," I begged. "Please don't do this! Please!"

Tarik strong-armed me, pulling me away.

"Please! Think about what I said," I shouted to Helaman, who stood stock-still, watching as I was dragged off. Then, without saying a word, he turned his back to me, walked to the tent, and disappeared through the door. And with him went all my hopes. Not only did he not believe me, but he'd handed me over to this twerp.

And now Helaman had the stone—the catalyst that would send me home! I had to get it back. Somehow, I had to get away from this guy and take back the stone.

"Listen." I tried to pull away from him.

"No! *You* listen!" Tarik jerked me to him so we were face-to-face.

I felt the sharp point of a knife pressed against my abdomen.

"I shall make you pay for embarrassing me in front of my father," he said.

And in that instant, I knew I was toast.

CHAPTER 7
Caught in a Snare

"Before I kill you, tell me what lies you have told my father." Tarik stood close enough to bite off my nose. I would have turned away, but I hardly dared breathe with his knife pressing into my stomach. I had no intention of telling him about the conversation I'd had with Helaman. Right now, I needed to do something about the knife.

My black-belt training took over, and I quickly stepped back so that the blade no longer pressed my middle. With my left hand, I grabbed the top part of his right wrist to keep the knife away from me. I tried to give him another snap-kick to the groin, but he'd seen that move before, and my foot only hit his thigh, knocking him off balance. Since he still had possession of my right arm, I twisted around, grabbed his arm, and wrapped it about his neck, bringing him down to his knees, teetering backward. Immediately, I gave him a hard shove to the ground.

And then I ran. I ran as hard as I could.

I saw movement out of the corner of my eye. Something or someone was charging through the bushes in my direction. I tried to run faster and not look back. All at once, Ximon was galloping beside me, nipping at my heels and apparently wanting to play.

Nunchakus! *Now* the dog appears! Where had he been all this time? It was just my luck to be stuck with a time-traveling buddy who had the brains of a brick. No way would I ever be able to blend into this time period with a Neanderthal dog by my side.

"Get lost!" I pushed him, still trying to run. The dog would have none of it. He playfully growled and chased after me. My only option was to outrun him.

It was a crummy option. Large, wolflike paws pushed on my back, knocking me down. Face-planting into the ground, I automatically rolled over. Ximon's gigantic paws pinned me.

"Oh, come on!" I tried to push him away, but the dog's slobbery tongue bathed my face.

"Your horse is on my side." Tarik came into view behind the dog's black-and-white spotted ears. I scrambled to my feet. Tarik reached out to grab me.

Ximon gave a low, guttural growl, teeth bared, ears pinned to his head. His neck muscles bunched together. Despite Ximon's challenge, Tarik claimed my arm. I could tell by Tarik's rigid stance that the dog scared him out of his ever-lovin' Ammonite mind, but he wasn't backing down.

The Great Dane and the man were at a standoff. Despite the fact that Tarik had a dagger, Ximon appeared to have the upper hand. At last, fate leaned my way. "Let go, and I'll call off my *horse,*" I said.

Tarik glared at me and then at Ximon. I felt myself relax a little. I didn't think he'd actually hurt me. Sooner or later Helaman would ask about me. And Tarik would not want Helaman to be upset.

As if he found touching me distasteful and beneath him, Tarik dropped his hold; however, he did not back away.

"It's all right, Ximon." I patted the Great Dane, hoping he'd forgive me for trying to lose him. When I saw the animal's tail wag, I knew all was forgiven. I heaved a sigh and faced Tarik.

"Look, I'm not a spy. I mean no harm to your father or any of your brothers. Honest. Let me and my dog go, and I promise we'll never bother you again." I prayed Tarik would give in. There was a long silence between us. I took a deep breath.

"Dog?" He finally uttered while glaring at Ximon.

I nodded.

He gave Ximon a serious once-over. "An entire family could feed on him."

I stepped in front of the animal. He might only be a dog, and a dumb dog at that, but he was my hero. And he was my—albeit unpredictable—port in this time-traveling storm. Not a feast for a family.

Tarik reached to grab hold of me once again, but Ximon, his teeth bared, charged and knocked Tarik on his rear end.

Snarling and snapping, Ximon grabbed hold of Tarik's right wrist guard and started dragging him away. I had to step in. Helaman would never help me or believe my story of coming from another time if I let my dog devour one of his men. And there was also the likelihood that at any moment, Tarik could thrust his dagger into Ximon and kill him.

"It's okay, boy. Come on." I tugged on Ximon's collar, trying to pull him off the blustering Tarik. Finally, the dog let go and stood beside me.

"I shall kill that beast!" Tarik leaped to his feet, incensed, ready to end Ximon's life.

I stepped between the dog and the man. "You can't kill him. He's mine." My mind tumbled over what I could possibly say that would keep Tarik from tearing the animal apart. I thought of when I'd first met Ximon. "He's my angel."

Tarik looked at me as if I were crazy.

Anxious to make him understand, I said, "Do you believe in prayer?"

Tarik shot me an even more quizzical look. Of course he did. He was a stripling warrior with stronger faith than I would probably ever have. But to him, I was a Lamanite spy who didn't pray. No wonder he looked confused.

"You see, I was in a tough spot and I prayed for help and . . . Ximon appeared." I continued. "And look," I pointed at the white angel shape on Ximon's chest. "He even has the markings of an angel on him."

"Angels don't have wings," Tarik muttered, though he didn't relax. Then he said, "What manner of *dog* is this?"

"A Great Dane." I relaxed a touch. At least Tarik was talking. Ximon leaned against me as if to protect me. "He really is harmless—except when someone tries to attack me. And he's not your dinner. He's a fighter." I patted the dog's head. "A warrior, so to speak."

"He is a wild beast." Tarik rubbed his arm. "And needs to be killed." He tightened his hold on the dagger in his hand.

"Look." I again put myself between Tarik and the dog. "He was protecting me. That's honorable, isn't it?"

Tarik stopped for a moment, giving me the perfect opportunity to keep talking. "Look, Ximon and I only have each other here." I stroked the dog behind the ears. His entire hindquarters wagged with his tail. "Don't take him away."

Tarik lowered the knife, staring at me. I couldn't tell what he was thinking, especially since I couldn't see his eyes in the dark, but he seemed to be thinking about everything I'd said.

It hit me that what I'd said was true. In this time period, it really was just me and Ximon. Maybe the dog was meant to be with me—my own personal guardian angel. So why had he run off when the tent flap had opened? The theory needed some work.

I thought about how the dog and I had come to this place together. I had a feeling we needed to go back together as well, which meant I had to keep him with me. I also realized that I would have to be obedient to Helaman's commands if I was ever going to see the stone again.

"I'll go peaceful-like to the stockade," I said, watching Tarik closely. "If you promise me I can keep my dog."

Tarik tilted his head as though weighing his options. He had to realize that he could kill the animal anytime he wanted but that my offer to go peacefully to the stockade and keep the dog away from him was a good deal.

He reluctantly nodded.

Then I realized my oversight and added, "And you'll tell Helaman everything that has happened."

Tarik chuckled as if I'd said something funny. And I realized that my request was impossible in his eyes. Of course Tarik would not tell Helaman I had nearly escaped from him. Nor would he tell Helaman I had gone peacefully to the stockade. He'd probably tell Helaman I was crazy and thought the animal was an angel. I'd only made things worse.

For a fleeting second, I was tempted to flip Tarik on his back again and leave as fast as I could, but as much as I hated to admit it, Tarik was key to my seeing Helaman—and the stone—again. What he decided to do next would be crucial to my survival and going home.

Like it or not, I needed him.

Sure, I could try to hide in the city, but it would be nearly impossible with Ximon by my side. I could try to hide in the wilderness. I could survive. I knew how to cook and defend myself, so no problem there. But when would I gain an opportunity to speak with Helaman again? He had the stone, my only ticket home. I knew I had to stay exactly where the prophet wanted. I would go to the stockade and hope that Tarik would arrange for me to speak with Helaman again. And that was all there was to it. But if I was ever going to see Helaman again, I needed Tarik's help. And that meant I would have to explain some things.

I had no idea if I could trust him; all I knew was that Helaman did. Helaman had gone to battle with him, had given him orders, and had trusted him to carry them out. If Helaman, a prophet of God, trusted this guy, and if Tarik truly was one of the stripling warriors, who had such tremendous faith, then I had to be able to trust him. But that didn't mean I had to like him. I would tell him only what I had to.

"Tarik," I said softly.

He gave me his full attention, looking at me warily.

"Look at what I have on." I pulled at the shoulders of my *gi.* "You must realize these are not the clothes of your enemy."

He said nothing. Crossing my fingers, I pressed on, "This is called a *gi.* And this belt," I said, as I pulled on it, "is a black belt. I'm a karate instructor. I teach people how to fight." As the words left my mouth, I realized that saying the word *fight* had probably been a mistake.

He stepped toward me as if I'd given him a challenge. Ximon growled. I blindly patted the dog's head, afraid to take my eyes off Tarik.

"Defensive fighting," I backpedaled. "I teach defensive fighting to those who need to protect themselves from harm. You've got to believe me. I mean, I've decked you twice." I waited for his reaction. He stood there like an immovable stone.

"Look," I tried to reason, "I'm not from this place. I just want to go home. If you tell Helaman what has happened and about the dog and stuff and if you ask him to talk with me . . ." I could tell by the *no-way-in-Hades* expression on his face that I was getting nowhere fast, so I pushed to the next level. ". . . I won't tell everyone I decked you. And you know I can prove it if they ask."

Now Tarik looked as though he'd like to growl and bare his teeth like Ximon had done. I hoped I hadn't bruised his ego too badly. A warrior's pride was his prize.

Tarik motioned for me to follow him. I had no other choice. If I wanted to go home to the people I loved, I had to follow.

We passed several campsites. No one was around. A calm blanketed the camp, tucking the occupants in. A hint of smoke, the tailings of extinguished campfires, filtered through the muggy, warm air.

I looked up. The stars above were so bright and near. The sky wasn't like ours at home. It was dark and clear, almost like in the planetarium, but much more so.

Oh, how I was homesick. I yearned to see Mom, to hear Gracie's voice, and even to see Colin's scruffy face.

Finally, we came to a large enclosure made of log poles stuck upright in the ground—a fence. Several guards carrying torches greeted us. One stepped forward.

"Tarik, you have brought us another?"

I looked closely at the guard who had spoken. He was an old, scrawny man whose pale skin sagged beneath his turkey throat. Raw-boned arms hung from his tattered tunic. He was toothless and so thin a slight breeze could topple him. He tried to heft the plank that barred the doors, but his chicken knees began to buckle, and his arms trembled. Tarik and the other guards jumped to his aid.

"I can do it," the old fellow barked. The others ignored him and hoisted up the plank, leaning it against the stockade wall.

"Ozi," Tarik said to the pouting, elderly man. "Helaman wants this one to have special care. Keep him isolated."

Ozi gummed his lips together as he nervously pointed to Ximon. "And the beast?"

"He comes with me." Tarik tried to grab Ximon's collar, but the dog quickly hunched down, growling and ready to attack. I should have known Tarik had no intention of leaving Ximon with me.

"I see." Ozi raised his spear. The weight of his weapon made him step back as he tried to gain his balance. Once he was solidly on two feet again, he brushed his long, thinning hair out of his eyes. Grasping his spear tightly and ready to attack, he said, "I can kill the wild boar if he bothers you."

The old man needed glasses. No way could he take on Ximon.

"It's a dog." I quickly stepped in front of the animal.

The old man lowered his spear, peering at the Great Dane I protected. Ozi stroked his sparse, long beard, twirling the ends around his gnarled finger. "His meat must be tough as a curelom's."

I remembered that word from the Book of Mormon and wondered what a curelom looked like.

Tarik nodded in agreement with the elderly man, then piped up. "Let him keep the animal. With the beast by his side, the other prisoners will leave him be." Tarik turned about and strode away, never looking back.

Since Tarik had tried to take Ximon with him, breaking our unspoken bargain, I didn't know whether he would keep to our deal or not. I clung to the hope that he would, since in the end he let me keep Ximon with me. My thoughts swung back and forth like a pendulum.

Ozi pushed and pushed on the door. It didn't budge. One of the other guards came to his aid, and it creaked open enough for Ximon and me to slip in. As I stepped aside to let Ozi follow, a guard grabbed me and clamped an iron collar around my neck.

"What the . . ." Panicked, I grabbed at the collar, digging my nails into my skin. The guard shoved me forward. I glanced back to see that another guard and Ozi, who carried a torch, were on my heels. They guided me to a pole planted vertically in the ground. A long chain dangled from it. The guard who put the band around my neck now attached the chain. The iron was heavy and pulled at the collar. Fear gurgled to my throat. Before I could say anything, the guards left, disappearing behind the stockade gate. The door closed and the plank slammed into place.

I gasped. My entire body began to shake. Darkness loomed everywhere I looked. I swallowed a lump that lodged in my throat and felt as small as a sparring glove. I backed up against the pole. Ximon whined and leaned against me. Even the dog sensed trouble in the shadows of this prison.

And I knew my every move was being watched.

CHAPTER 8

CRITICAL CIRCUMSTANCES

As I made my way to my father's tent, I could not help but think of the spy and the giant beast I had left behind in the stockade. The two were puzzling. I had never met anyone like the boy. Not only was his clothing strange, but his manner of speech was odd. He ran his words together, yet I understood his meaning. And he was small—puny as a field mouse. Perhaps the Lamanites left him behind on purpose because of his size.

But it had been a big mistake to overlook his ability to fight. The little mouse had been able to knock me down—not only once, but twice. And the second time I had been prepared for an attack. However, in my own defense, I was tired from battle. The spy had fresh energy. Still, the manner of his fighting and the smooth, thoughtful way of his actions were fascinating; it was as if he were casting a spell.

My thoughts turned to what the boy had said about prayer and how the animal had appeared to help him. Was it magic or a miracle? Did I believe the boy? I did not know. The dog did have a most unusual marking on his hide. I had never seen such an animal before.

I had heard rumors that the Lamanites practiced sorcery. Witchcraft. That could be the reason the boy had been able to flip me and why the dog had appeared to him. Yet, as I thought of the small one and how sincerely he had begged for the animal's life, I did not think such workings could be witchcraft. I had been around spell-casters before and had always felt the black darkness surrounding them. I felt no such sense of darkness. But there was something the boy was hiding. Of that I was certain.

I set my mind to learn more about him.

‡‡‡

In the darkness of the stockade, Ximon became restless, whining and nudging me with his nose. I wound my fingers around his collar. I had no intention of letting him slip away as he had when I'd opened the tent flap. But all of a sudden the dog ducked under my arm and twisted free of my grasp. He galloped off into the darkness, leaving me alone . . . again.

Some guardian angel.

I wanted to yell after him, but noise would only draw attention from the eyes I imagined were watching: prisoners who could see better in the dark than I could.

Left alone, I slid down the pole. A knot jabbed me, but I forced myself to keep my back against the rough wood. The pole was my only bearing in this sea of darkness. I wondered if the other prisoners were chained as well or if I was being staked out like meat. And where was that guard Helaman had asked to stay with me? As soon as I got the chance, I was going to tell Helaman how well his second in command followed his orders. *That is, if I live through the night,* I thought. I looked around me, seeing only inky blackness. A chill overcame me, and my teeth began to chatter. I had to be rational. Surely Tarik would not have left me in danger, or he would have to give an accounting to his captain. I needed to be calm and think. The best defense was a good offense. However, I had no idea who or what I was up against.

I considered my situation. It was the dead of night, and I had no idea who was lurking in the shadows. So what was my plan here? I remembered the ABCs of karate.

A: Avoid potentially hazardous situations.

Okay, so A was out. I was no longer being threatened with a knife at my throat or stomach, but now I was in a prison surrounded by bloodthirsty Lamanites or Ammoronites, whatever they were called, that I couldn't even see. Not a good situation for the girl from Salt Lake City. But I wasn't panicking yet.

B: Breath deeply, stay calm.

I took a deep breath through my nose and slowly let it out my mouth. A good breath of air usually helped clear the mind. It was too bad the surrounding air smelled of smoke, dirt, and tremendous body odor. I decided it could be worse, but at the moment I could not think how. To calm my nerves, I shook my hands and wiggled my stiff legs. That was all I could do as far as B went.

C: Communicate calmly and respectfully.

How could I communicate with people I couldn't see? How could I talk with people who had supported Ammoron? He was the evil brother of wicked King Amalickiah. Ammoron was seeking revenge for his brother's death, which meant his followers were probably bent on vengeance as well.

At least I didn't look like a Nephite. My Shoshone skin coloring might keep the other prisoners guessing as to which side I was on. But having dark skin had not helped the Ammonite warriors who stood by Helaman's side.

I stared into the darkness, straining to hear movement, or any sound for that matter. What I heard were distant snores. Now that was communication. Maybe all the prisoners were sleeping.

If I remembered my Book of Mormon stories correctly, most of the prisoners Helaman captured were sent to Zarahemla to help reinforce the city, so the prisoners sharing the stockade with me were probably the orneriest and meanest of the lot, since they would be difficult to take on such a long journey.

The thought was not comforting.

Odds were that most of the prisoners would probably just as soon chop me into pieces as look at me. I tried not to imagine watchful eyes. All I could do was ready myself for the attack.

Suddenly, something came at me in the darkness, scaring the life right out of me. I tried to leap to my feet, but I became caught up in the chain. I choked, coughing, trying desperately to get to my feet. Then I heard a whine.

Ximon!

As I stared in the direction I thought the whine had come from, I could make out his Great Dane form. "Where did you go?" I spat out a heated whisper as I rubbed my throat and crumbled back to the ground. The dog ignored my anger and dropped something beside me. I reached out to feel fur.

I stifled a scream that chased up my sore throat while I kicked the dead rodent away. Ximon went after it, like we were playing a game.

He deposited the rat at my feet again. The dog probably thought he'd brought me something to eat. I kicked the lifeless varmint again. Dead or alive, I hated rats.

Ximon started after the rat, but I latched onto his collar with both hands and dug my feet into the ground, dragging my rear in the dirt. The dog was as strong as a bear. He managed to get as far as the chain would allow. The iron band jerked against my windpipe. I gagged and coughed. Ximon immediately stopped. I let go of him and grabbed at the iron collar around my neck, gasping for air. I felt as though I'd been kicked in the larynx. It was a good thing I was sitting on the ground or I would have fallen. The dog whined and licked my face.

"It was very thoughtful . . . of you . . . to bring me dinner," I eked out. I crawled back to the pole. The Great Dane sat beside me as if to say he was sorry. Leaning my head to his, I muttered, "We need to have an understanding here, though. I don't eat rats."

Ximon's tongue hung from his mouth as he panted. His hot doggy breath fanned my face, and I pinched my nose. The beast was clueless, but that was okay. He was here with me. "It's the thought that counts." I patted him.

Ximon stretched out beside me, ready to sleep. Obviously, his feelings were not hurt by my rejection of his good deed.

Now he was going to sleep? I thought dogs were always on the alert and certainly a guardian angel should be. Just my luck; I was stuck with one who closed his eyes.

I curled my knees up to my chin and leaned my forehead against them. Bone-weary tiredness blanketed me. Despite my fears, sleep pulled at my eyelids.

And then I thought of my mother.

What was happening at the hospital? Was she all right? I thought of her lying in the hospital bed, looking so fragile, so vulnerable, and so very afraid. I clung to what I knew with certainty about my mom: she was a fighter. Even in bed, she was fighting for Gracie . . . and me.

Gracie! I knew she would be well looked after at Bishop Staker's, but I still worried. She'd be scared and wondering where Mom was, where I was. We'd never been apart for long. In some of the time-travel stories I had read, the person returned home to the same instant they had left. But could I count on that happening here? How did it really work? I hoped in my case it would work the same way.

But if it didn't . . .

I wondered if the bishop would tell Gracie about Mom's cancer. Surely he wouldn't. Surely he'd leave such news to Mom or even me.

But if I wasn't there . . .

I felt a lump form in my throat as I thought about events continuing on without me. What was going on back home? Oh, how I hoped the books were right. If I returned at the exact time I'd left there would be nothing to worry about. But if not . . . I knew I had to consider this possibility. I took some comfort in the fact that it was night and that it would be unlikely for anyone to have missed me yet. Gracie would be safe at the bishop's. I'd taught my karate classes already, so no problem there. Mom didn't know I'd returned to the hospital, so she wouldn't miss me yet.

Then I thought of my father. Our last conversation had ended with my trying to take him down. He'd bested me, though, and I had ended up on the ground. I had been in a daze, but I remembered what he'd said as he'd stood over me.

"Who do you suppose taught your mother karate?" His sharp words had surprised me. Mom had never mentioned that my father knew karate. Then I thought of his final words. "Ten years ago, your mother told me Gracie had died because of my drunkenness. That's why I left." With those words he'd turned and headed for his car. And as I sat a world away in a prison in Book of Mormon times, I wondered if he had been telling me the truth—had Mom neglected to tell me such important details? Had she lied to me?

No! Mom always told the truth. I had always been able to count on her. However, my father—a man who had left his family—was far from trustworthy. And why, if he loved me the way he said he did, hadn't he stayed in touch with me all those years? He lived in the same city! Who was telling the truth? The thoughts were too confusing. And I could do nothing to unravel the mystery here. I looked around.

Log walls as high as trees.

Prison doors timber-thick.

Iron chains heavy and condemning.

Despite my urgent need to escape and go home, there was nothing I could do. I was stuck until Helaman sent for me. All I *could do* was stay put.

✣✣✣

The sun was rising as I awoke with a start. I reached for Ximon. He lay close by. My neck was stiff and sore beneath the iron collar. I reached up and rubbed my fingers beneath the band. My skin was raw from the sharp edge. Who would have thought they had iron in this era anyway? Then I remembered that Nephi had taught his people to work in all manner of wood and iron. The skill must have been passed down through the generations.

Turning my attention to my surroundings, I looked around. Through the gauzy haze of dawn, I could see more clearly. The stockade was like a giant corral, barren of plants and buildings. Less than thirty feet away, dozens of tall poles were staked into the ground. Men were chained to them, like I was. Some of the prisoners leaned against their poles, some lay on the dirt. Most were still asleep. They were all filthy from war, covered with dried blood and mud.

As my eyes scanned the prisoners, my eyes fell on one in particular. Not more than twenty feet away from me stood a man that made my stomach drop to my toes. He looked like a sumo wrestler; he probably ate small girls like me as an appetizer. A few others stood behind him. It seemed he had a crew backing him up.

I studied the man. He, too, had an iron collar around his neck. Red paint covered one side of his platter-shaped face; his nose was flat against his cheeks. His hair was pulled tight into a ponytail. Bright blue and red feathers were braided in his hair. More red paint crisscrossed his massive chest. His loincloth hung around his enormous legs.

Before me was a Lamanite soldier . . . correction, Lamanite *soldiers;* all the prisoners leered in my direction.

One had long Dracula teeth; another had only one eye and a scar creasing his pie-shaped face. They were all painted and dressed similarly to Sumo guy and they didn't look happy to see me.

Hulks like Sumo were my worst nightmare. I could take on someone who was built like Colin or Tarik; they didn't intimidate me in the least, but big guys who look like they used nine-inch nails to pick their teeth . . . well, they made my spine buckle.

The only person who'd ever beaten me at a karate meet was a man who looked like Sumo. And he'd not only beat me, he'd broken my arm and bitten off a chunk of my courage in the process.

I couldn't take the stares any longer. "Hi there." I gulped, willing myself to stand. The iron band around my neck dug into my flesh. I ignored it, afraid that if I showed pain it would draw the enemy to look at my throat, which could very well be bleeding and might make the sharks start circling.

Sumo gave me the evil eye, reminding me of some the professional wrestlers I'd seen on TV: brawny men who looked like steam should billow from their noses.

"I'm only passing through." I tried to sound reassuring but only managed a squeak. "Just visiting, so to speak. Don't mind me."

Sumo lunged in my direction, but was jerked back by the thick chain attached to his collar and anchored to the pole. He yanked on the chain as if to break it, but the iron held firm. I knew if it hadn't been for the chain, I would have been roadkill.

Ximon scrambled to his feet, ready to protect me. When Sumo saw how big the dog was, he scowled and backed off, joining the other soldiers who still looked as though they'd love to spill my blood.

"Good dog." I nervously stroked Ximon's back, never taking my eyes off the men. Even though they were chained, I knew I had to watch them all the time if I planned on getting out alive. And it didn't help that I, too, was chained to a pole of my own. If they somehow got loose . . . all I could do would be to stand there like bait. I wanted to turn my back on them, but knew it wasn't a good idea. Mom had told me to always keep the enemy in my sights.

The gate swung open. In stepped Mariah and the guard, Ozi. Behind them were the other guards. In their arms were baskets of bread and gourds of water.

"He still lives—and the boar is still by his side." Ozi's voice sounded a bit defensive, as if he'd been scolded.

Mariah shook her head as she walked away from the elderly man who seemed all too happy to go with the other guards and feed the prisoners their morning meal.

Mariah walked cautiously to me, leery of Ximon. As she drew near, she said, "This animal is not a boar."

She held out her hand, an offering of peace to the dog. Ximon sniffed and licked her fingers. Mariah let out a relieved sigh, then said, "One of the guards should have stayed with you last night. I suppose it was Tarik's fault they did not." She gazed at me to confirm her suspicion. I returned her stare, not saying a word. It was not in my best interest to get Tarik in trouble. Like it or not, I needed his help.

Mariah shrugged and asked, "Are you hungry?" She handed me what appeared to be a corn muffin.

"Thanks." I took it and quickly chowed down. I hadn't eaten in a while, not since breakfast before Mom's operation. And with my worry for Mom, I'd had a hard time forcing down the toast. The corn muffin Mariah had given me was heavy but tasty. "This is good."

I glanced over at the group of prisoners, who were circling Ozi like bees over honey. Curiously, the prisoners did not appear to be hungry; they seemed to be joking with the old man. Mariah followed my gaze.

"Ozi has a way with the prisoners." Mariah turned her back to them and spied my throat. She yelled, "Ozi!"

The elderly man came over quickly, eager to see what her urgent cry was for.

Mariah pointed at my throat for him to see.

Ozi's eyes grew wide as he saw where the band had rubbed my skin raw.

"Unchain him so I can put something on the wound." Mariah looked straight at Ozi, as if daring him to question her authority.

Ozi grimaced and unlocked the band. It fell with a thud to the ground. His task accomplished, Ozi went back to the other guards and prisoners. I breathed more freely and rubbed my throat, feeling puckered skin where the rough edges of band had been.

Mariah took a cloth rag from her basket. "I do not have ointment with me, but this will help protect you from more injury when they refasten the collar." She gently tied the rag around my neck.

"I must go." She patted my shoulder. "But I shall return later with the medicine."

"Don't leave me." I knew I sounded pathetic, but I didn't care.

"I can do nothing." She looked down and gathered her shawl about her.

"Please." I took hold of her arm.

Mariah looked down at the hand that held her, then up at my face and hair. "In the morning light, you are not so warriorlike."

She must have noticed that I was small boned, kind of short, and well . . . feminine. At least *someone* noticed. Still, I nervously rounded my shoulders, wanting to keep my gender a secret awhile longer just in case I couldn't talk my way out of here. If the other prisoners suspected I was a girl, I'd be in even deeper trouble.

"Mariah, are you ready to leave?" Ozi had joined us and picked up my collar, preparing to lock my chains in place.

Out of the corner of my eye, I caught a sudden movement. Sumo!

He was headed right for us. Around his neck was the iron collar, but the chain dangled in his hand. And right behind him were Dracula and Scarface.

My heart drummed against my chest. A sheet of fear folded over me. I quickly scanned my surroundings, searching for the other guards. They were too far away to be of help.

There was no choice. They were too close now. Shoving my fear aside, I prepared to meet the attackers head on.

CHAPTER 9
NEW REALIZATION

As I walked with the troops that had been assigned to me, I thought of Father Helaman and the meeting I had left only moments ago. Though I knew Helaman was very busy, he had seemed unusually distracted. I believed his thoughts were with the spy we had captured. I had hoped Father would share his burden and tell me of his and the boy's conversation. He had never hesitated in taking me into his confidence.

But he did now.

And for some reason he had given me a most distasteful assignment. Sometimes doing what Father asked me to do was hard. I tried to reason why I, instead of someone else, had been assigned a mundane task like this. I was Father's second in command. I was supposed to be his right hand. I had twenty commanders under me. And those commanders led one hundred troops.

Had I done something wrong in battle?

Was I being punished?

Or did this have something to do with the boy?

A sudden realization dawned on me. I knew why I had been given this task. It was because the spy had beaten me. Father now thought of me as weak. My warrior status had been undermined by the mouse.

‡‡‡

Dracula-teeth knocked Ozi off his feet as he grabbed Mariah from behind. She screamed, kicked, and flailed about. The brute only laughed. I was powerless to help her; Sumo and Scarface were in my way.

As Scarface grabbed for me, Ximon leaped to the attack, biting the man's arm. Bright red liquid spurted into the air. Scarface shook off the dog and then kicked Ximon in the ribs.

The Great Dane yelped and swung back around to resume his attack. But the man had picked up a large rock and was ready. As Ximon rushed him, Scarface clobbered the dog over the head. Ximon fell to the ground and didn't move.

I was momentarily frozen in place as I looked at the still form on the ground, but in my peripheral vision I could see that Dracula had grabbed Mariah by the neck and was choking her. There was no way she'd be able to escape.

As I started toward her, I saw Sumo heading right for me, swinging his heavy chain. I ducked under his blow and charged Dracula. Without thinking, I gave him a tornado kick to the head. He went down heavy, like a sack of rocks. Mariah looked at me, astonished. I spun back around. Sumo was practically breathing down my *gi*. Glancing about, I saw Ozi swaying as he tried to stand, but he toppled over, the spear rolling just out of his grasp.

I needed that weapon. Dodging Sumo, I lunged for Ozi. As the old man tried once again to rise, Scarface leaped toward Ozi. In one mighty swipe, he picked up the elderly guard and held him high above his head, ready to slam Ozi to the ground. Such a blow would surely kill someone so old. I had to do something.

Grabbing the discarded spear, I rammed the blunt end into the back of Scarface's head. As Scarface crumpled to the ground, Ozi fell on top of him.

I quickly turned to face Sumo. He whirled the chain above his head, coming right at me. As he lunged, I raised the spear. Metal clashed against wood. The spear was ripped from my hold. Sumo then tossed the chain aside as if he would relish tearing me apart with his bare hands.

Fresh panic charged through my veins. I had to think, stay calm. The giant was big, fat—and slow. I was short and skinny, but I was much faster. He leaped toward me. I whirled around and kicked his head with my heel. The blow knocked him back only a little ways.

A wicked smile creased his huge face as he gained his wits and tore after me. As he charged, I jumped to the side and kicked the back of his knee. He lost his footing only for a moment. I intended to do a spinning sweep with my leg to complete the job and totally knock him down, but I was off balance and landed hard on my back.

That's when things went bad.

Sumo straddled me, clamping his thick beefy hands about my neck. I was suffocating. I clawed at his iron-like fingers and beat against his bulging muscles. He didn't flinch. Glancing up at his twisted face, I saw hatred in his eyes. A hatred I'd never experienced before in my life. Was this how I would die, at the hands of a Lamanite?

"Release him!" Someone barked a command. Through half-closed eyes I could see that beyond Sumo's shoulder, someone was standing over the hulk. It was Tarik, his dagger pressed at the man's throat.

Sumo didn't let up. Tarik grabbed Sumo's ponytail and pressed the blade against the fat man's thick jugular. The Lamanite finally, reluctantly, released me.

I grabbed at my throat and took giant gulps of air as I scrambled out from beneath his massive form. The bandage that Mariah had put on me before the attack was gone. It must have been ripped off in the fight. Two other soldiers stood by Tarik's side. He quickly assessed me, as if to determine whether the spy he was in charge of had been damaged.

I took this opportunity to scrutinize Tarik more closely. A band of red leather was tied around his forehead to hold back his thick, long black hair. The gash I'd noticed the night before when I'd first seen him in the lamp light had been cleaned, though not bandaged. The blood that had been smeared across his chest was gone. I couldn't help but notice he had nice-looking muscles. About his midriff was a wide, sheepskin waistband. Strapped to the band was the sheath for his dagger. Tarik still wore the wrist guard Ximon had grabbed onto the night before, which was now scraped and dinged. He wore leather-type sandals made of deer hide, but not like the ones worn by Native Americans of the West. These were tied tight to his legs and feet with thin leather straps. In the daylight, I realized with a bit of a shock that he was probably the most handsome man I'd ever seen. If I hadn't just been nearly strangled by a Lamanite, I would have smacked myself on the forehead. The guy thought I was a *boy* for crying out loud. And I couldn't very well develop a crush on someone who had tried to kill me the night before. *Twice!*

I quickly pushed the thoughts out of my head and nodded at Tarik, hoping he knew that I appreciated the rescue. He nodded back and went to join his men as they returned the prisoners to their chains.

"Are you all right?" Mariah sat beside me, feeling my forehead and checking to see if I was bleeding. Then she checked my neck.

"I'm okay." I rubbed my throbbing throat. "How's Ozi?"

The old man plopped down beside me, as if on cue. "I have never seen a fighter such as you." He patted my back and gummed his lips together. "You have saved my life. Your shadow I shall be for the rest of your days."

Was he serious? The earnest gleam in his old, bloodshot eyes told me he was dead serious. I was at a loss for words; I couldn't deal with him at the moment, though. Turning away, I looked for Ximon.

The Great Dane lay only a few feet away. I crawled past Ozi and over to my faithful companion.

"Ximon," I whispered. As I stroked his head I found a lump. "Oh, Ximon." I quickly checked for other injuries. No other wounds, but the dog didn't move.

"The animal is dead." Mariah had risen to her feet and stood over us.

"No!" Panic surged through me. Ximon had to live. He needed to go back home with me. We were in this together. I frantically felt his chest, searching for a heartbeat.

Beneath my hand I felt a faint thump. "He's still alive—feel!" I grabbed Mariah's arm and pulled her down.

She felt the dog's chest for a moment and then slowly said, "Maybe." A lock of curly brown hair escaped the threadbare scarf she had tied over her head.

"There's no maybe about it," I said firmly. "He's going to live." Then I remembered something. "I heard you say you know how to heal using plants."

"Never have I healed an animal," she defended, tucking her hair back into her scarf.

"Well, you can try, can't you?" She looked at me, studying me, and in that moment, I knew she understood how much I loved this animal.

"We must take him to the medicine tent." Mariah rose. "Ozi, come, help us with the . . ." She looked at me. "What manner of animal is this that you are desperate to save?"

The old man jumped into action before Mariah had finished talking and tried to heft the dog by himself; however, Ximon was too much for him to handle, so he stood there hoisting the dog's hindquarters.

"He's a *dog*," I answered as I lifted Ximon's front half into my arms. Mariah seemed surprised by my answer. I continued. "Great Dane to be exact. People think of Great Danes as the king of dogs where I come from. And the king of dogs is never eaten." I wanted to put a quick stop to people gawking at Ximon as if he were a porterhouse steak.

"Be calm." Mariah patted my shoulder. "I was only admiring the beast."

At that moment, Tarik walked up beside her. "Is there trouble here?" Tarik's men were close behind. They had safely chained up all the prisoners.

"Ah . . ." Mariah looked at me. "What is your name, boy?"

I really wanted to tell her I wasn't a boy, but the words wouldn't come. The misunderstanding about my gender had gone on too long. Explaining would only make me look like a liar and weaken her opinion of me. I had to play this out. Adjusting the weight of the animal I held in my arms, I answered, "Sydney Morgan, but you can call me Syd."

Mariah nodded and turned to Tarik. "Syd wants me to mend his . . . dog."

Tarik addressed Mariah."You should probably see to the boy as well." Tarik touched my throat, examining my neck. It made me nervous to have him so near, touching my skin. I wanted to push him away, but my arms were full of Ximon.

And then Tarik looked right at me. His eyes were an incredible royal blue and framed with thick, dark lashes.

Blue eyes. The Ammonites were of Lamanite heritage; everyone else I had seen had brown eyes. For a brief second, I thought I saw a look of concern, of caring, in those eyes, but all too soon Tarik's gaze turned businesslike. "Helaman would not want our spy to be hurt." He turned to walk away.

"Spy?" Mariah stopped him. "This boy is no spy. You should have seen the way he fought."

"I have never seen technique like unto his." Ozi struggled to hold on to Ximon's back end. "The boy saved my life."

"He saved mine as well," Mariah added. "You and your brothers could learn from him, Tarik. I saw him best you last night. Syd will stay with me. Tell Helaman what has happened." Mariah gathered up her empty food baskets. Then, looking at Ozi and me awkwardly holding Ximon, she added, "And find a blanket to carry the beast."

A couple of guards scrambled away and returned with a blanket. They must have taken it from a prisoner, because it was coated with dirt. They shook it off before putting it on the ground.

Ozi and I laid Ximon on the blanket. Holding onto the four corners, the guards easily lifted the dog.

I glanced at Tarik as I walked past him, hoping to see some sign of acceptance. I thought I saw a glimmer of admiration, but it was quickly replaced with a blank stare. I wondered what Tarik must think of me. I hadn't considered his point of view much; I was an alien who had crashed into his world, upset his cart. Maybe he was thinking he should have let Sumo kill me. But I couldn't quite believe this. I didn't feel the hate I had sensed in him last night. Today there was a subtle difference in the way he looked at me. Could it be respect? In a matter of minutes, a great deal had happened; perhaps now he thought of me as a warrior-brother of sorts. And maybe not. Either way, it was time to quit thinking about him.

My situation in this world was beginning to look more positive. I was leaving the stockade, and I had gained the admiration of both Ozi and Mariah. Heck, Ozi had promised to be my shadow for the rest of my days—which really gave me no comfort—and with Mariah's help, perhaps Ximon would be healed. Yes, things were looking up.

As we passed through the prison gates, I glanced across the valley and saw an army of soldiers marching away. As I stared at them, however, I realized they weren't just soldiers. They were stripling warriors!

At their head, Helaman rode on a white stallion. The warriors were leaving Judea. With a sinking feeling, I realized that with Helaman gone, my chances of returning home went down drastically; this meant more delay in helping my mother, in finding out the truth about my father. But mostly it meant more time away from the people I loved.

Helaman couldn't leave now.

"Mariah?" I pointed in their direction.

Upon seeing the warriors, she whirled around to Tarik. "He is leaving now?" Mariah was as surprised as I had been. "Without the prisoners? Without more troops?"

Tarik nodded. "Our Lamanite brethren have fled. We must strike fast to save Antiparah. Most of my brothers' wounds were not as serious as we first thought. They go to follow and support our leader."

Starting to panic, I wondered whether Helaman had taken my stone with him. I knew chances were slim that he'd left it behind. And the only person who would know for certain would be Tarik. Yet I didn't think it was a good idea to ask him outright. Instead, I asked, "Why didn't you go with him?"

Tarik clenched his teeth, as if I'd reminded him of something distasteful. Staring at me with those blue eyes that now held no admiration, no emotion at all really, he said, "Do you not think my first loyalty is to my father? Do you not think that I wanted to go with him above everything else?"

I was a little taken aback. I hadn't meant to offend him. I needed the stone. But I wasn't going to let him intimidate me. I did not turn away from his stare.

"I am here because Helaman ordered me to look after *you,*" he spat out accusingly.

Now I understood why he was looking at me with lifeless eyes. No wonder the little admiration I'd seen had vanished as my words tormented a sore spot. Tarik was a stripling warrior, not a babysitter, but he was stuck with me. At that moment all I wanted to do was tap some ruby slippers together and go home.

Instead, I walked on, feeling numb and hopeless.

CHAPTER 10
Fellow Soldiers

As we walked to Mariah's medicine tent, I began to feel less optimistic about things. I looked at the still form in the blanket and felt fear knot my stomach as I wondered if Ximon would die. I walked close to the dog, hoping he would sense my presence and gain strength from knowing I was near.

Glancing back at the other soldiers who dutifully followed, I noticed that Tarik's little band of brothers didn't exactly look friendly. Except for Ozi, none smiled, but marched in a tense, solemn rank, as though waiting for the mere flick of Tarik's wrist to spur them to action. That was okay. They'd certainly come to my rescue in the stockade, and for that I could endure the blank stares.

We finally came to the tent. Mariah ushered in the soldiers who were carrying Ximon. Tarik, Ozi, and I followed. She quickly laid out a mat for the animal.

"I need a fire," she told Tarik, who, along with the other soldiers, immediately left the tent.

I knelt beside the Great Dane. His black coat, splotched with various sizes and shapes of white dots, was warm to my touch. I ran my palm over the white angel shape across his hide, wishing with all my heart I had the power to heal him. "You're going to be all right, boy." Resting my hand on his ribs, I felt him take small breaths. In a peculiar way, he had been an answer to my prayer; now I prayed for him.

Mariah searched through several baskets, picking up different herbs and putting them into a pot. As soon as she'd gathered everything she wanted, she slipped outside the tent.

Now only Ozi, the dog, and I were left. I looked at the elderly man who knelt on the other side of Ximon. Ozi's kind eyes crinkled with a slight smile. In his gaze was heartfelt appreciation, which made me mighty uncomfortable. Maybe I really had saved his life and maybe I hadn't, but he was acting as if I'd saved the world.

"You are no spy." As his head shook, his thin gray hair tousled about. "But you are not one of us, either." He looked down on Ximon. "So, you are a Great Dane." He stroked the dog. The old man's scarred and gnarled hand was gentle as he caressed Ximon. "The beast will be fine."

"I hope so." I smiled at the old man who had pledged his life to my safety. He was an odd little fellow—and a major complication if he really was committed to being my shadow the rest of my days. I suppressed a small smile as I wondered if he would have made the pledge so readily if he knew he'd have to follow me through time.

I decided we needed to set things straight. "Ozi," I said. At the mention of his name, he looked up. I didn't know exactly what to say, but I plunged ahead anyway. "I didn't save your life. You would have fought him off."

"Nah." He gummed his lips together.

"You've fought in many wars, haven't you?" I waited for his reply.

"I have seen many." He nodded.

"So in battle your fellow soldiers watched your back; and they didn't expect you to be their constant companion the rest of your life. Besides, you know it was just luck I happened to deck the man who had you." I hoped he would agree.

"Not luck." His gaze grew serious. "I never have seen such fighting."

He'd said that before, just after the fight. I knew that karate was an ancient martial art and that surely the Japanese were practicing it during this time in history, but it was unlikely that these two cultures had crossed paths. Of course, Ozi had never seen the sparring and fighting I had used to protect us.

"Do you want me to teach you?" Maybe this would encourage him to give up the notion of following me.

"I am too old to teach." His stared off as if remembering his younger days. Then he looked at me and firmly stated, "I shall be eternally in your debt."

It seemed that reasoning with him was not going to work. I didn't want to be rude, but I needed him to understand that I couldn't have him following me everywhere. I thought of something. "You know, Ozi, the troops depend on you, too."

"They are young and have no need for an old man." Then he looked at me with a sudden expression of understanding. "I shall not be a pest to you but merely a loyal servant." He staggered to his feet. "I must speak with Tarik and say good-bye to the stockade guards." He nodded and left. As I watched him go, I sighed. I'd gained a friend for life . . . or at least for my Book of Mormon life.

Mariah came back into the tent empty-handed. "How is the animal?"

"About the same." I studied Ximon. His breathing was still shallow, and he hadn't moved.

"I am steeping a tonic for him, though I am not certain it will work. Perhaps the Almighty will smile down on us and be merciful to the beast." She gave me a comforting smile, then looked at my throat. Her brows bunched together. "I was going to put ointment on you, but I think something else will work better." Mariah went to the back of the medicine tent. I couldn't tell what she was doing, but when she returned she held a leaf of what appeared to be part of an aloe vera plant. She scored the leaf with her fingernail then rubbed the clear, slimy insides on my throat. "This will heal your skin."

"Thank you," I said. I remembered the time I had burned my finger and Mom had put aloe vera on my reddened skin; the next day there had been no evidence of a burn. The aloe vera would probably heal the skin on my throat in the same way.

Mariah smiled, rubbed my arm, and left.

For a moment, I had Ximon to myself. I leaned down to his ear. "Stay with me. Please." I inhaled his dog scent and felt his shallow breathing fan my cheek. I stroked the top of his head as I waited for Mariah to return.

The tent flap opened. I straightened up and saw Tarik holding the flap. He stood just inside the door.

With rags protecting her hands, Mariah entered the tent after Tarik, carrying a pan of steaming liquid. She settled down beside me, setting the pan in front of Ximon's nose. The vapors smelled of sage and allspice, though I knew the brew was probably not made up of those herbs.

"This should bring him around," she said.

"Thank you," I replied.

"After what you have done for me, I am honored to help your Large Dane." Maria pointed at Ximon.

I smiled at her reference to my dog. Well, he was large.

"When he awakens, make him drink the brew. It will give him strength." She patted my shoulder. "Now, forgive me; there are others I must tend to. Many of Antipus's men were badly hurt in battle, and some of Helaman's boys, who were not well enough to leave with him this morning, need more care."

"Of course." I was embarrassed that I had taken up so much of her time and had kept her so long. "Please go. If there's something I can help you with . . ."

"No. Stay here." Mariah gathered a few more herbs and hurried out. I expected Tarik to follow her. He didn't.

"I'm sure you have important things to do as well. I promise to stay here with my dog," I told him.

"I know you will," he said. Then he sat on a crate by the door and folded his arms. He had no intention of leaving.

I suddenly felt annoyed. He had made it clear that he wasn't very happy about being left behind to stay with me—so if he knew I wouldn't leave, why didn't he go do something else? He sat on the crate, looking at me like I was a bug in a bottle.

"Look, Tarzan . . ." I'd suddenly had it with him, good-looking or otherwise. Right now, all I cared about was Ximon.

"My name is Tarik." A scowl crossed his face. "Who is this Tarzan?"

"Someone who would never let me get the drop on him." The instant I said the words, I regretted them. I knew I'd hit Tarik where it hurt most.

His scowl deepened. He didn't reply—just looked at me. I could tell I had burrowed under his skin like a thorn.

Finally he said, "The more you speak, the more you condemn yourself as a spy." He shifted to the edge of the crate.

Tarik waited for me to reply. No doubt he was planning a good comeback. I bit my tongue so I wouldn't say something I'd later regret. It was time to do some backpedaling here. "You must believe me when I say I'm not your enemy."

He just stared at me. I thought about what I had just said. Why should he believe me? I'd never given him a reason to. Since the moment we met we had fought. Our relationship was more than a little strained.

Turning away from Tarik, I concentrated on Ximon. The dog still hadn't moved. Seeing the animal lying there as if he were dying made me think of Mom.

By now she would believe I was at school or with Gracie. What would she do when people told her I was missing? She'd be panicked; what if it made her cancer spread more quickly? I needed to get back to her. And that meant I needed the stone.

I glanced at Tarik. His expression had not changed. What was the matter with me? Here I was arguing with him and trying to belittle him when all along I needed his help.

Clearing my throat, I said, "Tarik, did you meet with Helaman this morning before he left?"

He didn't answer; he merely gave me a *now what?* stare.

"You probably did, since he gave you orders to keep an eye on me and everything. Did you happen to notice if he carried a strange-looking pack with him?"

A look of *what-are-you-up-to* shone in his eyes.

"The pack is mine; and if I had it, I'd leave here and never bother you again. I promise. Cross my heart—" I motioned an *X* over my chest "—and hope to die." I put my hand up in a pledge. A flicker of a smile pulled at his lips. The ice was beginning to break. "Did he take the pack with him?"

Nothing.

The flicker of a smile went out.

"See, if you were to bring the pack to me, my dog and I could sneak off. You wouldn't have to tell Helaman that I beat you twice last night. You know Mariah and Ozi will bring up the fight at the stockade when he returns." I really didn't mean to rub this in, but my mother needed me. If I was ever going to get back to her, I needed that stone. And I'd do anything to get it.

Tarik stood. Looking down at me, he said, "I told Helaman what you wanted me to do last night. He made no reply. And after seeing you fight this morning in the stockade, I do not wish for you to leave. What Mariah has said is true. My brothers and I could learn much from your way of fighting. I will do everything in my power to keep you here."

CHAPTER 11

WITH MUCH CONVICTION

"What?" The spy named Syd leaped to his feet. "I can't—"

"If you truly are not a spy, as you say," I said, cutting off his objection, "you will not refuse to help us." He looked about to continue his protest, but after a few moments, he sat back down beside the beast.

We did not speak further; I sat in silence watching Syd tend to his beast. I could learn to tolerate his presence, especially if he did not speak, and especially if he would teach me and my brothers how to fight like he had. What a force we would make if we knew how to spin as he and kick so high. Where had the little fellow learned such a skill? Deep down, I admired him, but I did not want him to know it. Syd had a strange way about him, and his words were always biting. Before this morning, I had thought looking after him menial work, but if my brothers and I could learn his way of fighting, my trouble would be worthwhile.

I wondered if Father Helaman and the troops had reached Antiparah yet. I prayed the fighting would not be fierce and that none of my brothers would be killed. I had wanted very much to go, but after what I'd witnessed this morning, I understood that my otherwise distasteful assignment was of great value. Father would be pleased to know our spy could serve a purpose.

My attention was drawn away from my thoughts as I saw the animal's paw move out of the corner of my eye. And then the dog, who was as big as a burro, opened his eyes.

"Hey, boy!" Syd stroked the animal's head. "How's the noggin?" He gently patted between the dog's white-spotted ears. I was a bit taken aback. The boy's mannerisms were almost womanly. I needed Syd to teach my commanders his way of fighting—and to teach them, he would need to earn their respect. If they saw him nursing this beast in such tender ways, they would never listen. I had to warn Syd about his mannerisms. The troops could never see this side of him.

"Make him drink Mariah's medicine." I left my perch and stood over Syd.

Syd tilted the pan toward the dog. The beast pulled back and looked up at him, not wanting anything to do with Mariah's brew.

"Come on." Syd coaxed and pushed the pan closer to the dog. "You missed lunch, and it's close to suppertime. You have to be hungry. It's not that bad."

He cooed to the dog like my mother did to me and my little brother when we were ill. "Stop fussing with the animal. How do you know it shall not sicken him?" I said under my breath.

Syd glared at me. "You're not helping."

The dog attempted to get up but fell back.

"Oh, dear." Syd gave the dog a hug. A hug! For a dog? There was much work to be done with this boy.

Syd tried again to make the beast drink. "You really need to have some of this." He scooped liquid into the cup of his hand and poured it over the animal's black lips. The dog licked away the moisture. Syd dripped more on his lips. The dog licked again. He kept this up until the beast closed its eyes and fell back to sleep.

"I don't think he should sleep, especially if he has a concussion." Syd stroked beneath the dog's chin, trying to keep him awake. My eyes were drawn to the marking on the animal's chest, the one Syd claimed looked like an angel. Certainly this dog did not have magical powers or he would not be lying here, near death. Yet, I had to agree, he was different. I looked at the boy. They were a pair of misfits that had found one another.

Syd continued to stroke the dog's head. I rolled my eyes. My patience spent, I grabbed the boy's arm and pulled him to his feet. He needed to act like a warrior, not a nursemaid. "The dog should rest after drinking Mariah's treatment."

"Let go of me! Are you insane?" Syd's large brown eyes lit with anger.

"Rest will allow Mariah's tonic to work on the animal." Why should I explain this? I was becoming soft, watching his caring ways. "You must come with me."

"Why?" Syd pulled back.

"Because I have much to do, and I need you to stay within my sight."

Syd glanced back at the dog. Out of curiosity, I did as well. The animal's breathing had improved. Still Syd seemed reluctant to leave and tried to pull away.

I roughly guided him toward the door. Trying not to give him a chance to balk again, I pushed him out of the tent.

"Who do you think you are, pushing me around? Have you forgotten what happens when you do that?" Anger claimed Syd's face, wrinkling his forehead. He obviously did not care for being manhandled, but I did not care for his girlish manner.

"Helaman ordered me to look after you." I took hold of his arm. "I have not forgotten your ability to fight, but I also know that your desire to be accepted by Helaman is stronger than your desire to stay here with your . . . dog, so you must do what I say."

Syd looked tempted to argue, but then he turned his head toward the sound of footfalls approaching. looking up, I saw Ozi walking as fast as his wobbly legs could carry him. His thin hair and beard wafted at the sides of his wrinkled face.

"Commander!" he said, out of breath as he came to stand in front of me. He gave me a respectful nod. "Have I arrived on time?"

"Yes." I nodded back and told him, "Stay with the animal until we return." Then I began to walk away, thinking Syd would follow.

He did not.

It appeared that Syd had no intention of following. I had hoped he would accept leaving his precious dog with Ozi.

"I shall take good care of the boar . . . dog." The old man stroked his long, thin beard, nodding at Syd. In turn, Syd patted Ozi's drooping shoulder. The boy showed a startling amount of tenderness to the older man. This contrasted sharply with the way he argued with me over everything. Syd turned and walked toward me.

I shifted my gaze to the campfire, where my little band of troops sat. Syd stood beside me, waiting. After a moment of silence, I said,

"After Ozi left you in the tent this morning, he came to me and asked to be assigned as your personal guard." I faced Syd, wanting him to understand that this was an honor.

I continued. "Ozi deserves respect. But as you could see for yourself—with the prisoners stealing his keys—he is not as quick as he once was. I told him to tell the stockade guards he had been reassigned, and I also gave him permission to be your aide from now on."

"Good. I like Ozi." Syd shot me a defiant look as though to say, "in comparison to you."

I showed no reaction.

"So, where are we off to?" Syd asked.

Not giving an answer, I began walking. He followed. My troops stood at attention as we approached. One picked up the bag I needed and ran up to me, eagerly awaiting my command. "Here, sir, I have it!"

"Good work." I took the bag and began walking.

Syd glanced at the eager warrior who had quickly returned to the fire, then reluctantly followed me. I could tell he wondered what I was about to do and where I was going, but I decided against telling him. The boy needed to learn his place, needed to learn that I was in charge.

We reached the hilltop and turned north. Last night when we'd stood at this point, we'd turned south and seen the stripling warriors gathered in the small glade. They were gone now. The stockade was west of us, so I'd never seen anything farther north.

For the first time, I saw Judea. But all I could really see was a dry moat and a huge dirt wall that surrounded the city. On top of the wall was a timber fence about the height of a tall man. At key points, towers were positioned on the palisades to give guards a good view of anyone who approached. On top of the towers were tall poles. I remembered reading about this in the Book of Mormon. Captain Moroni had built these fortifications around all the Nephite cities. They had given the Nephites excellent defense for a while. Now, however, many of their cities had fallen into Lamanite hands, and these mounds of earth and deep, dry moats had become major obstacles in regaining their cities. I stopped walking and took in the scene. It was surreal to see everything with my own eyes.

Tarik had walked halfway across the pathway bridging the dry moat to Judea when he realized I'd stopped. "Now what causes you to wait?"

"Just looking." I hurried to his side, marveling at my surroundings as I tried to keep up. Curious, I asked, "Have you ever met Captain Moroni?"

"No. But I am devoted to him and his cause." Tarik gave me a sideways glance.

"His cause?" I knew what Moroni's cause was, but I wanted to hear Tarik tell me.

"Freedom. Have you not heard of his title of liberty?".

"Of course," I replied.

His look turned curious. "So," Tarik said. "Tell me what you know of the title of liberty."

This was my chance to impress Tarik with what I knew and to show him I was not a threat—that I truly was on his side. "Well, some people fell away from the Church, and they chose to follow King Amalickiah."

"So a Lamanite spy knows Lamanite history!" Tarik chuckled and rolled his eyes.

"Look, you know this story too. Does that make you a spy?" I asked, hoping he'd be reasonable.

He relaxed a touch.

"Anyway, Amalickiah stirred up the people with contention and preached all sorts of false doctrine. Many in the Church fell away, and this really upset Moroni because he'd just fought an awful war for them only a few years prior. I mean, he'd given up so much and fought so hard—of course he was upset. He became so angry that he ripped his coat, tore part of it completely off, and wrote on it. And that became the title of liberty. He put on his armor and placed the standard on a pole."

"Then what did he do?" Tarik gave me a skeptical look, just waiting for me to trip up.

"Well," I had read this part of the Book of Mormon so often that I'd memorized certain passages. I knew exactly what to say. "He prayed."

Tarik nodded, and I could tell by the smile that tugged at the corners of his mouth that he was a little impressed.

I continued. "He prayed that liberty would rest on his brethren. He said, 'Surely God shall not suffer that we, who are despised because we take upon us the name of Christ, shall be trodden down and destroyed until we bring it upon us by our own transgressions.' Or something like that."

Tarik scratched his brow, and I thought I saw the flicker of admiration in his eyes again. He asked, "And what did the title of liberty have written upon it?"

"Oh, that's easy." Then suddenly my memory failed. "Uh . . . I know this . . . I do." I stared at the ground as if the words were written there. Nervously, I glanced up at Tarik. He was patiently waiting. And then the words came to my mind with the full impact of their meaning. With conviction in my voice, I said, "'In memory of our God, our religion, and freedom, and our peace, our wives, and our children.'"

"Maybe . . ." he paused, his eyebrows raised. "Maybe you are not a spy. Are you a believer?"

"I am," I replied as earnestly as I possibly could.

Tarik looked at me for a moment as if trying to make up his mind. Then, just as I thought he would say something nice, he turned and started walking again. I followed, wondering if I had made any impression on him at all. I thought I had. I thought I'd made a darn good impression—hopefully good enough that he'd help me find my backpack.

We passed through the log-walled fence that ran along the city's perimeter. On the other side was the city of Judea. War had taken its toll on the light-brown adobe buildings. Some of the thatched roofs had fallen in. Weeds grew near the walls. Below the entry was what I assumed to be the market square. Night was coming, and the large area was empty except for several tired women in tattered clothing standing at the well filling their water gourds.

Instead of walking down the slope into the city, Tarik turned and walked the narrow path at the top of the city's earthen wall. I followed.

Coming to one of the towers, he slung the bag the soldier had given him over his shoulder and climbed up a ladder. Again, I dutifully followed. A guard stood at attention at the top of the ladder. As we crawled to our feet, Tarik nodded to him and asked, "Are you ready?"

The guard bowed.

Tarik set down the bag, but before reaching in, he turned to me. "Would you like to open it?" He motioned toward the bag.

More than a little perplexed, I reached in and pulled out some heavy, coarse material. I tugged, pulling out more and more of the same piece. Tarik helped to hold it. And finally I came to the end.

"What is this?" I asked. As I studied the cloth, I saw Hebrew writings on it. And then it dawned on me what the cloth was. Many had flown from the towers of Nephite cities.

A shiver raced down my spine.

Chills rippled over my skin, raising the tiny hairs on my arms. I was touching one of the flags patterned after Moroni's original.

I was holding a title of liberty.

CHAPTER 12
PREMONITION

I stood in awe as I watched the title of liberty being raised on the tower pole. Warmth filled my heart. With the task completed, Tarik and I made our way into the war-torn city. Worried people bustled about, trying to put their lives back together after fighting off the Lamanites. Tarik and I received some wary looks as we walked down the street. Many gawked at my clothing; others appeared frightened and shied away. Still others boldly looked at us, and I knew they were wondering if we were the good guys or the bad guys because of the dark color of our skin. Certainly word had gone out that the sons of Helaman had helped to save these people; it seemed that more than anything else, they should show appreciation.

We entered a large adobe building, which appeared to be a hall or grand meeting place. Reed mats were spread on the ground for the wounded. The scent of blood tainted the air. Moans echoed throughout the cavernous room. Mariah busily gave instructions to men and women alike, seeing to the needs of the injured. These soldiers must have been the ones fighting with Antipus. They were Nephites and therefore had fair skin. Bandages were wrapped about heads, chests, and legs. Many men had their arms in slings. I tried not to stare, but I'd never really thought about the wounded of the Lamanite and Nephite wars. I'd read about the thousands who had been killed, but I had never really dwelt on the fact that there had been wounded. Mom's Doctor Foster and the nurses at the hospital were sorely needed here.

I looked up from my thoughts and was glad to see a familiar face in the room. Mariah stood a short distance away, mixing a poultice of some sort.

Mariah looked up and saw us. She walked over and asked, "How is the king of dogs?" She gave me a warm sisterly smile.

"Better," I told her. "Can I help you here?"

She looked surprised at my offer, and I realized warriors probably didn't help nurse the injured. That was probably women's work. She smiled and said, "My nursemaids can see to them." She glanced to Tarik.

"My brothers . . ." Tarik scanned the wounded, searching for some of his men. No Ammonites were among the wounded.

"They are well." Mariah motioned for us to follow her. She led us to a different room, not so large. "This room is free from drafts. Antipus's men insisted the boys have it." Inside were the few stripling warriors that Helaman had left behind while he battled for Antiparah. They were a ragtag bunch. Those who didn't have bandages around their middles were bare-chested. Their skirts were made of animal hides dyed various reds, browns, and blues. Most wore headbands. As we entered, some stood on makeshift crutches. Others rose up on their elbows. Their head wounds were covered in a gauze-like material. Smiles brightened their drawn faces.

"Have we taken Antiparah?" one of the youngest warriors anxiously asked. The others joined in on the questioning.

Tarik motioned for them to quiet down, then he addressed the young boy who had started the rally. "Jacob, I have not yet received word of the battle."

"Sir, why did you linger here with us?" Jacob asked, obviously confused by the fact that this high commander had remained behind. One soldier glared at me as if he knew it was my fault.

"The captain asked me to stay for other business and to make sure you mischief makers were not lazing about, forgetting your duty." Tarik smiled at them. The boys chuckled.

Tarik became serious. "We should hear news from them by this evening. When I learn of the outcome, I shall share it with you." With that he stepped into the crowd and began talking with the wounded, empathizing with their pain and bolstering them.

"How are you?" Mariah came to stand beside me, glancing at my neck. "Your throat is still red."

"I'm fine." I didn't want her to worry. The tone in her voice and the way she spoke made me think of my mother once again. "Mariah, did you see Helaman this morning before he left?" I asked.

"Only for a moment, and at the time, I did not realize he would be leaving. Why?"

"I gave him something before he left, and—"

She held up her hand. "Oh! I found an object I think belongs to you." Mariah scurried into the other room and was gone for a few minutes. Finally she returned and handed me my mother's small leather purse. I'd been so focused on getting the backpack I'd forgotten about it.

"I found this pouch in the medicine tent this morning before taking your breakfast to you in the stockade. With all the trouble there and my coming here, I was delayed in returning it to you. Surely it is yours."

I latched onto the thin strap. "Yes, thank you so much." I knew I should probably check to see whether everything was still inside, but if I pulled out the cell phone or anything else not familiar to these people, I'd have even more explaining to do. I wondered if Mariah had looked through it. I glanced at her. She was watching me. She hadn't said anything, so I decided to change the subject. Besides, I desperately needed to know about the pack. "Did Helaman have my backpack with him this morning before you came to see me?"

"Backpack? I do not know what this is." She crossed her arms, looking at me seriously. "Could you describe this for me?"

Slipping the strap of Mom's purse over my head, I mimed the size of the bag. "It's about this big, black, and has two big straps that come from the bottom and meet up at the top, close together like."

Mariah nodded. "I see." She appeared to be thinking. My hopes were high, when abruptly she shook her head. "No. I do not remember such an object. Last night Helaman lodged in the next building so he could be close to his wounded sons. Maybe it could be there. Come, I shall take you." We were just leaving when Tarik joined us.

"Where are you going?" he asked.

Mariah gave him a rather curious look. "Not far. Only a building away."

He followed us, and I saw suspicion in his eyes—again. It seemed I would never win Tarik's trust—even after all I'd told him of the title of liberty, and fighting the prisoners to save Ozi and Mariah. After all that, he was still wary of my motives.

Stepping into the small building where Helaman had slept, I was struck by the simplicity of the furnishings. A small wooden table, a spindly stool, and . . . the backpack!

I scrambled to it and unhooked the clasp. I gaped in the bag. It was empty.

"No!" Distraught, I fell to my knees.

"What troubles you, Syd?" Mariah hurried to me, kneeling to gaze at me at eye level.

"It's gone." I clutched the pack to my chest.

"My brother-in-law is marching to battle. He would leave behind what he does not absolutely need." She brushed my bangs away from my eyes. "What is it he has taken?"

Tarik stood behind her, and I could feel his gaze taking in the scene, studying me.

"The pack had some information I needed so I could return home," I uttered.

I realized I'd told a half-truth by saying the pack had information in it. But I couldn't very well tell the whole truth: that I needed the stone to transport me home. If I told Tarik about the stone, I'd have to tell him how I got it—and I'd also have to tell him that Helaman thought I was a thief. There was no telling how much I'd have to keep explaining.

Tarik folded his arms, distrust darkening his stare. Watching him stand there looking down at me, I felt like a child. I knew he expected me to stay and teach the warriors my fighting techniques, but this wasn't my century, wasn't my battle. I belonged home with Mom and Gracie.

At that moment, a winded warrior rushed in, covered in trail dust. He immediately went to Tarik and stood at attention. His hair was windblown, and he looked like he'd been riding a horse for quite a while. "Sir." He inhaled deep gulps of air.

"Isaac!" Tarik asked, "How goes the battle for Antiparah?"

"The city is ours, sir." The lad's tired face split into a smile of pure joy. "The Lamanites abandoned it. We entered unharmed."

Tarik placed his arm about the boy's shoulders and gave him a brotherly hug. The soldier's bloodshot eyes became misty. "Come, give me a complete report." Tarik guided the tired boy outside, leaving Mariah and me behind.

"This is good news!" Mariah grabbed my arm. "Surely the Lord watches over them."

I clutched the pack to me and didn't say a word. The Lord was indeed watching over His stripling warriors.

But what about my mother?

What about Gracie?

What about me?

Did the Lord know my circumstance? Did He care? My family was in desperate need, just as much as these people were. Why had I been sent to this era at a time when my mother so greatly needed my help and support? Why was I here? They didn't need me here. They had plenty of soldiers to do their fighting. But Mom . . . she depended on me to be there for her and Gracie.

Mariah noticed how quiet I'd become. "What troubles you, Syd? With no battle to contend with, I am certain Tarik will help you."

"I don't know about that," I said under my breath, but Mariah had heard me.

"Are you two still squabbling?" Her gaze searched my face.

I nodded.

"It is just his pride. You are very much alike, you and he. Both young men who are willing to fight for what you believe." She drew my arm into hers. "Come." She rose to her feet.

I followed, still clutching the pack under my other arm. We went outside. The sun was setting. Brilliant oranges and pinks blazed across a darkening sky. The air was humid. But through the humidity, a breeze brought with it the scent of the sea. I wondered just how close we were to the ocean. I didn't know much about the geography of the Book of Mormon, mainly because no one really knew for sure where the cities actually were . . . are . . . had been. There were logical theories, but in the end, no one really knew.

"You must be hungry, with only a piece of cornbread all day. You sat with the dog for hours." Mariah had a calming way about her. I was again reminded of my mother. I wanted to go with Mariah, to be fed and put to bed, to forget all about my troubles. But a full stomach and sleep would not make my troubles go away. What I needed to do was go to Antiparah and find Helaman. And I was more than willing to head out on my own—except I didn't know where Antiparah was.

I needed a guide.

I needed help.

"Mariah," I slung the backpack over my shoulder next to Mom's purse. "Do you know where Tarik and the soldier might be?"

"They are probably with their warrior brothers, sharing the good news." She nodded to the building where she tended to the wounded.

"Excuse me, please, but I really need to talk with him." I left Mariah and dashed up the steps, hurrying inside. Among the others stood Tarik and the soldier who had delivered the message. Their faces glowed in the dimming light. Smiles were served all around. Their pain had been forgotten for just a moment with the news of Antiparah.

Tarik saw me. I motioned for him. He excused himself from his men. As he neared, I wondered just how I was going to convince him to help me. How was I going to chisel past his mistrust?

"What is it you want?" he asked.

I wasn't going to beg in front of other people. I motioned to go outside. We stepped out into the day's fleeting light.

"Before you speak, I have a message for you." Tarik said. "Isaac brought a message from Helaman for you and me."

I had a feeling that this would not be good news. I braced myself for what he would say next.

"Helaman has requested I take you to him immediately." Tarik was all business. "You have time to see your dog, but then we must leave."

Relief shot through me. Heavenly Father had heard my prayer. He did know of my plight.

Tarik started back to the building but stopped. "I must tell the others that I am leaving. What was it you wanted?"

"It doesn't matter now." Though I was greatly relieved things had so easily fallen into place, trepidation bit at my heels. I didn't know why, but the trepidation quickly turned into a nagging premonition that something bad was about to happen.

CHAPTER 13

Into the Darkness

Tarik and I, along with the soldier who had delivered the good news regarding Antiparah, returned to Mariah's medicine tent. We found Ozi sitting cross-legged on the ground out front, his thin beard puddled in his lap. I knew that Ximon must be doing much better or Ozi would not have left his side. The old man's eyes were closed, and he appeared to be asleep. Oddly enough, the sight of him gave me comfort. I liked Ozi. I really did. I just didn't know what I would do with him as my bodyguard.

"How is the injured creature?" Tarik asked Ozi as we neared.

"Fine," the old man replied as he opened his red-rimmed eyes and gave me a smile. "He is weak, but he shall regain his strength."

Mariah walked out of the tent. Ximon followed on wobbly legs. The Great Dane's head hung low. He was probably suffering from a king-sized headache.

I knelt down and hugged the black-and-white speckled dog. His long pink tongue licked the side of my face and left a trail of slobber behind. I wiped away the moisture. "I'm happy to see you, too."

"Mariah." Tarik took charge of the situation. "Syd and I are to leave for Antiparah."

"Not without me." Mariah folded her arms, challenging his authority. I loved her *think again, flyboy* attitude.

"Helaman wants to see him as soon as possible." Tarik nodded at me. "You and the troops will follow in a few days. But Syd and I must leave now." Tarik glanced at me, and I knew by the determination in his eyes that he expected me to back him up.

"Do not concern yourself with the beast. I shall watch over him," Ozi interjected, trying to comfort the worry he must have read on my face. He had read me wrong. Though I was concerned about the dog's well-being, I was pretty sure he was out of the woods now. I was more worried that I might need the dog with me to go back to my own time, to go home. If Ximon remained behind with the others, my return might be impossible.

"Surely Ozi and the dog can come with us," I said to Tarik.

"The dog is too weak." Tarik shook his head and leaned close to my ear, whispering, "Ozi will never be able to keep up."

I glanced at the others. Mariah remained standing with her arms folded. The tired soldier who had just arrived from Antiparah stood perfectly still, as if wanting to overhear our quiet conversation. Ximon leaned against Ozi, and the two looked to me as though they were holding their breaths, awaiting a verdict.

I turned to Tarik. "They will follow soon?" I asked.

He nodded, and his blue eyes showed relief that I was not going to make an issue out of this.

I mulled over my situation. There were two things that bothered me here: I hated being separated from Ximon, and, though I needed Tarik to show me the way to Antiparah, I really didn't look forward to being alone with him. Although he'd been friendly while we'd hoisted the flag up the tower pole, he had reverted to being suspicious of me.

Besides, once we arrived in the city I needed to be alone to find answers to the questions plaguing me. For instance, did Helaman still have the stone? And if he did, how was I going to take it from him? What if he wouldn't give it back? All the scenerios I could imagine would be complicated by having Tarik hanging around and nearly impossible if Ximon and Ozi were tailing me. So, maybe it would be good to go on with Tarik and without them. I could lose Tarik, but the dog and Ozi were another matter.

I knew that in the end, the pros and cons of the situation didn't matter much. I had to go along with whatever Tarik wanted. "Ozi, please take good care of my dog."

Ozi patted Ximon. The dog licked the elderly man's age-spotted hand.

"I shall see to them both." Mariah began collecting the baskets that littered the outside of her medicine tent. "And I will make certain the boys are cared for as well. Even though some have serious wounds, they will want to follow Helaman." She paused in front of Tarik. "It goes against my nature to say this, but you are right. We shall follow as soon as your warriors are strong enough. And now, you two should eat before starting on your journey."

So it was settled. I was to go alone with Tarik. But as the time grew closer for us to leave, my concerns over Tarik were trumped by other thoughts—worries about how I would find the stone, thoughts of Mom and Gracie, and the foreboding feeling that something was about to go wrong.

✝✝✝

The sky was filled with thousands of twinkling stars smiling down on us. The scent of ocean floated through the clear air. The sorrel I rode obediently followed Tarik's bay. And despite the fact that I'd never ridden before, I quite enjoyed it. It still hit me every few hours that I was really here with one of the stripling warriors, and that we were on our way to meet with Helaman, the captain . . . the prophet.

I wondered why he wanted to see me of all people. I wondered if he had realized that what I had told him in Mariah's tent was true. Maybe he'd had a revelation or a vision and he now knew I didn't belong here.

The more I thought about why, the more I was convinced Helaman wanted to thank me and return the stone. This relieved my mind a great deal. The panicked urgency, which had haunted me since my arrival, was replaced with the hope that I'd soon be home with my mother.

Tarik stopped the young bay he rode, waiting for me to ride up alongside. "Are you all right?" he asked.

"Sure," I said, even though my bottom hurt from the crude saddle, which was merely thin leather tacked onto a wooden base. I wondered what Colin would think of this saddle. He'd tried to make one the year before in his leather tooling class. He was forever explaining every step to me. I had half-listened, not seeing the relevance. If I had only known.

I looked at Tarik. His head was cocked to the side, and he was listening. Tarik was concerned about something, and this set the teeny-tiny hairs on the back of my neck at attention.

"What is it?" I asked.

His face was cast in shadow, but I could tell that his eyes scanned the horizon and that his jaw was clenched tightly.

"Stay close," he said. "Stay alert. And keep quiet. If something happens, do exactly what I say, when I say it."

Nunchakus. Here I thought I was home free. Just a little trip to visit Helaman. The danger was supposed to be over; the enemy long gone. "I don't understand. I thought the Lamanites had fled."

"Once they left Antiparah and Judea, where do you think they went?" He spoke as if he were talking to a child, as if I should have known better.

I hadn't thought about where the Lamanites went after fleeing one city for another. It made sense now. We were riding right into danger. I thought of the premonition I'd had before leaving Judea. I should have taken it more seriously.

Tarik urged his horse to start walking. I did the same. He continued talking in hushed tones. "Most of the Lamanites will have gone east to Cumeni, but there is the chance some have traveled north."

I thought of the prisoners who had attacked me that morning. Friends of theirs could be making their way to Judea to free them. They could be on the same trail we were on.

My knees dug into the sides of my horse. I suspected the animal I rode was an older steed because it stumbled every once in a while. I wondered what the animal would do if it needed to go faster, if it actually needed to run. I prayed I wouldn't find out and that we'd arrive at Antiparah without incident.

⁂

The boy was acting like we were on a big adventure. Syd had truly not thought of the possible dangers of our journey until I had whispered them to him. That I was stuck with him in the jungle was troubling. Would he even know enough to run away from an advancing jaguar? Though Syd knew how to fight, he had apparently not learned that even the best warrior had his limits. He had undoubtedly not realized as yet that the Lamanites had no code of honor when it came to battle.

Why was this boy so important that Helaman would have me risk our lives by traveling at night and without troops? I could not think of an answer. My leader knew I could take care of myself, but the boy? Perhaps this was a test of some kind.

But a test for who? The boy or me?

‡‡‡

We rode for hours. The only noises heard were the soft plodding of our horses' hooves on the rich jungle soil, the swish of branches from the exotic trees towering over us, and an occasional bird squawk or owl hoot. Even though I was scared out of my skull, and my knees and bottom ached, the lull of riding teased my eyelids shut. On the brink of sleep, my arms and legs sometimes twitched so hard I'd jerk upright. I knew Tarik was watching me and probably silently laughing his head off.

How could I sleep with the threat of a Lamanite attack looming and the goal of reaching Helaman and the stone so critical? But as I thought about it, I hadn't really slept for several nights. I had stolen a couple hours' sleep in the stockade, but that had been restless. For a nanosecond, I was too tired to care about any of it. I yearned to lay my head on a goose-down pillow.

To keep myself awake, I thought of Gracie. Had the bishop taken her to school? Did he read her stories from the Book of Mormon when he tucked her into bed? Was the Staker family letting her help fix supper and encouraging her with "Great job!" and "Way to go!"? And what about Colin? Was he being nice to her or were he and his football cronies making fun of her? I was wide awake now. He'd better be nice to her, or when I returned—if I returned, he have to deal with me.

New subject. Now I thought of my father. Was he watching over Mom? Had he gone to see Gracie? My mind drifted to the possible lie my mother had told. If she had lied to my father—and that was a mighty big *if*—she must have had a really good reason.

I suddenly remembered the little half-lie I had told about the stone.

But I *had* had a good reason. I had to get home. Again, the nagging voice in my mind came. *What if she had had a good reason to lie? What then?*

There could never be a good enough reason to tell your husband that his drinking had caused his own daughter to die. So I wasn't going to think about it. It had always been Mom, Gracie, and me against the world. My father had chosen to live a separate life all this time. And that was where he was going to stay. I took a deep breath to calm myself.

The horses plodded on and on. I made a concerted effort not to think of home, family, or anything else I could do nothing about right then. I concentrated instead on what was ahead of me: more and more jungle.

The trees were different here, taller than any I'd ever seen and so thick. A wind picked up, tossing the branches wildly overhead and kicking loose topsoil into the air. I had to squint to keep the dirt from blowing into my eyes.

Once again, my old friend sleep tried to overtake me. I ignored it the best I could; every once in a while I'd think of Tarik watching me, monitoring me. Then I'd straighten.

"We should rest," he said as we approached a stand of trees.

"Helaman is waiting," I replied. I didn't want him to know that my knees ached, my bottom felt like I'd done a thousand squats, and that my entire body yearned for rest.

"Yes, and you should be awake when you see him. You can barely stay on your horse."

He was right.

Just as Tarik was about to dismount, the night was pierced by a war cry. Tarik immediately kicked his steed into a run. I leaned close to my own horse and raised my foot to kick it into action, but I did not move quickly enough.

Out of the darkness, savage hands latched onto me and threw me to the ground. My mind switched into karate mode, so that when I landed, I rolled up on my feet and took a defensive stance against my attacker.

He was gone, swallowed by the night. I was being taunted by my captor, played with like a mouse before a cat is about to eat it. Suffocating blackness closed in around me. My heart kicked against my ribs. A chill seized me as if a ghost had passed through my body.

Peering into the shadows, I saw nothing, but I knew he was out there. I heard a twig snap in the opposite direction my attacker had disappeared.

Correction—*he* wasn't out there; *they* were out there!

Every nerve in my body tingled. I clenched my teeth together and stepped one foot back, ready for an attack from either side.

Another piercing war cry sounded from above. A feeling of dread filled my soul. I looked up to see a huge Lamanite, leaping from a tree limb. He dropped in slow motion, a mass of war paint and muscle. I could see a fiendish glint in his eyes that zeroed in on me . . . his prey.

CHAPTER 14
SOOTHSAYER

The Lamanite knocked me to the ground. I had every intention of doing a tuck and roll, but when I landed, he was already on top of me, his reflexes shockingly fast. He wrenched my arms behind me and hog-tied my hands and feet together.

My face planted in the soil with my arms nearly pulled from their sockets, I tried to break free, twisting and turning, but there was no escaping the ropes.

I had been captured!

My pulse sledgehammered in my ears. I sucked in long, deep breaths. Hating the feeling of vulnerability, I craned my neck to have a better look around and gain my bearings. Blinking grains of dirt and sand from my eyes, I saw several Lamanites circling, eager to make mincemeat out of me.

Their faces were painted red and black. On their heads were animal headdresses: some wore jaguar heads, some boar heads, and some deer. Clutched in their hands were crudely crafted spears with obsidian tips as well as bows and arrows.

My attacker spit on the back of my neck. Spittle slid over my skin. "Traitor!" He cursed as he kicked my ribs. "Dirty Christian! He is one of them. I recognized Helaman's second in command. This must be another 'stripling warrior.'"

I rolled into the mind-numbing pain and onto my side. However, when I rolled over, my black belt came untied, and the front of my *gi* fell open. The Lamanites suddenly stopped and stared. I glanced down and saw that my lacy Cross Your Heart underwear was showing.

I tried to roll back onto my stomach, but my attacker stamped his foot in my tender side, pressing his weight down hard. "What manner of dress does our traitorous Ammonite wear?"

He reached toward me. I tried to flinch away from his grubby hand. Clawing my shoulder, he tried to pull at the strap, but the elastic snapped from his fingertips back to my skin.

While he was caught by surprise, I squirmed from beneath his foot, moving as far away as I could while my wrists and feet strained against the unrelenting bands, tearing my skin. I could not get away. I could do nothing.

Nothing except pray.

I closed my eyes. *Please God, tell me what to do, what to say.*

Someone grabbed a fistful of my short hair, jabbing jagged fingernails into my scalp and pulling me back. I came eye-to-eye with the man who had spit on my neck. This close up, I could see that his face had a large purple birthmark covering part of his forehead, one eye, and part of his cheek. He placed his dagger at the top of my hairline.

An idea came to me. "I have a message for King Ammoron," I lied. I had no message, but I did have knowledge.

The man wrenched me back farther. Glaring down on me, he stuck his face so close his bulbous nose touched mine. The intense pain from my scalp and neck was amplified by the shooting ache in my cramped arms and legs.

"Liar!" He spit as he spoke.

I blinked away the spittle and said, "I know who killed Ammoron's brother, King Amalickiah." I prayed I had remembered correctly and that the Lamanites at this time were unsure of who had killed their king. I was betting that the Lamanite who could give the name of the killer to Ammoron would win his favor and that these men were more than a little eager to be their new king's favorite with any news they could beat out of me.

"The Nephites killed him. That is no secret." He scowled.

"I have a name," I added.

He stopped, gave me a confused look, then dropped me back to the ground, smashing my nose. Pain streaked through to my eyeballs. Blood rolled down my upper lip.

Then I heard him step away, probably to consult with the others on how they would get me to talk before killing me. I only had a few minutes to make my escape. I frantically worked on the ropes binding my hands and feet.

Suddenly, I felt other hands reach out to touch my own. A new panic surged in me. Was this a new attacker?

"Shh!"

A knife slipped between my wrists, cutting me free. I quickly turned about.

Tarik hugged the ground. "Follow me," he whispered.

Wiping the blood from my lip, I glanced at the group of Lamanites who were huddled together as if discussing a football strategy. However, there was one Lamanite lying on the ground close to us. Tarik must have taken care of him before rescuing me. No wonder he'd been able to sneak up unnoticed.

Hurriedly crawling into the bushes, we were finally out of their sight. Jumping to our feet, Tarik and I took off running toward his horse, which he'd left a couple of hundred yards away in another stand of trees. My flip-flops fell from my feet. Turning to retrieve the blasted things, I saw that the Lamanites were in pursuit. No time to fetch my sorry excuse for shoes.

I ran like I've never run before in my life. Pain needled my feet and gnawed at my side, but I kept going. Stealing a quick look behind me, I saw they were bearing down on us, leaping over bushes and rocks as if they had springs for legs.

Tarik jumped on his horse and offered me his arm. I grabbed hold and with all the strength I could muster, I swung up behind him.

The horse took off as if a gun had been shot. Tarik leaned forward; I hugged him as tightly as I could. If I fell, I'd be dead. We became one with the horse as the animal darted between the thick trees. When the trees thinned, we found ourselves on a beach. There, the horse gained speed as its hooves splashed through the water and dug into the hard-packed sand.

Time moved slowly. The horse ran on and on for what seemed hours until Tarik pulled up on the reins, slowing the beast to a trot. After a while, he guided his dutiful steed back into the jungle along the shoreline and slowed him to a walk.

Predawn light filtered through tree branches and hanging vines. Birds twittered and chirped, and every once in a while, I swear I saw little monkeys swinging about, staring at us. They must have been spider monkeys. I'd read about them in science, but had never actually seen one.

Coming to a stream, Tarik stopped his tired horse, swung his leg forward over the animal's neck, and leaped off. He reached up and helped me down.

My *gi* fell open again. I automatically reached for my black belt, but it was gone, lost forever with the Lamanites. The evidence of years of work and discipline were gone—like my life in modern times. Without saying a word, Tarik wrapped my *gi* around me. He cut a length of rope from the coil tied to his saddle. After tying it around my waist, he left my side and guided his horse to the water's edge, allowing the animal to drink.

Tarik moistened a piece of cloth and came back to me. He began wiping the dried blood from my face. "When were you going to tell me you were a woman?"

"Never. But I guess my Cross Your Heart gave me away."

He appeared puzzled. "I do not know your meaning, though I suppose you refer to the strange contraption you wear over your chest. I knew you were a woman when you leaned against my back."

Now I was embarrassed. If I hadn't been so scared I wouldn't have hugged him so tightly. Of course he'd never seen a bra. People in ancient America didn't wear bras, let alone Cross Your Heart brand.

"Why did you not tell Helaman or me of your gender?" He peered into my eyes as if he could see the truth in my pupils.

I raked my fingers through my short, windblown hair, knowing full well anything I said would sound lame. Finally I blurted, "I thought it would be easier if you didn't know."

Tarik's gaze didn't change, and at that moment, I would have gladly taught karate nonstop for a solid week with the most bratty kids in the dojo just to read his mind.

His horse raised its head, water dripping from its chin. Tarik grabbed the reins and led his trusty bay to a tree, tying him up.

"What else have you not told us?" His tone was edged with anger. We were back to square one.

"I was only trying to do what I thought was best!" I defended. Tears of frustration threatened to overtake me, but I willed them away. I knew I needed to tell Tarik what was going on. No more half-truths, no more half-lies.

"I don't belong here," I said.

"Neither do I," he growled.

"I mean, not just here." I motioned with my arm at our surroundings. "I mean, here." I looked up at the sky and back at the ground. I quickly glanced at Tarik. He did not understand.

"Look . . ." I began to pace as I talked. "See the backpack?" Suddenly I realized I didn't have the backpack or Mom's purse. They were on my horse! And there was no telling where the animal had gone during the ambush. "The backpack and my mother's purse were on my horse," I told Tarik slowly.

"Your horse probably bolted for home." He leaned against a boulder and folded his arms. "Go on."

Realizing it was futile to worry about the backpack and purse, I continued. "It sounds absurd, but it's true, I assure you." I wrung my hands together, hoping he'd believe me. "I'm from the future."

"Future? Where is this town?"

"No. It's not a town or a place." Or was it a place? After all I'd been through, I wasn't sure anymore. "It's more like a time. My hometown is called Salt Lake City." I stared at Tarik, hoping beyond hope he might comprehend a little of what I was about to reveal.

"You live in a lake of salt?"

"No. Well, there is a lake nearby that does have salt in the water, but that's not what's important." I looked at the sky and rising sun. The scene was hopeful, and it helped me gain the courage to continue. "When I first had that backpack, there was a stone in it. The stone looked like quartz, only more clear. When I touched it, Ximon and I were overcome with a brilliant light, and when the light went out, we were in Mariah's tent."

"Why did you not tell us of this stone before? You said only that there was information in the backpack." Tarik had caught me in my half-truth.

"I know, but in a way, the stone is information, which I think will send me home. I didn't know if I could trust you and Mariah. Now you've saved my life. And I really should have given you the benefit of the doubt, but I was scared. And when I found the stone missing, I had nothing to back up my claim. That's all." I'd run out of breath.

Tarik stood and rubbed his smooth chin, a mannerism he must have picked up from watching Helaman stroke his beard. He asked, "Who has this stone now?"

"Helaman. When I showed it to him, he became angry. He claimed I had stolen a priceless treasure and said the stone was actually one of the sixteen stones of the brother of Jared."

"What?" Tarik paced, rubbing the back of his neck beneath his thick mane of black hair. He stopped. "Why did Helaman not slay you then and there?"

"Because I think some part of him believed me, but he wasn't sure."

"I heard you tell the Lamanites you had a message for King Ammoron." Tarik grabbed both of my shoulders. "And that you know the name of the man who killed Amalickiah. Only a traitor would have offered such information to our enemies."

"I wasn't really going to tell them," I said quickly.

"Good, because I would have had no choice but to kill you if you had spoken his name." Tarik clenched his teeth as he stared at me.

"Really, I wasn't going to tell them." Against my will, I began trembling, but Tarik maintained his grip on my arms.

"How *do* you know his name?" He was not going to let this go.

"I know who killed Amalickiah because I read it in a book. This book tells all about the people who live in this land. It tells of *your* people, the Anti-Nephi-Lehies, who changed their name to Ammonites. It tells how your fathers made a covenant with God to fight no more. I know that to prove their devotion, they buried their spears, bows, and arrows."

Tarik released his grip on my arms, but he did not take his eyes off me.

"I know your mothers taught you to have faith that Heavenly Father would watch over you and that because of your faith not a single one of you was killed in the battle near Judea."

He remained quiet.

"I told this to Helaman. In fact, I told him he would take Antiparah without a fight."

"Stop!" Tarik came to stand beside me. "Only a soothsayer would know such things. Only a soothsayer could fight the way you do and see what is yet to be."

"I'm not a soothsayer!" I yelled. "I know how to fight because I'm a black belt in karate. I've already told you that. And I can't see into the future; I *know* what will happen because I read it in the Book of Mormon."

Tarik just looked at me.

No expression.

No movement.

"You have to believe me," I pleaded.

He looked down to the ground, then back up at me. "I cannot. You have lied from the moment we met." Tarik wasn't letting up.

"I know it seems like it, but I didn't really lie to you; I just didn't correct your assumptions." Then I thought about what I'd told the Lamanites. "And when I told the Lamanites I had a message for King Ammoron and that I knew who killed Amalickiah, the only part that was a lie was that I had a message. I was just stalling for time."

"So, do you know the name of the man who killed Amalickiah?" Tarik was testing me.

"Of course. Captain Teancum sneaked into Amalickiah's tent in the middle of the night and killed him with a javelin."

Tarik's face was expressionless. I couldn't tell if he was impressed, mad, or amazed.

Tarik's horse whinnied. He turned from me and jumped up onto a nearby boulder.

"They are coming. We must leave."

"But . . ." I needed to hear him say he believed me.

Tarik untied his horse and swung up into the saddle. Leaning over and extending his arm to me, he said, "Soothsayer, spy, believer, or otherwise, I do not know who or what you are, but I do know you need my help. Come, I will take you to Helaman. He will deal with you."

Frustrated and sad at the same time, I was tempted to turn my back on him. I clenched my teeth so as not to spout off what I really thought about the situation and Tarik's stubborn refusal to believe me. But I had no desire to confront the Lamanites again, and I did want to see Helaman.

I grabbed Tarik's arm and leaped onto the horse.

CHAPTER 15
A Stripling Warrior

As my horse, Spirit Chaser, galloped swiftly over the ground, I noticed that Syd did not hug me as tightly as he had before.

No, not he—she.

She appeared uncomfortable now that I knew of her secret. She had hidden it so well. I was puzzled, though. What about her fighting skills? How did a young woman learn to fight as she did? My admiration of her ability increased. I had marveled at her abilities when I thought she was a boy, but now I was astonished. What manner of woman was she? I wanted to learn more.

She had told such a strange story; she had said she was from a lake of salt and that she had read about my people in a book. By "book," I supposed she meant some type of scroll. True, she knew our history, but she also knew things that most did not—that Teancum had killed Amalickiah. And she claimed to know what had happened at Antiparah before the captain and his troops arrived there.

How was this possible?

She spoke of a stone Helaman took from her. Obviously he did not trust her story; why else would he have thrown her in the stockade? However, he had assigned me to watch over her. If he had given me such a task, he must have believed her somewhat.

Did Helaman know that he was a she? He must not have known, for he never would have sentenced a woman to stay alone in the stockade.

Then I remembered that Helaman had asked me to have a guard stay with Syd. And I had neglected to do so. Maybe he had known that she was a woman.

Remorse filled me as I recalled that night; Syd's animal would not follow me away from the stockade as I had ordered. I had become angry not only with the dog but with Syd as well.

I had left her in the prison with only her animal as a guard.

I must meet alone with Helaman. I knew I must tell him of my neglect and of Syd's secret as well.

⁂

We arrived in the city without further incident. Tarik met with Helaman alone, leaving me outside the door of what I assumed was Helaman's office. This building, like the ones in Judea, was made of adobe but rose two stories tall. The room Helaman was in was on the second floor. The hallway walls were stark. As I leaned against the interior wall, anxiety filled me like water filling a pitcher. But trailing close behind the anxiety was hope.

I clung to a slim chance that in a few minutes I'd be safe at home. The thought calmed my nerves. I fingered the rope Tarik had given me to keep my *gi* top closed. Noticing my wrinkled clothing, I knew I looked pretty scruffy. I brushed the dirt smudges off the black material of my *gi* and finger combed my hair.

Tarik had given me some crude deerskin sandals to wear since I'd lost my flip-flops. I wasn't sure where he'd gotten them, and they were more than a little too big, with about an inch sticking past my toes, but at least I was no longer barefoot.

After what seemed like an eternity, Tarik came out. "Good fortune," he said as he walked past and motioned for me to go inside. I assumed he meant "good luck." There was an odd smile on his face, as if he knew a secret no one else in the world knew. Ignoring him, I took a quick breath and stepped over the threshold.

The room was simple, with a few hand-carved chairs, a large animal hide on the floor, and a table, which Helaman sat behind. On the surface was a crude map of the region.

No longer dressed in armor, Helaman wore a tan tunic and blue outer robes. His red, sandy hair was pulled back to the nape of his neck. He had trimmed his rust-colored beard. Helaman's intense, shining eyes—which I had thought were a rust color, but now held more of a copper hue—stared at me. Though he held a war map in front of him, Helaman's entire presence spoke of his prophetic calling.

He rose to his feet. I was awestruck.

"Tarik tells me you two met with some trouble on the way." His deep voice was matter-of-fact. He walked toward a window which overlooked the city.

I followed. "Yes, but we handled it."

"He said you told him some of the peculiar story you related to me in Judea." Helaman gazed out the window, not at me.

"Yes." I wondered what else Tarik had told Helaman. He had been in here long enough to give the man my entire life history—except Tarik didn't know my history. He only knew that I was from the future . . . and that I was a woman. Maybe Tarik had told Helaman this. No, there was no maybe about it. He would definitely have told him.

"Your guess regarding Antiparah was accurate." Helaman looked directly at me, waiting for my reply.

"I didn't guess." I stood my ground. I knew he was testing me. "I know what happened. Just like I know what will happen in the days ahead. It's in the *book.*"

"Perhaps," he replied. "Do you still insist your book is at home in the future?"

At first I wanted to say yes, but then I realized something. "Actually, you have it."

Helaman tilted his head and looked at me carefully. "I have it?"

"Yes." I moistened my chapped lips with my dry tongue, then continued. "As I said before, I know that Chief Judge Nephihah had your father give the records to you. You are the record keeper for the Church right now."

He sighed, still watching me carefully. "My having the record proves nothing. What has happened here in Antiparah is not in the records." His rust-colored eyebrows pressed together as he studied me.

"That's because you haven't written it yet." I watched as skepticism furrowed his brow, so I hurriedly continued. "Actually, what you write about Antiparah is in the message you sent to Captain Moroni. You told him Ammoron wanted a prisoner exchange for the city. And you basically told Ammoron to stick it in his ear. And when you arrived here, you found the Lamanites had already gone."

"It is true. I have written such a letter. The messenger took it this morning." He seriously studied me, and I worried he would call me a spy again or send for the guard.

Instead he said, "Stick it in his ear?" Helaman chuckled. "This is a term I am not familiar with. But I understand the meaning." And then Helaman relaxed and motioned for me to have a seat.

He did not resume his seat behind the table but sat beside me. "I would like you to know that the Lord revealed to me that Antiparah would fall without a fight. I did not learn it from you. However, you are a great mystery to me. I do not know what to make of you. You truly believe you are from a different time?" He gazed at me.

I nodded.

He continued. "And that I should know this because of my priesthood calling?"

"Yes." We were finally getting somewhere.

"Many things are revealed to me." He half-smiled. "Some I wish I did not know." He paused in reflection, then went on. "But I am not the one who controls such revelation. I am the receiver, not the giver. Do you understand?"

I nodded, but I really didn't understand. He was supposed to know everything, see everything. He was supposed to help me go home. Surely that was why I was sent to him.

"The Lord has not confirmed your story to my heart as of yet." Helaman leaned back in his chair. "And that is why I still question you. You have answered wisely, as only one who knew such things would. And yet . . . I hesitate."

"But . . ." I bit my bottom lip. "What can I do to make you believe me?"

"Pray." He offered the solution, and it was obvious. I should have known that one myself.

"Yes, I have and will continue to." I needed him to understand that I was sincere and a believer. "Prayer is what saved Tarik and me on our journey."

"I know." He smiled.

"I'll continue to be prayerful, sir, but maybe in the meantime, maybe you could return the stone to me?" There, I'd said it. This was the taboo subject that could jinx everything.

"Ah, the stone." He grew quiet, as if trying to remember where he'd put it.

"You still have it, don't you?" Panic raced through me.

"Of course." He appeared a little upset by my question. "I would never endanger such a treasure. But I am still perplexed as to why you had it. I have inquired of the Lord but have not yet received an answer. Be assured, the stone is in a safe place." Helaman leaned forward, his elbows on his knees. Then he looked back at me. "When the Lord tells me the time is right, I will give the stone back to you. But only if it is His will. Until then . . ."

"Until then, what?" I felt frustrated. "What else? I need to go home. My mother may be dying. My sister needs me. My father . . ."

"Fear not." Helaman patted my arm. "Little One, you are not alone in this trial. The Lord will watch over your mother, sister, and father as well. They are in God's hands."

"Do you promise?" I bit the inside of my lip.

"I promise." He placed his arm around my shoulders. "The Lord will reveal to me when the time is right to give you the stone. Until then, you can be a great help to my sons."

"I'll do anything you ask." I knew in my heart that Helaman was still testing me, and I was more than ready to roll up my sleeves and get to work. Tarik had probably told Helaman I was a girl and that I should do womanly chores. I'd do anything as long as Mom and Gracie were all right and as long as the stone would soon be in my hands.

"I saw you flip Tarik on his back, and I have heard about the incident at the stockade." Helaman rose and walked to the chair behind the table. "My sons must face many more battles. They are young and inexperienced, but they are fearless. They have won but a single battle. Many sore battles lie ahead of them. Their faith has preserved them and will continue to shield them, of this I know. But the battles will be fierce. Because of their inexperience, they will suffer many injuries." Helaman's face was cast in worry.

My mind jumped back to Judea, when Tarik and I were in Mariah's medicine tent watching over Ximon. Tarik had told me he'd do everything in his power to make sure I stayed here to teach him and his warrior brothers how to fight. I had been so focused on trying to find a way home that I had dismissed the idea as absurd—but what if I could help?

Helaman looked me square in the face. "You are a great fighter; you can teach us many things. I extend to you a calling to teach my sons your way of battle. In so doing, you will become a stripling warrior."

At first I felt like a major mistake had been made, but then my heart soared. To be called to such a position boggled my mind. As a little girl I'd daydreamed about what being a stripling warrior would be like. But I didn't know if I could accept the call. I had been asked to be a stripling warrior—a title only given to boys.

I realized that Helaman must not know. He never would have asked me otherwise. A girl would never be asked to teach warriors to fight.

I stared back at the man who held my fate in his hands. Trying to read his body language was impossible. He patiently waited for my reply. His eyes took in everything: the twitch of my cheek, my nervous hand-wringing, and my restless legs.

Should I tell Helaman that I was a girl? After Tarik's reaction to finding out that I was a girl, I worried what Helaman would think. How would he react to the fact that I'd kept this a secret so long? What would he do? What if he decided he could never return the stone to me and I was stuck here forever?

It was better for everyone if they thought I was a boy. I would fulfill the calling I had been given. A calling to help the Nephite cause. My duty was to accept and aid the warriors and Helaman the best I could while I was here. And that meant keeping the fact that I was a girl a secret. And then another thought hit me.

Did I have what it would take to actually be a stripling warrior? Did I have the faith they had? I mean, I believed in God. I believed in Jesus Christ. But did I believe enough to face death? Nothing was certain. In fact, the only thing I did know for certain was that I needed to accept this call.

And there must be a reason.

Could I be strong enough to find out what that reason was?

I was unsure. What I did know for sure was that I still had to live behind the guise of being a boy. I looked at Helaman and, as I nodded my head, said, "I would be honored to teach your warriors, sir."

CHAPTER 16
A Different Kind of Danger

I quickly left Helaman's headquarters, afraid the longer I stayed, the more opportunity he would have to learn my secret. Dashing along the hallway and down the stairs, I escaped into the humid afternoon. The stairs and clay road were wet. The scent of freshly fallen rain should have been refreshing, but it felt oppressive. The air was heavy with moisture, much as my life felt heavy with trouble.

"So . . ." Tarik was leaning against the building near the exit, waiting for me.

"You knew what he was going to ask me to do, didn't you?" I didn't stop to wait for his reply and tore down the steps.

"I did." He followed me to the bottom, where his horse was tied and waiting.

"Why didn't you tell him I'm a girl?" I knew I shouldn't blame Tarik, but someone had to take the blame for everything going haywire in my life. Why not him?

"I expected *you* to," he countered.

"Yeah, well. I didn't. I couldn't." I looked up at him, and he had the nerve to smile. "Quit that."

"Quit what?"

"That smiling thing." My emotions tangoed inside me. I wanted him to be serious. Didn't he realize the gravity of this situation?

"I never noticed before, but your eyes sparkle like the topaz from the mountains of Antionum when you become angry," Tarik said as his smile broadened.

For a second I was speechless. My face felt hot, and I knew my cheeks must be scarlet. "What's with you?" I asked. "Are you coming on to me?"

"Coming on to you?" He rubbed his firm, masculine chin. His blue eyes studied me, earnestly seeking understanding.

"Yeah, as in care for me, you know . . ." I didn't want to explain this to him. "Because I gotta tell ya, we're not going there. I like that idea about as much as I like watching football."

"Football?" Tarik tilted his head and looked at me earnestly, which only made him more attractive.

I tore my gaze from him; I was still blushing furiously, annoyed at myself for having gone down this road. "Oh, nunchakus! Forget football. That's completely beside the point, and I don't want to explain it." And then I did. "It's a stupid game where men dress up in weird costumes, with helmets and bulky shoulder pads. I mean, what are they thinking? Who cares about a little pigskin ball, and who cares about running it down the field before the other team? I mean, where's the thrill in that?"

"You appear to be upset." Tarik had that tolerant tone in his voice again.

"You bet I'm upset!" I ranted. "I'm stuck here in this time. My mother could be dying, my little sister is living with strangers." That wasn't exactly true. "Well, she knows the Stakers, but it's not the same as living with family. And then, there's my father, the reformed drunk . . ." Tears clouded my vision as I thought of my father standing over me outside the hospital. I didn't want his words to repeat in my mind. I forced back the tears.

Tarik was standing too close to me. He reached to put his arm around my shoulders, but stopped as a a small group of men walked past us. He waited until the men were out of hearing range and said, "I never thought about your having a family."

"Yeah, well, I do." I looked at the young man beside me and saw only kindness in his eyes. He really seemed to care. "And I miss them."

Despite everything that had happened in the past few days, Tarik gave me a hug. A mother and small daughter walked toward us, baskets and gourds in their arms. Tarik quickly dropped his arm from my shoulders. I smiled at the woman as she passed.

I was suddenly overcome with an overwhelming urge to tell Tarik about my fears, to lean on him for strength. As if reading my mind, he said, "I am sure you miss them. But it is important that you are here now." He started walking, leading his horse. "Helaman and I both think the Lord sent you here for a purpose. I want to learn all I can from you."

"Learn all you can from me? Don't you care what happens to me or my family?" I asked, refusing to follow him.

"I care for you." His voice was etched with brotherly concern as he placed his hand on my shoulder.

I didn't want him to act like I was his sister. All the family I wanted was back in my own time. But when I realized how I wanted him to act, I felt intensely annoyed by the entire situation. Was I having a meltdown or what? Five minutes ago I'd been upset that Tarik was acting like he liked me. And now . . . I was more confused than ever. I said, "Well, don't do me any favors." I shrugged off his hand and started walking, not knowing where I was going or what I was going to do when I got there.

"Favors?" Tarik was by my side. The horse gazed at me over his master's shoulder as he clopped along beside us. Oh, what the animal must think.

"You know." I stopped and glanced up at Tarik. His intense blue eyes looked back at me. I remembered how attractive I had thought he looked when I'd first seen him in daylight. He stood waiting for me to finish my thought, and I wondered for a split second how an ancient guy had managed to be so good-looking.

I shook my head. This was the guy who had stuck a knife to my throat, the guy who'd thrown me into the stockade . . . the guy who had rescued me from the Lamanites.

"Just don't feel sorry for me, okay?" I muttered under my breath.

"I would never feel sorry for someone who can flatten me in the blink of a hummingbird's eye." He smiled, and something in my stomach flip-flopped. I did my best to ignore the feeling.

"Yeah, well, speaking of that, since you didn't tell Helaman I'm a girl, I have to teach you and your friends how to defend yourselves." I hadn't meant to sound quite so accusing. I was surprised when Tarik did not lash back.

"Let us not argue over who did not tell Helaman. He did not ask, and I did not tell. On our journey here, I was determined to tell him. However, I realized I could not burden him with this knowledge. My warrior brothers are good men, but they would never tolerate having a woman teach them how to fight. It is best for everyone not to know." He looked over my face, and I knew he feared that if Helaman knew of my gender I would not be allowed to teach his brothers.

The intensity of his gaze brought a flush to my cheeks. He took hold of both my hands and looked at them for a moment. His touch was gentle. "I will take the blame of not telling Helaman."

I didn't want him to feel like he needed to protect me now that he knew I was a woman. I quickly pulled my hands from his. "It's my fault. I should have told him. And I will tell him when the time is right."

"Very well," Tarik said, looking at me with the hint of a chuckle pulling at his mouth. "I will do as you wish."

We walked in silence for a while, the horse close at our heels. I didn't know what to say. I needed time to sort things out.

Finally Tarik spoke, "When I first met you, I never noticed your womanly features. However, when I watched you care for your dog, I noticed your womanly ways and wondered. But now, after talking with you, I know that you truly are a woman."

What was he talking about?

"You have high cheekbones, and your hands are thin. Some men are built that way as well, but it is the things you say that give away your gender." Tarik shrugged as if conceding something. "You speak out of both sides of your mouth and can never make up your mind as to whom you are upset with."

"Excuse me?" I glared at him. "I do not speak out of both sides of my mouth. For one thing, that's physically impossible to do, and for another thing, I do know *who* I'm upset with."

"See." He wiggled his brows and smiled.

I rolled my eyes and started to walk away. But I stopped. I realized that he wasn't trying to make me mad; he was teasing me. *Was* he coming on to me?

"I'm letting this drop for now," I said slowly, shrugging my shoulders. "But that doesn't mean I agree with you. It means we have a lot of work to do." Trying to take my eyes and mind off of Tarik, I glanced about.

There were small homes on all sides of us, and I saw many women and children in front of them. Some women were weaving while sitting outside their front doors; others worked in their small gardens next to their houses, and children played on the hard-packed clay streets. "Where do we go from here?" I asked Tarik.

"My brothers are camped outside the city." Tarik took my cue to get serious and guided his horse and me through the city streets. We walked up a mound of dirt much like the one leading out of the city of Judea. At the gateway, we stood and surveyed the scene before us.

Less than a mile away a pale blue ocean loomed on the horizon. The refreshing scent of ocean hung in the air. Being from Salt Lake, the closest thing to ocean I'd ever smelled was on hot summer nights when the Salt Lake smelled of brine. This air had a fresh, inviting smell to it.

Beyond the dry moats surrounding the city stood a lush jungle. Camp had been set up there among the trees; eventually all two thousand stripling warriors would stay there. Most of them had already arrived with Helaman. The others—the wounded we had left in Judea—would arrive with Mariah and Ozi, possibly as early as tomorrow. I was anxious for them to arrive—anxious to see Ximon again. I missed the dog, though I'd only known him a few days. We'd been through a lot together. We were a team, that dog and me.

"Come." Tarik leaped on his horse and reached to help me. "You must teach us to fight."

I took hold of his arm and looked up into his clear, warm eyes. My heart gave a little lurch. He might have beautiful eyes, but I knew that he was dangerous.

With him, I was in danger of losing my heart.

CHAPTER 17
A Greater Call

We rode into camp. Tents both large and small nestled in the jungle glade and made a city. Multicolored banners for each squad flapped in the breeze. Only a few soldiers were about.

Tarik nodded to them. They greeted him warmly, and I could tell they wanted to speak with him, but they held back out of respect for his status. Tarik stopped in front of a long, narrow tent.

"This will be where you stay." He climbed off his horse and helped me down. His hands lingered at my waist a moment too long, and I stepped away.

"That's a big tent for just me." I had a bad feeling about this.

"The commanders will stay here as well." Tarik tied his horse to a nearby tree. The tent had a rough drawing of a hawk on the door flap. I glanced at the other tents. They too had drawings on them: bears, large cats, and so forth.

"Since you will teach the commanders, you are to be considered as one of them." Tarik smiled at me.

I stared at the tent.

Tarik tugged several bags off his horse. Holding them in his arms, he looked at me.

"Is there a smaller tent where I could stay by myself?"

"No," he said rather curtly. "If you were given a tent to yourself, it would show favor for you over the others. Because you are an outsider, the others would not take kindly to this. But if you live with them, they might grow to accept you."

"Why do they have to accept me? If they don't like me, they won't get too close. You know, there's a certain amount of respect you have for someone you don't know." Tarik had to understand that it was totally inappropriate for me to share sleeping quarters with the commanders.

"I do not think that is the type of respect you desire. I am the commanders' leader. And you are part of my team, so you must sleep here. You must gain their respect and devotion, and to do that, you must live amongst them."

I let out a long breath. The entire situation was impossible.

"Syd, it is the only way." Balancing his hand-stitched bags on one arm, Tarik reached out to console me but drew back his hand as if thinking better of it. "Once you teach the commanders your way of fighting, they shall teach their squads. You must develop a good relationship with them."

"But . . ." Everything he had said made sense. Still, the thought of living with a group of men was more than a little overwhelming.

"Do not fear." Tarik started for the tent. "You may sleep on the mat next to mine. No one will bother you."

With my sleeping mat close to Tarik's, the matter of the other men would be resolved, but there would be a new problem. Tarik. I mean, was this right? What would Bishop Staker say if he knew I was sleeping next to a boy? Not to mention a boy that had the bad habit of giving me butterflies.

Then again, though, the whole scenario of me spending any time at all with the stripling warriors was just a little out of the ordinary. It was true what Tarik had said; they thought I was one of them. It would cause problems if I acted otherwise. Being in close quarters with Tarik seemed like less of a concern when I looked at things in that light. I took solace in the fact that the Lord knew my situation. I would keep my focus on who I was and the reason I was here—the calling I had been given by Helaman.

Tarik went inside the tent and I followed. Inside, the tent was dark and musty, and it took my eyes a while to adjust. Finally, my eyes focused on a path down the middle. I could see what appeared to be handwoven sleeping mats on the bare ground, each with a bundle near it, which I imagined to be the few belongings of the commanders. These guys traveled light. Tarik dropped his bags on one mat.

"Will Helaman stay in the city?" I asked. It would make me feel better somehow to know he was nearby.

"Sometimes he stays in the city." Tarik pulled a sleeping mat away from the others and placed it between his and the door. "This is where you will sleep."

I nodded, then continued with my questioning. "What do you mean 'sometimes'?"

"Helaman stays in the city, but sometimes he visits camp, and there are times he goes with the scouts, so he sleeps in his saddle. Why?" Tarik picked up a spear from the ground near his mat, handing it to me.

"Just curious." I took the weapon.

Tarik stood looking at me for a moment and then started for the tent flap. "Women who speak out of both sides of their mouths always have double meanings to their questions."

"Of all the . . ."

He strode outside with me dogging his heels.

I dashed in front of him and planted my feet, sticking the weapon in the ground. "You know, it's rude to walk away when someone is talking to you."

"Rude?" Tarik shrugged and pulled the spear from the ground, handing it to me again. "That was not my intention. We must leave now to meet the commanders. They await us on the beach."

"What?" When had Tarik had time to arrange this?

As if reading my mind, he said, "While you met with Helaman, I sent word for the men to meet me there. Your lessons are to begin posthaste."

"Now?"

"Yes, now." Tarik passed me.

I felt a little queasy. I needed to prepare: I needed to know what they knew, how they fought, what weaponry they had at their disposal. I was far from ready to meet the commanders.

Tarik trudged farther and farther away, assuming I'd follow.

And what else was I to do? Back home I'd never allow a guy to take the upper hand. But I wasn't back home. I was here—in a different time, a different place, where customs clashed with what I knew. I had a lot to learn . . . but I also had a lot to teach. Finally, reluctantly, and with more than a little apprehension, I followed the stubborn warrior.

As we stepped from the jungle onto the beach, I thought I saw movement out of the corner of my eye and turned to see who had followed.

No one was there, but several sea swallows soared overhead. I gazed down at the shore. Greenish-blue water lapped at a white, sandy beach littered with seaweed. Seagulls flew overhead. Twenty commanders who looked to be between fifteen and nineteen years old were scattered about. When they saw Tarik, they immediately stopped what they were doing and came to him.

"Glad you could join us, Tarik," said a tall, muscular guy who had a warm, friendly smile. A quiver of arrows was strapped to his bronzed back, and his bow was slung over his shoulder. "Now tell me; why are we here?" He looked me over. "And who is the runt?"

I deleted *friendly* from my mental file on him.

"Enough, Abraham," said Tarik, then he turned so the others could hear. "As you have heard, Chief Captain Helaman is very proud of the way we fought; however, many were wounded in the battle for Judea. He has sent someone to help sharpen our skills so that we might avoid more serious injuries. This is Syd, from a land far away called Lake of Salt. He has a way of fighting that the chief captain has never seen before, and he wants all of us to learn this skill. If we learn it well, we should be able to avoid some injuries."

"Even you?" asked a huge, hefty fellow whose round face was accented by a knife-shaped nose. He brandished some type of weapon made of an animal's jawbone in his thick hands. His leather headband was wider than the others' and covered his entire forehead. Boulder-shaped shoulders made him a mountain of a man. He snorted.

"Even me." Tarik nodded. "I have seen Syd fight. If we learn his skill, we will surely overcome the Lamanite army and push them to the land of Desolation and even beyond." Tarik stepped into the ranks, leaving me as the center of attention.

Again, I got the funny feeling that someone was watching me from behind. I quickly checked and saw only the bushes swaying in the breeze.

I turned back and looked at the men, who waited for me to do something. For a moment, I wasn't sure what to do. The one Tarik had called Abraham was staring at me, sizing me up. A warrior whose name I didn't know stood off to the side, apart from the others. He leaned on a wooden club embedded with obsidian pieces. He was of medium build and had a fairer complexion than the others. He must be part Nephite. I couldn't take the time to assess the others. They were waiting for me to say something . . . to do something.

I knew I had to start with the basics. Falling back on what I'd been taught by my mother, I barked, "I want you to put your weapons down for a while and form four lines of five people."

No one moved. Tarik looked at me like I had gone crazy, which only spurred me on.

"You do know how to form a line, don't you?"

They all looked at Tarik, and he gave them a nod to do as I said. Reluctantly, they stepped into formation, but no one gave up his weapon. They seemed pretty attached, so I decided not to make a big deal of it. Surely as they exercised, they'd put them down.

"All right now." I took a deep breath. "We're going to do ladder drills."

They continued staring at me. This was not going to be easy.

Grabbing a stick, I walked out in front of them and drew four lines for each group spaced about five feet apart in the sand.

"What I want you to do is this: the first person in each line will run up and touch the first mark for his line, then run back to where he was standing, then run to the next mark and go back and so forth until he has touched each mark. Then he'll go to the end of the line so the next person can take his turn. Okay?"

Blank stares.

"Go!" I yelled.

Tarik slowly walked up to his line and touched the sand.

"You're supposed to run as fast as you can. Move it!"

Tarik snapped to and did exactly as I asked. The others slowly followed suit. I noticed that those at the end of the line ran much slower. In fact, the medium-built fellow with the obsidian club chose not to run at all, but walked and looked at me defiantly.

"You have a problem with this exercise?" I asked him.

He didn't answer, just stood there.

I tried to think of how to handle this situation. If I let the guy get away with insubordination, I'd lose control—which I only had because of Tarik and the respect the men had for him.

I needed the men to have respect for *me.* Was I asking too much too soon? All I knew was that I couldn't let this guy best me. "Okay. What's your name and rank?"

"Baram, commander of squad three." His voice was low and deep, almost a growl.

"Well, everyone, because Baram, commander of squad three, doesn't seem to care for ladder drills, you all are going to run as fast as you can down the beach to that driftwood. That's about a half a mile. Once you return, I want you to run backward to the log. And after that, you're going to do it sideways."

The commanders looked to Tarik as if to say, *Is he for real?* Tarik turned to me with a questioning look on his face. But then he inhaled a deep breath and took off. The others followed, some less enthusiastically than others. Baram, commander of squad three, was the worst. It was apparent that he intended to make me prove myself. The warriors were fast runners, and in no time they reached the driftwood and were heading back.

I tapped a stick in my hand, trying to think through the situation more thoroughly. I dropped the stick, and as I was crouching down to pick it up again, I heard another noise—and it was coming closer. Footfalls rushed toward me from behind. Someone had decided to take the insubordination to a new level. I waited until my assailant was close and then swung about in a tornado kick, aiming for where I thought his head would be.

I missed.

I realized with a start that my assailant was a little kid. My foot had only brushed the top of his head. He was still coming at me. I whirled about and stopped.

The kid gritted his teeth together, grabbed the stick from the ground, and jabbed at me. I smacked down his arm, knocking the stick from his hold. Then I kicked his front leg so he was off balance. Whirling about, I hooked his head behind my knee and fell, bringing him down. I quickly sprung to my feet and stood over him.

"Lib!" Tarik yelled as he stopped beside me, out of breath.

I glanced around. All the commanders had followed Tarik and now crowded around us.

"You know this kid?" I asked Tarik.

He nodded.

"So, who is he?"

The hefty commander, who looked like he could crack a brick with his pinky, piped in. "Tarik's little brother."

The boy's eyes narrowed. "I am not little. Take that back, Dagan." Lib quickly wiped his nose with the back of his hand, then started after the one he called Dagan, who was ten times his size. And in that moment, I thought of Gracie and decided that I liked this kid. Despite incredible odds, he was willing to take on anything.

Tarik grabbed his brother's arm and pulled him aside. "Be still."

"Why did you attack me?" I asked Lib.

"My brother is second in command, not you," the boy replied, his voice full of indignation.

Suddenly a tiny spider monkey scurried from the brush and climbed up on Lib's shoulder. "You brought Jukka?" Tarik asked. "Does Ima know where you are?"

Lib hesitated a moment, then said, "Yes."

I'd seen that expression before. Gracie always hesitated before she stretched the truth. This kid was lying. It didn't bother me though, mainly because it was so very obvious. Lib pulled the monkey down from his shoulder, setting him on the ground.

Tarik looked at me. "I have seen you use that technique before. How do you move your legs in such a manner?"

My mind went to the first time I had met Tarik, remembering how I had kicked his legs out from under him. "It's a sweep kick. The exercises I had you do are to help strengthen your leg muscles, to make you more coordinated so you can do it."

I turned to the group of men. "What you saw me do is just a small part of what you will learn if you follow my instructions. I can teach you how to fight men five times your size or five times your number, and you'll still win if you learn these moves. But that means you need to do the exercises."

"Maybe we should run down the beach once again?" Abraham asked the others. Looking at them, I saw less wariness, a little respect and, best of all, a hunger to fight like me. They took off. Lib started to follow, but Tarik snagged him, bringing him back.

"Return to camp. Ima will be worried." Tarik gave his kid brother a stern look. "Give me the sign."

Lib huffed, then reached as though to shake his brother's hand but instead took hold of his forearm. Tarik took hold of Lib's forearm as well, and they shook. I assumed that this was a sign of good will and of keeping a promise.

Once they let go, the monkey crawled up on Lib's shoulder again. Lib turned about and begrudgingly headed back to the jungle.

"Your brother is a bit young to be a warrior," I said as I watched the boy disappear behind some brush.

"He is only eight years old and not a warrior, but a pest." Tarik rubbed his chin and smiled as he too gazed at the brush where Lib had disappeared.

"Is Ima your sister?" I asked, wondering how many siblings Tarik had.

"No. I have no sisters and no more brothers." He sighed a little. "*Ima* is another word for mother. Her name is Bella, but we call her Ima."

He looked at me as if thinking some far off thought, then said, "I should catch up with the others." He took off down the beach.

I glanced back to the brush. The scruffy kid was trying to hide in the bushes, but his monkey gave him away. The creature sat like a sentinel on Lib's shoulder, where everyone could see.

The kid was keeping an eye on me. It made me think of the time when my mother had first started her karate studio, and how I'd sneak downstairs to watch her. I wanted to learn karate so badly that even when she threatened me with grounding, I'd still take every chance I could to watch. Spying on Mom teaching karate became a game for me.

I knew that this could not become a game for Lib. I couldn't have a little kid distracting me or the warriors. These boys were going to war—and the consequences were life and death.

CHAPTER 18

The Others

Walking back to camp, I wondered if I had accomplished anything. Fortunately, Lib had given up spying on us before the boys finished their exercises. Tarik left the group near the end to make certain that his brother had returned home.

I sighed and shook my head. The commanders' exercising had gone great compared to their sparring. They seemed to listen and even tried to do as I told them, but once they set aside their spears, swords, and other sharp things, sparring became a free-for-all—an all-out Ammonite brawl. I knew they were trying, and as I thought about how they had sparred, I realized that not long ago these boys had been farmers. I consoled myself with the fact that although they were undisciplined as soldiers, they yearned to be great warriors.

I had started with the basics. However, these guys needed remedial work. They were worse than the youngest karate kids on their first day. So what came before basics? I knew the answer. Nothing came before basics—thus the word *basics*.

"That went well." Tarik stepped beside me, interrupting my thoughts. He had returned from taking Lib to camp.

I was confused. "What went well?"

"No one killed you." He smiled.

"That's true," I said halfheartedly and kept walking.

"Perhaps . . ." Tarik huffed, trying to make me stop, ". . . they were a little unruly."

I didn't want to be cheered up; I wanted a solution. *Keep walking,* I told myself. *You're frustrated and tired, and you're going to say something you'll regret.* So of course, I spoke. "What I'd really like to know is, how in the world did you all manage to survive battle?"

Tarik looked at me, bewildered by my harsh tone.

"Really, I need to know." I stopped walking.

Tarik became somber. He stepped closer to me, invading my personal space. "Battle is different. Have you ever come face-to-face with a man who wants to kill you?"

"Yeah, remember? I'm the one you held the dagger on—twice."

"I was merely threatening you. I had no intention of killing you, especially the second time." He brushed the incident aside.

I thought of Sumo. "What about the stockade rumble? Oh, and the Lamanite who hog-tied me." Then I added with more conviction than before, "And I was only able to defend myself because of my training, which brings me back to my original question. How in the world did those boys survive battle?"

"If I recall, I saved your skin both of those times. And to answer your question, those boys survived battle because of their faith," Tarik replied calmly, watching my face, waiting for my reaction.

He was right. He had saved me. And after today, I knew with more certainty than ever that faith could be the only reason those warriors had been spared. How could I have forgotten? *Faith taught to them by their mothers.*

"Well," I said with a half smile. "Do you think you could lend me some?"

"Sure." He looked around as if he'd find it behind a tree or under a rock. "I left it somewhere around here."

"Very funny." I smiled, relaxing a little. I couldn't believe he'd pulled me out of my sour mood. But a part of me wondered if maybe it would be better if I just stayed mad. I had no desire to leave part of my heart in Book of Mormon times. "Seriously, we have a boatload of work to do."

"Boatload, huh?" Tarik's blue eyes sparkled with sincerity as he said, "The boys have much ability, and with you teaching them, we shall become a mighty force."

I appreciated his optimism, but I still didn't know where to go from here. I started walking again.

He caught up. "We can teach you something as well."

"And that would be?"

"How to hold a sword, throw a spear, or use a bow and arrow." He placed his hand on my shoulder, stopping me. "Soon we must go to battle for the city Cumeni, and your defensive fighting will serve you well, but you must also know how to kill."

"No," I said, taken aback. My karate training was not a precursor to murder.

"I misspoke." Tarik rubbed his brow, staring at the ground, then he looked at me. "You need to be *prepared* to kill. That is why I had to save you in the stockade brawl and why the Lamanites captured you. You hesitated to kill. The Lamanites will *not* hesitate to kill you, and you must be prepared to do what you have to do to survive."

I knew I could learn to handle crude spears. I'd already had training with swordplay in karate, so that wouldn't be a problem. I hadn't used a bow and arrow before, however. But I hoped that by the time the boys were ready to go to battle, Helaman would return the stone to me. This was their war, not mine. I was honored to help with what I could, but my war was back in my time, taking care of Gracie and helping my mother beat cancer.

Still, while I was here I needed to think of a way to reach the warriors. I thought of how poorly things had gone during the first training session. If things didn't change I would likely be in ancient America until I was old and gray. And then I'd have to go to war alongside them . . . and kill. Just like Tarik had said.

"I can tell you have not given the matter much thought." He started walking. "Helaman asked that I teach you how to use our weapons before the next battle."

"He did?"

Tarik nodded.

I was surprised by this news. How long did Helaman expect me to stay? "So he knows I won't be finished training by then?"

"Of course."

"But . . ."

"You will be prepared. I am a good teacher." Tarik winked at me, and my resolve melted just a little. For a moment, I forgot the tremendous responsibility I had been given, forgot I had been misplaced in time, forgot everything except for his royal blue eyes.

"Tarik!" someone yelled.

"Over here," he called.

Tall, lanky Abraham came into view. He looked at Tarik and then at me as if assessing the situation. He finally said, "They are here, Ozi and the rest. Arrived early. They bring good news."

⸸⸸⸸

Abraham and I went to greet the new arrivals.

"So, where did Father find the scrawny runt to teach us?" Abraham was not one for tact. He spoke as he thought and when he thought.

"Judea," I answered. I did not need to justify Father Helaman's decision to have Syd teach us. Abraham was my lifelong friend . . . and rival. We were constantly competing and constantly sparring. If our parents needed to find us, they only needed to look for one to find the other.

"I did not see him in Judea," said Abraham, as if he did not believe me.

"You were taking care of your squad, and then the next morning you left with Helaman." I hoped this would put an end to his queries.

"So that means the runt was there the night the battle ended."

I nodded.

"Forgive what I am about to ask, but how do you know he is not a spy?" Abraham appeared genuinely concerned.

"That is why Father had me stay behind—to question him and find out his history." I had to say this in a certain way or Abraham would know something more was afoot.

"And . . ." Abraham wanted more.

I thought of Syd hugging me tight as we'd ridden on my horse to escape the lamanites and of the way the sun had found light streaks in her short black hair.

"Believe me, sh . . . Syd is not a spy." I had to quit thinking of Syd as a woman or I was going to slip and give her away.

I told Abraham how we had been captured by the lamanites and how I'd had to rescue Syd from certain death. When I told Abraham how Syd had stared down the enemy even though they held a knife on her, he seemed more accepting.

"Good to know the boy is loyal to Helaman and our cause," Abraham said.

I was relieved to hear a more friendly tone in his voice. Syd could use all the help I could give her. There might come a time I would not be there for her. Steering the subject away from Syd, I asked, "You said sixty more of our brothers have arrived?"

Abraham nodded and led the way. "You can almost smell Jershon, our homeland, on them," he said in wistful remembrance.

"I must take an accounting of their trip, assign them to a squad, and then report to Helaman." I listed my duties aloud, hoping Abraham would assist.

"May I be of help?" he asked, as I had hoped.

I nodded. But as we walked toward the new troops, I wondered how willing Abraham would be to help if he knew I was withholding the truth about Syd from him.

‡‡‡

When Tarik left with Abraham, I hung back. I needed a little time to myself.

Time to think.

Time to worry.

I could tell by the way Abraham had been staring at me that he'd just as soon I turn Lamanite.

I understood why it would be difficult for Abraham and the rest of them to accept me. I had to gain their respect. There was no way they would learn unless they respected me enough to listen to me.

My mind drifted to what Tarik had said about battle. *Could* I could really kill someone? I remembered a conversation I had had with Mom when I had told her I wanted to be a police officer. After we had discussed the matter for a while, she had looked at me and said, "Honey, I think it's wonderful that you want to be a police officer. I want you to answer a question for me, though. Other lives will depend on you as a police officer; and in some situations, you might have to take someone's life to preserve other lives. Can you honestly tell me you could kill someone? Because if you can't you have no business being an officer."

I had thought about the question and answered her, saying, "If another officer were threatened, I know I could."

"And what if it were you, honey? Could you do it then?" I knew Mom had a valid point. It was easier to sacrifice for or stand up for someone else. However, I had ignored the wisdom of her question and answered, "Of course, no problem."

She had lifted my chin so we were staring right at each other and said, "I hope you're telling me the truth, because you're the only one I'd be worried about. I don't know what I'd do without you." Then she had given me a big hug. The memory was so fresh I could almost feel the warmth of her arms.

Please, Lord, watch over my mom, I prayed. I felt overwhelmed with old and new responsibilities. Even though I was warm, I shuddered and began walking toward the tent. As I drew near the tent, Ximon loped up to me. I immediately wrapped my arms around his neck. His long, thin tail whipped back and forth.

"The beast is glad to see you," said Ozi. He wobbled a little, carrying Mom's purse and the backpack with him. Tarik had been right—the horse must have returned home after our Lamanite attack. As Ozi handed the belongings to me, his feeble arm shook.

"Thank you," I said as I took the load. Ozi appeared more tired than ever. But despite his haggard appearance from traveling all day, his eyes were keen. He continued in his gravelly voice. "Are you well?"

"Yes, very well." I squeezed his shoulder. "And you?"

"I am as well as a curelom." He took in a deep breath.

"Just what is a curelom?" I'd heard him refer to this animal before, and I knew they were mentioned in the Book of Mormon, but I had no idea what they actually were.

"They are much the same as cumoms."

"Okay . . . and what is a cumom?"

Ozi gummed his lips together, then said, "Bigger than an elephant, and shaggy maned."

I thought for a moment, and then it dawned on me. "Are you talking about a woolly mammoth?" I had heard debates on this subject in seminary. Some people believed that the woolly mammoth came over with the Jaredites on their barges; others thought that the animals had gone extinct long before the Jaredites. I tried to think of what the

Book of Mormon said. I recalled that the Jaredites had cattle, oxen, cows, sheep, and even horses and donkeys. And I vaguely remembered there was a mention of elephants during King Emer's time.

But mammoths?

"Mammoth, no; they are no more." Ozi shook his head. Thin strands of his hair tousled about his scalp like a dandelion gone to seed. "Except perhaps in Ablom."

"Where is Ablom?"

"North, past the land of Desolation, past the Agosh Plains. Ablom was my homeland."

"Why do you think there might still be mammoths there?" I was more than a little curious.

"When I was a boy," he began as his gaze turned dreamy, "I often went hunting with my father; once we saw an entire herd."

"What happened to them?"

"I know not." Shaking his head, he said, "They are ill-tempered animals. You never want to be in one's path."

"Well then, if they are still around, hopefully they'll stay north." I said.

At that moment, Mariah came around the tent. "Syd, it relieves my mind to see you well." She glanced at my neck where the iron collar had rubbed. I knew that it must look better because she smiled. "I was also concerned for the large Dane. The journey was hard on both him and Ozi, but I see they are both revived after laying eyes on you."

The old man looked offended that Mariah thought the journey had tired him.

"Others need my attention now, however." She started away.

"How are the wounded boys?" I asked.

"Some traveled well, some did not." Mariah's face turned grim, filled with concern. In her heart, I knew Mariah had adopted all of Helaman's stripling warriors, all two thousand of them. "I am just glad the others have arrived," she added. "It will give the boys more time to heal."

"Others?"

"Yes." Mariah's face brightened as she eagerly told me. "Sixty more Ammonite brothers have joined us. And they brought word that more troops are coming."

I suddenly remembered more details about this time in Book of Mormon history. If the sixty Ammonites had already arrived, that meant six thousand more Nephite troops from Zarahemla would soon be here; so that was why Helaman knew I wouldn't be finished training his stripling warriors. The Lord must have given him a revelation that more troops were coming.

I felt overwhelmed. For the warriors to overtake the city of Cumeni, there was too much to do and no time to do it.

CHAPTER 19

For the People They Love

My meeting with Helaman was brief. Much occupied my captain's mind. We did not speak of Syd, only of the fresh troops who had arrived. I did not tarry with him long; I wanted to speak with Ima before she met Syd.

Ima was a wonderful mother who worried for my well-being much more than she should. Upon arriving at her cooking tent, I found her cutting corn from a cob with the sharp edge of a deer's jawbone. On the fire bubbled one of her soups. She looked up as I entered. Her round, cheery face brightened to the color of a red dawn when she saw that I had arrived.

"My warrior." She set the bone and corn cob on the stone slab used for cutting and came to me with open arms. "Helaman told me he left you behind in Judea to tend to some important matter." She wrapped her soft, ample arms around me and hugged me tightly.

"Ima . . ." I protested, thinking of my commander status. Then I thought better of it and hugged her back.

"What was this important matter?" She stepped away and gazed up at my face.

"The lord has sent someone to help us—a boy who comes from a faraway land." I kissed her cheek. "Ima, he is special. He will help protect my warrior brothers from harm in battle." I wanted her to know some of the story, so she would make Syd feel welcomed.

"The lord sent him?" she questioned as she hurried to stir the bubbling pot on the fire.

"Yes, I believe so," I answered.

"I must meet him." She set down the wooden spoon and started for the tent flap.

"Wait." Sometimes Ima overwhelmed people, especially those she deemed to be heaven-sent. "I shall send for him straightaway."

She placed her calloused palm on my cheek and gave me a loving pat. "He will be welcome here, my son. I shall treat him well." She wiped a bead of sweat from her brow.

"Oh, and he has an animal." I was uncertain how to describe a dog as big as a horse in terms my mother would understand. "He calls it a great dog."

"Is it harmless?" she asked while setting to work on the corn once more.

I would not say Ximon was harmless, for the beast had attacked me on the night I escorted Syd to the stockade. But as I recalled, the beast had not broken the skin, and he well could have. "The animal fights in battle with Syd, but to you, I believe he will be harmless."

"I shall treat the young man and his dog as family. Have no fear, son." With a corn cob in one hand and the jawbone in the other, she reached up and kissed me as I turned to leave.

⁂

When Ozi, Mariah, and I walked into camp, everyone was eating and sitting around various campfires by their tents. Mariah wanted Ozi and me to go with her to the cooking tents to pick up our food. I convinced the elderly man to go with her. I thought it would be best if I ate with the commanders. Besides, I needed to put the backpack in the tent. I slung Mom's purse strap over my shoulder and nestled the purse against my hip. I wanted it with me from now on. It was one of my few physical links to home.

After storing the backpack in the tent, I went to the commanders' campfire with Ximon nearly hugging my legs. He was making it obvious that he was not planning on letting me out of his sight again. The feeling was mutual. Having Ximon near gave me hope that indeed, we would eventually go back home where we belonged.

We found the commanders eating stew out of clay pots. Tarik noticed me first. He stopped eating long enough to say, "The cooking tents are beyond that grove of trees. I'm not sure what the dog can eat."

Everyone looked up then. Disbelief hung on their faces as they spied the animal beside me. I decided this would be the perfect time for introductions—and the perfect time to stop anyone from thinking Ximon would make a tasty meal.

"Boys, meet Ximon." I patted the dog's head. "He's not just a dog. He saved my life, and he may save yours. He will be a big help in battle. Treat him with respect."

I heard grumbling and a few moans. But I knew that with Ximon by my side, the boys would be a little more mindful of me. The dog would keep them on their Ammonite toes. That would be a good thing.

"Ima's tent is the first one. She cooks only for the commanders, the nursemaids, and Helaman. She is waiting for you." Hearing Tarik say the word "Ima" and the tone of respect in his voice caused another pang in my heart for my own mother.

At first I had thought it odd that Tarik's mother was here in the thick of the fighting. But I knew that if Mom were given a choice, she would be here with me as well. Besides, even warriors needed a cook. Everyday things still went on during war. Things like eating, doctoring, and personal hygiene. I knew I needed to learn more about how this last item went down in ancient times—and soon. I hadn't bathed since I'd arrived.

My stomach growled. I nudged Ximon, and we headed to the grove of tall ceiba trees. Tarik had told me the name of the stately trees as we had journeyed. A wonderful smell filtered through the grove. Was it bread? No. Something similar though. I took another sniff and detected a hint of meat.

Past the trees, I found a village of small tents cozily situated in a rough circle. I wondered which one the heavenly aroma came from. I also wondered how many other mothers besides Ima had come to cook for their sons. My stomach rumbled in protest. I needed to eat. Tarik had said his mother's tent was the first one.

Stepping over the threshold, I found Mariah and Ozi waiting to be served from a very short, round Nephite lady who was obviously the cook. The skin hanging from her arms looked soft as marshmallows.

Sweat rolled down the sides of her plump face. She looked tired—understandably so, as she was standing by a large fire pit. The fire was now merely hot coals. Among the coals were large, flat stones on which rested a huge metal pot.

The woman was plainly dressed in an apron and long tunic, which was dampened with perspiration under her arms and down her sternum. Her brown hair, peppered with gray, was braided in one long tail and hung almost to the back of her knees. It was the longest braid I'd ever seen. Her face split into a happy smile when she saw me.

"The new boy! And his . . . dog!" she exclaimed as she quickly handed steaming bowls to both Ozi and Mariah while keeping an eye on Ximon. Ozi tried to pass me his bowl. His generous offer was touching, but I couldn't take his food. I knew he had to be terribly hungry from his long journey.

"No need, Ozi," the woman said. "He gets the special bowl." She quickly wiped her hands on her apron and rummaged among a huge stack of baskets which filled one entire side of the tent, until she found an unusual bowl made of red clay, not brown like the others. A speckled cat was drawn upon it. The woman ladled a generous helping of stew and handed it to me. "My Tarik said you and your beast would be coming. I saved the guest bowl just for you."

I smiled and took the bowl. So this was Tarik's mother. I never would have guessed because of her lighter skin. She looked nothing like him. But then I noticed her eyes . . . royal blue. This was definitely Tarik's mom. At that moment, Ximon sniffed at my food.

"Do you think that your beast . . ." She eyed Ximon. "Do you think he would eat some soup? I understand he has seen battle with you." Without waiting for an answer, she began rummaging again among the stacks of baskets until she found a rather large gourd. "There is not much left, but enough to give him nourishment." She scooped up the tailings, scraping the bottom as she poured the remains into the gourd.

I took it from her.

"Bella's stew is not only delicious, but I think it has healing powers." Mariah sniffed the steam rising off her stew. Ozi was already spooning his stew into his mouth as he walked to the door of the tent and stumbled outside.

I wanted to shake Bella's hand and thank her properly, but I held the clay bowl in one hand and the gourd in the other, so I bowed and said, "Thank you. I'm sure this will help him."

"You need something to eat with." Bella pulled a wooden spoon from her apron. "Keep this and the bowl with you. Every warrior is responsible for his own gear."

"Have you eaten, Bella?" Mariah asked before we left.

"Ah, I eat as I cook." Bella waved good-bye, then said, "Oh, do not forget the cornbread."

I had not seen the other pot resting in the coals. In it were the last few pieces of cornbread. Bella set a square on top of the stew in each of our bowls, except for Ximon's.

"Come join us, Bella," said Mariah. "I am certain your poor back needs a rest."

Bella thought for a moment and then tugged off her apron. "A few minutes would be nice." She followed us outside.

Ozi had disappeared; I imagined he had gone back to Tarik's tent thinking I'd go there. Right now I preferred a little female company, though. Especially considering where I'd be sleeping that night. We came to a grouping of rocks. Mariah claimed one, Bella sat on another. I took the one on the other side of Tarik's mother. Ximon was anxious to eat and danced about as I set the gourd on the ground.

"That is a most unusual animal." Bella eyed Ximon.

"You should have seen him fighting off the prisoners in the stockade," Mariah chimed in. "He nearly died."

I ate some of the hot stew and was pleasantly surprised by the taste. There were mushrooms, chunks of various squashes, onions, corn, sweet potatoes, and tender pieces of meat, all swimming in a broth. The soup was every bit as tasty as anything I'd ever made. "What spice have you used in this?"

Both women stared at me with the most astonished looks on their faces. Bella finally answered, "The secret is a leaf of red zapote."

"It's a very earthy, woodsy taste." I took another spoonful, savoring every drop. I noticed Bella watching me. I said, "It's fantastic."

"Why, thank you, young man." She seemed hesitant, but added, "You are a most curious fellow." She eyed me even more closely.

I just smiled and bit into the cornbread. Heaven. "You have to give me the recipe," I said, licking my lips.

"Recipe?" Bella looked at Mariah, then back to me.

"You have to tell me how you made this so I can make it." As the words left my mouth, I realized my error. Men and boys did not cook in this time period. Cooking was strictly women's work. And since they thought that I was a boy, no wonder they looked at me as if I had grown three heads and a wart on each nose. I had to remedy this. "I think my mother would like to know so she can make it for us."

"Oh," Bella sounded relieved. "Certainly. I would be happy to tell your mother. I thought you said *you* wanted to make it."

"Well . . ." All I had to do was tell the truth. And I could do that. "My mother's ill."

Concern wrinkled Bella's forehead. "You poor dear." She patted my arm. And for a moment, emotion churned within me. Bella's loving pat on my arm opened the flood of emotions I'd been able to hold in check until now. Tears clouded my eyes.

"There, there." Bella placed her ample arm about my shoulders. Mariah came to kneel in front of me. "You never mentioned your mother before. What ails her?"

They would never understand cancer. I paused a moment, and said, "She has lumps growing inside her."

Bella gasped.

Mariah patted my knee. "I have something for that."

I really didn't think so, and my doubt must have shown on my face, for Mariah said, "When you are ready to return home, come to me, and I shall give you a precious root." I doubted such a remedy would work in my time, but I made a mental note to talk with Mariah before I left anyway.

"You should be at home with her." Bella stroked my hand. "A mother needs her son." Her words were kind.

I thought of Mom and hoped that she wasn't too worried about me. Stress would be the worst thing for her right now. I had to trust what Helaman had said—that the Lord would watch over her. I hoped the Lord would help her not to worry.

"So you're here so that you can be near Tarik?" I asked Bella.

"Yes." Her eyes were filled with reflection. "I pleaded with Captain Helaman to allow me to come. Then I convinced him with my cornbread." She winked at me in the same way Tarik had. It made me wonder about her husband. Did he wink like that?

"Is your husband here as well?" I questioned.

Bella withdrew her hand. The caring smile left her face, replaced by a worried look. "Mehujael is at home."

Mariah, who sat on the rock on the other side of me, spoke up. "He and the other Ammonite fathers made a covenant with God that they would fight no more. They have stayed home to tend their crops."

"Yes, they made the promise." Bella picked up the telling of the story. "The prophet Ammon converted Mehujael and his people. Mehujael's own father was killed while kneeling in the battlefield beside him as they prayed for their Lamanite brothers. My husband's covenant was sealed with his father's blood. He will always keep his word to God, even if it means death."

Her conviction and faith were strong. I could feel the love she had for her family. I wondered how she and her husband had met. "Were you there?"

"Oh, no," Bella replied, smoothing her apron. "My people live near the land of Jershon, where Ammon had my husband and his people settle. Our courtship is quite a story, but you must eat."

"Why didn't you leave Lib with your husband?" This was none of my business, but I was curious as to why such a caring woman would bring a child to war.

"Oh, I did leave him," Bella huffed and then chuckled.

"Lib," Mariah added. "That one has a mind and will of his own. He appeared in Judea a day or so after Helaman and his troops arrived. Imagine traveling all that way alone at such a young age."

"He and his brother are much the same." Bella nodded. "As soon as Helaman suggested that the young men in our village fight so their fathers could keep their covenant, Tarik was the first to sign up. Lib tried, but I would not allow it. Tarik was the one to talk him into staying home. My Tarik has always had such a gentle way about him. He could talk a jaguar into purring."

Obviously, Tarik's persuasive power hadn't held for long because Lib had followed. I thought of the two times that Tarik had threatened my life. He had never impressed me as gentle. But then I thought of how he had helped me off his horse after saving me from the Lamanites, how he had wiped dried blood from my face, and how he had flirted with me after my meeting with Helaman. Yes, there was gentleness in him.

"Where's Lib now?" I questioned, looking about, expecting to see him and his monkey materialize.

"That boy will be the death of me," Bella sighed. "He gobbled down his food and mumbled something about doing exercises before he and Jukka raced off. What are *exercises?*"

Mariah shrugged.

"It is using your muscles to strengthen them," I told her, trying to keep it in terms she'd understand. The kid had overheard me talking with the commanders. I had to admire his spunk.

I looked at Bella and then at Mariah. These two women would be my solace. I wanted so much to tell them I was a girl and that I was from a very different place and time. I briefly wondered whether if I told them, they'd be able to convince Helaman to return the stone to me. But in my heart I knew I couldn't tell them.

The Lord wanted me to help the stripling warriors. And after listening to Bella speak of her husband and knowing that each one of the warriors came from a home and a family that had sacrificed so much for their faith, I felt my determination to do as Helaman had asked strengthen.

I couldn't help Mom right now, but I could help these boys fight for the people they loved.

CHAPTER 20
The Agreement

I lay wide awake on my mat—Tarik on one side of me, Ozi on the other, and Ximon snuggled against my feet—listening to a remarkable choir of snores. How Ozi ended up between me and the door, I didn't know. Now that I was awake, I knew I'd never fall asleep again with this racket going on. Ozi was the worst. Not only did he snore, but he had some gurgling action going on. Mom never snored. Gracie did on occasion, but her snoring was nothing compared to the commotion going on inside this tent. I was grateful for the little sleep I had stolen, since I had retired before anyone else.

Glancing over at Tarik, I noticed he didn't make any noise but slept soundly. Cautiously, I crawled past Ozi over to the door. Ximon awoke and followed me as I slipped out.

Louder snoring came from the other tents. How in the world was I going to get any rest?

With Ximon by my side, I started down the grassy forest path leading to the beach. I decided that sleeping on the beach and listening to the rolling waves was preferable to having my ears assaulted by that nasally chorus.

As I walked, I grabbed Ximon's collar, hoping he'd guide me safely through the trees surrounding us. The bushes reached out, grabbing at my *gi.* Twigs brushed my face, and, for a moment, I wondered if a Lamanite could be prowling in the trees, stalking me. I was so tired my mind was playing tricks. Step by silent step, we made our way.

Diverting my thoughts from images of Lamanites, I thought about how I could bring order to the commanders' sparring.

Repeating the techniques might bring more order. I had to keep after them to listen and to do what I asked them to.

I stepped out from the protection of the trees onto the beach. The face of the moon appeared. Its silvery glow sparkled over the ocean of darkness as small rolling waves whispered up to shore. The ebb and flow of the water was hypnotizing. Being an inlander, I truly appreciated such a glorious sight. It looked like heaven, and I had the sudden urge to swim.

Shedding my *gi,* but leaving on my underwear, I raced down to the water's edge, hesitated a moment, and dived in. The cold water swallowed me; it felt wonderful and wasn't as cold as Utah Lake. I realized these waters were closer to the equator. I looked to shore and saw Ximon sitting alone on the beach. He wasn't fool enough to swim. I didn't swim long, a little afraid I'd become too tired to walk out.

Shivering as I hurried to my clothes, I wished I'd brought a towel. After tugging the pants over my wet legs, I quickly slipped my arms into the top, all the while scanning my surroundings, hoping no one had seen me. I knew I couldn't do this all the time, but I really had to take a bath once in a while, even if it was in the ocean. My skin felt salty and slightly sticky.

Shoving my feet into the soft doeskin sandals Tarik had given me, I realized Ximon had disappeared. He had probably gone back to camp. I sighed. I knew I couldn't really sleep on the beach. Sand was everywhere, and probably sandmites as well. I was so tired now I was certain the guys' snoring would not keep me awake.

Leaving the beautiful scenery behind, I headed toward camp. In the moonlight the huge trees appeared even more foreboding, their branches outstretched and vines hanging from them. They looked like floating ghosts. As I walked, I swore I could hear someone tailing me. *Stay calm,* I told myself. *Simply confront.*

Quickly turning about, fully expecting to see someone, I was relieved to find I was alone. The wind rustled the branches above as I stood stock-still, waiting, listening.

Gooseflesh prickled my skin. I felt as though a wraith had passed by me. The urgency to run to camp swung me around—and right into a person.

Tarik growled some Hebrew term I'd never heard before.

Once I realized who it was, I hugged him with relief. The warmth of his body was like a cozy comforter to my cold, wet skin. After a moment, I stepped away, and cool air rushed between us. Ximon was with him, and I wondered if the dog had retrieved Tarik.

"What are you doing out here? And why are you wet?" he scolded as he glanced over me, taking in my wet hair, damp skin, and shivering body.

"I couldn't sleep, so I went for a swim," I explained between shivers. "Did Ximon wake you?"

"No. I rolled over and found you were gone. The dog met me on the path." Tarik reached out and brushed wet bangs out of my eyes.

I shivered.

He put his arm around my shoulders, rubbing my upper arm to warm me. As we walked toward the tent, I said, "I like your mother."

"Good. I do as well," he said as another chill overcame me. He hugged me closer.

"She told me about your father, Mehujael."

"Yes?"

"And that he refuses to fight because of his promise to God."

Tarik said nothing.

"I think you and the other warriors are the most noble people I've ever met." I was sincere.

"That's good," he replied.

I had hoped he'd say something more, something along the lines of "I think you're pretty great, too."

"I just gave you a compliment," I said.

"A compliment?"

"A tribute." I hoped he understood what I meant.

I stopped walking and looked up at him. The moonlight glanced over his sculpted face, and I thought once again that he was one of the most handsome guys I'd ever seen. He leaned his head down to mine. He was so close—kissably close.

There was no way I could think like this. Irritated at myself for my romantic thoughts, I blustered, "Well?"

"Well, what?" His breath fanned my face.

I stepped away and raked my fingers through my damp hair. "Never mind."

"Syd, what should I say?" He was earnest.

"I don't know." I felt silly for making a big deal out of this now. "When someone compliments you, you should say something nice in return."

"I do not think you are angry over a tribute." Tarik exhaled a long breath. "I *do* want to honor you with tributes—tributes of your courage, of your skill in fighting." Tarik paused and looked into my eyes. "And also of how beautiful you are." He reached up again to brush his hand against my cheek.

I felt myself blush in the darkness. No one had ever called me beautiful before—well, besides Mom. Then Tarik said, "But I cannot endanger your teaching the commanders. Right now, they are more important than my feelings for you. If I jeopardize their respect for you, they will not accept your help as a teacher. If anyone saw us . . . together . . . We cannot risk anyone finding out you are a girl. We cannot risk being alone in the night ever again." I knew that what he said made sense, but a tingling flashed over my skin. *He felt the same way I did.*

Who would have thought that the first guy I'd fall for would be from 66 B.C.? I knew that these were crazy, dangerous thoughts, especially when my future depended on clear thinking.

I swallowed the lump that had been growing in my throat and mumbled, "Perhaps we should go back to the tent."

"Yes," he said quietly.

We walked in silence. Reaching the tent, we entered. Ximon had beaten us back and was snuggled up to Ozi. Both of them were sound asleep. Tarik and I lay down on our separate mats.

We both turned on our sides, facing away from one another.

It was many hours before I fell asleep. As I finally drifted off, I could still feel the touch of his hand on my cheek.

✢✢✢

I awoke to find an empty tent. Grabbing Mom's purse and running a hand through my hair, I hurried out. Ozi and Ximon were waiting for me near the cold campfire.

"You slept well?" asked Ozi, whose wrinkled face looked like a dried-up apple in the early morning light.

"No," I said hoarsely, not really wanting to talk yet. The dog and old man followed me to Bella's cooking tent.

Bella gave us corn tortillas. Her gaze was hard to meet, knowing I was fast developing a crush on her son—while she thought I was a boy. I mumbled a thank you and left.

Heading for the beach, where I knew the commanders would be waiting, I glanced back at Ozi and Ximon. They were still following and looked at me as if to say "Now what?" I waved back at them and kept walking. Once we were on the beach, Ozi settled in the shade of some palm trees with Ximon.

"Let's get to work," I called to the commanders. Most of them ambled over. Tarik had not arrived as yet; neither had Abraham.

Baram came to stand beside me, which I thought was a little odd. I didn't want to confront him. Not today. I quickly glanced over to Ozi. He had fallen asleep in the shade. Ximon watched over the elderly man.

I turned my concentration back to the group before me. "Today I'd like to teach you the warrior art of the Leopard." I noticed Baram had remained standing by my side instead of going back to stand with the others. I went on, ignoring him. "This is a very aggressive, powerful fighting style, which relies on speed."

Suddenly, Baram flew into motion. "Like this?" he yelled. Using his club as an anchor, he launched a kick at my side. Immediately I spun into action, deflected his attack, and jabbed my elbow into his back as he passed by me. He went down on his knees for just a moment. Baram looked livid. He grabbed his club, which was embedded with sharp obsidian, and jumped to his feet. With a dark gleam in his eyes, he swung his club. He meant to kill me.

Mom's words came to my mind: "Do not rely on your own strength; rely on your opponent's weakness."

With Baram's arm stretched back, his entire torso was vulnerable. I quickly did a spinning side-thrust kick and rammed my heel into his side. He doubled over, dropping his club. I managed to toss the hefty club away from us. If he wanted to duke it out, at least now our fight would be fair.

Baram drew a concealed dagger from his belt. So much for fairness. He hurled himself at me. Ready for such a double cross, I swiftly stepped to the side and parried his attack with the outer part of my arm, chopping his wrist to make him release the dagger. Striking his arm twice, I pinned it to him. Quickly slapping his throat, I did a step-through, open-hand strike and knocked him to the ground. Snatching up the dagger, I pressed the blade beneath his chin.

True fear twitched the corners of his eyes; but I knew I could not draw blood. I would not hurt him. He glared up at me, expecting me to deliver a blow. But karate was not about killing. Flipping the dagger so it stuck in the sand, I stared down at him. "If you want a piece of me, you'd best pay attention during class."

Turning away from Baram, I realized Tarik stood near me. Beside him was Abraham, and behind them were the rest of the commanders. Tarik confiscated Baram's dagger and helped the humiliated warrior to his feet. They glared at each other until Baram slunk to the back of the crowd. Looking at the other commanders, I saw respect in their eyes.

As everyone settled down, I glanced at Ozi and Ximon. They had not stirred. I smiled. So much for my personal bodyguard coming to my rescue.

Things went better from then on. Baram stayed at the back of the class. He reminded me of a pouting juvenile delinquent; I could see him scrutinizing my every move, just waiting for me to make a mistake. But that was all right; it would keep me on my toes.

The commanders put down their weapons to exercise this time; I was impressed. I knew this was hard for them. Weapons were an important part of life here. After watching the men in camp the day before, I understood why they had been reluctant to put the weapons down. The boys carried them everywhere they went, ready for an unexpected attack.

Their sparring improved. We worked on gripping, footwork, and strikes. I drilled them hard, making sure they targeted their opponents' torso and thighs, with no strikes to the knees, neck, or groin. I didn't want them crippling each other before an actual battle.

I tried to discourage them from grappling, wrestling, or clinching. And although they wanted to learn how to do sweeps, I first wanted them to concentrate on how to disarm and release as fast as they could.

When the sun shone straight overhead, I gave the warriors a break for lunch. Tarik motioned for me to walk with him along the beach. His expression told me that there was something he wanted to talk about. He told the others to go on to the cooking tents without him.

Ximon galloped over to me. Patting the dog's head and rubbing behind his ears, I glanced over to Ozi, who was still sleeping against the tree trunk. "We're going to have to do something about Ozi. He follows me everywhere; he's bound to find out I'm a girl."

Tarik glanced at the old man. "I understand. Perhaps I should tell him that Helaman wants him to guard the prisoners again. They had to bring the prisoners from Judea. He will not want to, but at least he will be gone part of the time. Be patient with him. He is very devoted to you."

"Thanks," I said. Tarik smiled slightly, the same smile he'd given me the night before. He looked about to say something more, but then he turned and headed toward Ozi. I sighed. Being so close to Tarik was difficult. I knew that having him train me to use a sword and a bow and arrow would be just about unbearable. I needed to speak with Helaman.

As Ximon and I walked away, I wondered what Tarik had been about to tell me. I almost turned back around but decided that if it was important, he would tell me later. I headed to the cooking tent and tried to think of where Helaman might be today.

Suddenly Lib jumped right in my path; the spider monkey clung to his shoulder and squawked a chimplike jargon. Ximon lunged forward, trying to nip the creature.

I grabbed hold of the dog's collar and asked Lib, "Was there something you wanted, Lib?"

"I need to speak with you." He wiped his nose with not only the back of his hand but his forearm as well, as the monkey crawled to his head, grabbing chunks of the boy's hair. Ximon strained against me to get at the critter; then suddenly he stopped, turned toward camp, and broke free of my hold.

I glanced down the path, watching as the Great Dane disappeared near the cooking tents. Wonderful aromas drifted my way. It seemed that Ximon's desire to eat was more powerful than his desire to play. I was curious what wonderful food Bella had made.

"Come, eat with me, and we can discuss what's on your mind." I started down the path.

"I heard . . ." his voice came from behind me. "I heard you and my brother talking last night. You are a girl."

I stopped dead in my tracks.

So I *had* been followed. I immediately swung around, checking to see if anyone had overheard. No one was about.

The kid smiled up at me with a smug look on his face, and I swear his flea-bitten monkey did, too.

"I don't know what you're talking about." Lib couldn't know my secret. I turned and started for the tent again. But then I stopped.

There was no use denying it. He knew.

Lib was a threat to everything now: to teaching the warriors, to my going home where I belonged. I could not chance his telling what he knew.

Swinging around to face the little twerp, I watched as he clutched the monkey to his body like a football and began running away. Nunchakus! I took off after him, catching up as he slowed down for Abraham and Dagan, who were walking up the path.

He dodged between their bodies, escaping me.

"What . . ." Dagan tried to get out of my way, but his wide girth made it impossible.

Abraham latched on to Lib. "What are you doing?" he asked, looking first at the child, then at me. I saw that Abraham had that friendly, deceptive smile on his face, the one that had fooled me when I'd first met him.

"We're playing 'catch me if you can.'" I grabbed on to Lib. "Thanks for the help." I hustled the boy away from them and went in the opposite direction. The monkey leaped from Lib to me. His sharp little claws dug into my neck as he clung on. I walked deep into the jungle, away from everyone, before speaking.

Sitting on a log, I kept a tight grip on Lib's arm. The monkey jumped off and scampered up a tree. I looked at the kid, who smiled wickedly.

The little blackmailer.

"Look . . ." I was suddenly at a loss for words. Finally, I asked, "What do you want?"

He swiped his tongue over his chapped lips, as if I'd offered him a treat of some kind. Growing quiet, he looked at me seriously. "Teach me how to fight."

"You're too young." I let go of him.

"I can fight like the rest of them." Grit was in his voice, earnest desire in his tone.

What could I do? What could I say? I taught karate to kids much younger than Lib every day back home. But those kids were not about to go to war. If I said no, Lib would tell everyone I was a girl. If I taught him, he could get killed. Great choices. But I also knew that if I didn't teach him, he would likely find a way to go to battle anyway.

Lib was determined. And right then, sitting there looking into his eyes, I realized he didn't remind me of Gracie at all.

No, he reminded me of myself.

I rubbed my eyes; my tired, burning eyes. And I looked again at the kid who mirrored me at this same age, except . . . he *was* a boy. He had me cornered. I could do nothing. "Okay."

He let out a loud shout and started jumping around. The monkey became excited too, chattering up a storm.

"Quiet down," I said as I took hold of Lib's arms and bent down so that I was at his eye level. "I'll do this, but you have to promise me something; you have to take an oath that you won't tell anyone I'm a girl."

"You mean, as my father did when he promised he would not fight his Lamanite brothers?" Lib's eyes seemed to bore right through me. He knew how serious this was.

"Yes, like that." I was tempted to smile but didn't.

He reached with his right hand and took hold of my upper forearm as I'd seen him do when he promised Tarik he'd leave my first training session with the commanders. But I did not see the glint of mischief in his eyes as I had seen before. I took hold of his forearm. As we shook arms, Lib said, "I swear not to tell that you are a girl."

He was so fervent, so serious. I replied, "We have an agreement."

CHAPTER 21
MEN'S VOICES

Ozi was very unhappy to be reassigned to guard the prisoners. When I told him we were short of men and he could be with Syd whenever he was off duty, he seemed to be comforted. The elderly man knew something was different about Syd, though I was sure he did not realize the difference was that Syd was actually a woman. With Ozi on his way to the new stockade, I hurried toward the city. I wanted to tell Syd what I planned to do next, but I had to make certain Helaman would be in agreement with my decision first.

As much as I hated to admit it, Syd was right. She could not stay in the commanders' tent. She had to sleep somewhere else.

Not only to keep her secret safe, but to keep a safe distance between the two of us.

‡‡‡

Climbing the steps of the building where I had met with Helaman, I saw Abraham walking out with his bow and quiver of arrows slung over his shoulder. He squinted up at the sun, then down the stairs at me. I didn't want to talk with him, deciding that the less I said the better off I'd be.

"Where is your four-legged friend?" He stopped me before I could go by.

"With Bella. It seems he prefers her cooking to being with me right now." I hurried past.

"Where are you going?" Abraham asked as I hurried away.

Without turning, I said, "Looking for Helaman."

"He is not here." Abraham sighed. "He is gone on a scouting trip."

"Nunchakus." I turned around and went back down the stairs.

"Is your message important?" Abraham followed.

"Yeah." I didn't look at him, afraid he'd be able to read my mind.

"Well, you might catch him." Abraham pointed to the thatched roof of a building. "He saddles his horse at the stable."

"Thanks." I reached to give Abraham a thank-you pat on the arm but stopped myself. Fortunately he didn't seem to notice.

"We need to talk when you return to camp," he called after me.

"Why?"

"Look for me on the beach," he added as he strode away.

I hurried down the dirt road and wondered what Abraham wanted to talk with me about. Maybe he wanted more practice sparring, though he was catching on faster than the others. I really didn't think he had a problem. Maybe he was a perfectionist.

Nearing the stable, I tried to think of how I would tell Helaman that I couldn't have Tarik train me.

Walking up to the stable door, I heard voices. Helaman was speaking with someone. When the person spoke, I recognized the voice.

Tarik!

I leaned against the wall and listened.

"Sir, I have stationed Ozi with the prisoners."

"That is fine." That was Helaman.

"Also, sir, I believe Abraham should train Syd on how to use a weapon."

"Why, is there a problem?"

There was a long pause, then Tarik replied, "No, sir, I believe Syd has the capability to be a great bowman. The bow is not my best weapon, however, and Abraham is an expert."

So that was why Abraham wanted me to find him when I returned. Tarik must have already primed him to take over my training.

"I see. Do what you believe is best." Helaman again. "Tell Abraham to start right away, though. Time is in short supply. Anything else?"

"Yes." Another pause. "I think it would also be better if Syd lodged with my mother and little brother."

"Why?" Helaman's gruff voice questioned.

"Uh . . ." More pausing. I was curious what excuse Tarik would give Helaman.

"For the men to pay him the respect he needs, Syd should have some distance from them."

Exactly what I had said when Tarik was so determined to have me stay in the commanders' tent.

"With him gone, the men can complain all they want to me, and I can set them straight."

Helaman must have been busy with his saddle or something because no one spoke for a long time. Finally Helaman answered, "All right, but why put him with your mother and brother?"

I had the same question.

"Sir, with his rank, Syd cannot lodge with the other troops."

"Of course not, but we could give him his own tent. Your mother is so busy cooking and chasing Lib that another person in her quarters would cause her grief."

"I spoke with her this morning. She thinks Syd would be a good influence on my brother."

"Very well. Let it be so. However, upon my return, I want a full report from you and Sydney as to the troops' readiness to fight."

The sound of horse's hooves on packed clay clued me in that Helaman would soon ride out. I'd lost my chance to say my piece, but it turned out I hadn't needed it. I slipped around to the other side of the stable where Helaman couldn't see me and waited until the pounding of hoofbeats faded away.

I was, for the most part, relieved that Tarik had spoken with Helaman about where I should lodge—and that the fact that I was a girl had not slipped out. But I was also a little annoyed that Tarik had taken matters into his own hands without saying anything to me. And the thought of spending so much time with Lib was a bit daunting, especially now with him blackmailing me into training him. It might be better if I had my own tent. I'd seek out Helaman when he returned and see if that could be arranged.

As I crept from my hiding place, I spied Tarik striding down the road. I ran to catch up.

"So, you decided for me where I should stay?" I said as I neared him.

He glanced behind and stopped. "I decided for *me*."

"What?" His answer was a surprise. I hadn't been prepared for that response.

"With you sleeping near me last night, I could not rest." He sighed.

"Well, why didn't you move?"

"I did not want to wake you." He looked over my face as if committing it to memory. "I knew you had trouble sleeping." His eyes became kind and caring. "You were so tired. You look much better today." He reached as though to touch my cheek but stopped.

Any annoyance I'd felt was gone. How could I stay annoyed with someone who looked at me in such a way?

I was tempted to tell Tarik that his little brother knew I was a girl. But standing there on the clay road with the sun beating down on us, I saw the crease of worry on his brow and realized Tarik had enough problems without my adding to them. He was second in command with over two thousand and sixty troops depending on him; he didn't need to worry about everything.

"If you overheard me talking to Helaman about your moving in with Ima, you must have heard about Ozi, and about your training with Abraham as well." He turned and started walking.

"Yes." I followed. "I heard. Thanks for taking care of Ozi. Do you really think I could be skilled with a bow and arrow?"

"You would be good doing anything you set your heart on." He smiled. "So yes, I do believe you would make a fine bowman."

"I'd never thought of myself as the Robin Hood type," I joked. He looked at me a bit confused. I continued. "You're not trying to keep me away from hand-to-hand combat, are you?"

"I must admit the thought crossed my mind." He stopped. And I did too. A fringe of my bangs fell into my eyes. He pushed it aside with his finger. "Though I know combat will find you. War is war." He stood gazing into my eyes, weakening my knees and quickening my breath. I willed myself to stand there, breathing in his nearness. I didn't know what to say. Finally, he spoke. "We must fit you with a helmet, and wrist and shin guards. A shield and spear would be good as well."

"Tarik, I don't plan on being here that long. As soon as Helaman returns, I will speak with him about going home."

"You haven't trained the warriors. They need you." His pleading eyes searched mine.

"They are better now than they were yesterday. Tarik, I want to help the warriors. I really do. I'm torn between wanting to help here and going home to my mother and little sister. You have Captain Helaman. Mom and Gracie only have me," I said. Surely Tarik would be able to understand my situation.

"I understand the loyalty you carry for your loved ones. But war does not stop for family. Please teach my warrior-brothers more of your skill before you leave us."

I thought again of what Helaman had told me: the Lord would look after Mom and Gracie while I was here. They would be all right. I just needed to work on my faith. But I knew that the longer I stayed, the more important it was going to be that I keep my distance from Tarik. The more my feelings became tangled up with him, the more difficult it would be to leave when the time came.

CHAPTER 22
A Summons

The days went by quickly, filled with my teaching the commanders in the morning and training with Abraham in the afternoon. At night, Ozi would always stop to see how I was doing and tell me how his day had gone. He seemed to be gaining more strength. His legs didn't wobble, nor did his arms shake as they had. He was a kind old man, and I loved him as I would a grandpa. I enjoyed thinking of him as a surrogate grandparent. At home, I didn't have grandparents. Mom's folks had died when she was young. And I really didn't know if my father's parents were still alive.

Several times I caught Tarik watching me during the day from a distance. If he had been Colin, I would have been annoyed that he was keeping an eye on me, yet with Tarik, his watchfulness gave me comfort.

During our progress reports with Helaman, Tarik would stay in the same room with me. However, once the meeting drew to a close, he'd take off like a sprinter, claiming he had something urgent that needed his care. I was a bit disappointed by this but also relieved. I had enough to do without complicating my mind with thoughts of our relationship . . . a relationship doomed from the start.

My move to Bella's tent turned out to be the best thing for everyone. No snoring and no close quarters with Tarik. For the most part, Ximon got along fine with Jukka, Lib's spider monkey. Many times the monkey rode on Ximon's back as they played.

Being away from the main troops also allowed me to secretly train Lib. After dinner, we'd go for a walk back to the same secluded grove of trees where I'd agreed to train him. I was pleased to discover that the boy had potential and learned quickly.

Then one day, while in the midst of my bow training with Abraham, Helaman sent a messenger to fetch me. My arms ached from the draw of the bowstring and my fingers were sore. But my aim had improved, and nine times out of ten I could hit my target. I immediately gave up my practice and ran with Ximon by my side most of the way to Antiparah and the building where Helaman stayed.

I noticed a horse tied to the hitching post when I arrived. The black mare had been ridden long and hard; a film of lather showed on her flanks, dried mud clung to her hooves, and trail dust covered the saddle, except where someone had sat. A chill skidded up my spine. What did this mean?

"You have been summoned as well?" Tarik stepped beside me and patted Ximon. The dark blue of Tarik's eyes was more intense than ever when he smiled. The sun glared down on his ebony hair, held back from his face by a leather strap. For a brief moment I allowed myself to admire his bare chest and muscular arms; I wanted him to hold me.

"Yeah," I answered as I tried to distance myself. Like a mantra, I mentally repeated, *I am a warrior.* Finally, I asked, "What do you suppose this is about?"

"I am not certain." He followed me. "I had been helping Dagan with his squad. They are having trouble with the 'snake circle' you taught them to disarm the enemy."

"It can be a challenge." My mind flashed back to teaching the technique in my mother's dojo and how, even under those favorable circumstances, the students had had trouble.

"Do you think the leaders are improving?" Tarik opened the door to the building. I stepped past him and was followed by Ximon.

"Yes, they're much better," I had to admit. In the last couple of days the grumblings I'd endured in the beginning had entirely disappeared. Even Baram seemed to listen intently.

We had arrived at Helaman's door. Men's voices could be heard. Tarik looked at me. I looked at him. He shrugged and knocked. A Nephite soldier I'd never seen before opened the door. He wore a metal breastplate over his tunic and held his helmet under his arm. At his waist was strapped a large scimitar. He was of Nephite descent, but the dust of the road clung to his skin so thickly he appeared brown-skinned.

I stood there looking at him, wondering who he was. He warmly shook Tarik's forearm, drawing him inside. Finally gathering my wits about me, I nodded a hello to the Nephite as I stepped into the room. Ximon followed with his head down, not looking at the stranger. He settled next to the wall, as if to keep out of sight.

Helaman had been sitting behind the table and rose as we entered. He came to stand beside Tarik and me. "Captain Gid has just arrived with fresh supplies from Zarahemla."

So this was Gid. I'd often wondered what he looked like; he was so briefly mentioned in the Book of Mormon. I reached out my hand and said, "Nice to meet you."

The soldier merely stared at me. And then I remembered I was just a little miss—mr.—nobody. I joined Ximon next to the wall.

Helaman went on, oblivious to the awkward moment. "Gid's troops are waiting on the outskirts of Cumeni. We must prepare our boys to leave as soon as possible."

My heart skipped a beat, then tripled in speed. The time had come. My training was over. Everything I had taught the commanders, and hopefully everything they passed on to their troops, would now be put to the test.

I prayed they were ready.

And then, I prayed that now the training was over it was time for me to go home.

CHAPTER 23
PREPARE YE EVERY NEEDFUL THING

Captain Gid had worked out a plan, and we spent the better part of the afternoon talking strategy. I hoped that by the end of the day I'd be in Salt Lake.

"Ammoron has left the city," said Captain Gid. "His troops' provisions are low. I left my army on a bluff overlooking Cumeni. With your warriors we can easily fight our way into the city."

Remembering the story of how Cumeni had been taken, I said without thinking, "But if they are low on provisions, do we really need to fight our way in? Couldn't we just wait them out?"

Captain Gid once again gave me a look that said, *and you are . . . ?* I couldn't blame him. Here I was, the new warrior on his Nephite block, telling a battle-scarred soldier how to capture a city. I glanced over to Helaman.

He looked between me and Gid, then turned to Tarik. "What do you think we should do?"

Tarik studied me, and I couldn't tell what he was thinking. I tried to send him a telepathic thought to go along with me on this. I knew what I was talking about. Tarik glanced at Gid before turning his full attention to Helaman. "Captain Gid knows firsthand what has happened at Cumeni."

Why wasn't Tarik listening to me? I wanted to interrupt him, but knew such an action would be insubordinate. Gid already didn't seem to like me. I couldn't cross the line of army protocol.

Tarik kept his gaze on Helaman. "It may be best to go in while they are weak and before they can regroup and become stronger.

However, it may be wise to meet again once we are on Cumeni soil so that we can assess the situation."

Well, at least he didn't totally shoot down what I'd said. I could tell that Gid wasn't all that happy with the compromise. He clenched his teeth and kept his attention focused on Helaman, ignoring me—the intruder.

"To meet once we are there would be wise," Helaman said, laying a hand on Tarik's shoulder. "Prepare the troops for immediate departure. Meet me and Captain Gid in front of the stable."

Helaman turned to Gid. "You must freshen up and eat before we leave."

"To freshen up is for weak-kneed women," Gid growled, but smiled for his friend. "Though some of my sister Bella's cornbread would be good."

I was surprised. If Gid was Bella's brother, he was also Tarik's uncle. Why didn't Tarik call him uncle? Why did Helaman act as if the two were not related? Then I realized it must be the custom of rank in their army. No wonder Tarik had sided with Gid; at least he had left the door open to the idea of waiting. I realized that Tarik had been as diplomatic as he could have been under the circumstances.

"Very well." Helaman clapped the man on the back. "I am certain Tarik will be happy to take you to Bella's tent."

"Syd," Helaman called to me. "Please stay a moment."

Joy replaced my apprehension; maybe now, at last, he would return the stone to me. It all fit. I had finished training the commanders. Ximon and I were together. We could be home in a matter of seconds, no need to go to war, no need to deal with my feelings for Tarik. The time had come for me to go. I wanted to take Tarik aside and tell him good-bye, but he and Gid were out the door before I could speak. A pang of sorrow pricked my heart; I would never see Tarik again. But I pushed the feeling aside; I was going to see my mother.

Helaman closed the door and motioned for me to have a seat. He sat on the chair behind the table, looking at Ximon. Then he called the dog. Amazingly the Great Dane went to him as if they were long lost friends. Rubbing behind Ximon's ears, Helaman said, "This is the animal that escorted you here?"

Did he mean to this time period or to this building? I'd never thought of Ximon escorting me to this time, but now that I thought about it, if it hadn't been for the Great Dane I might be home right now. And the dog had followed me to the meeting. It didn't matter which instance Helaman referred to, because it was true on both counts. I nodded.

"On the night we met, you mentioned we would take Cumeni, but you neglected to say how." Helaman turned his attention away from the dog and directed it to me.

This was not how I'd pictured the conversation going. I'd already told him he'd take back Cumeni and the city of Manti. Besides, he had direct revelation from God. He didn't need me.

Helaman quietly, patiently waited for my reply.

Again I was prompted to tell him what I knew. I plunged ahead, praying what I remembered was right. "It is true the Lamanites are low on provisions. If our warriors, along with Captain Gid's troops, surround the city by night we will be able to stop supplies from reaching them."

So far Helaman was with me, but the hard part was coming. Drawing on my Book of Mormon knowledge, I forged ahead. "We will need to keep the Lamanites surrounded for many nights."

Helaman nodded, but said, "As you can see from the meeting we just held, my friend Captain Gid is a man of action. He will not care for such a strategy." Helaman studied me as he spoke as if he were a professor and I were his student. He continued. "Gid is a true soldier who wants to end this war quickly. I rather doubt he will have the patience to wait. What do you think?"

"He probably will hate waiting. And I'm sure he's going to hate this as well: our troops must sleep on their swords in case the Lamanites try to sneak out and kill them in their sleep."

Helaman's right eyebrow jumped up. He nodded though. "Gid would welcome such news. Soldiers want their swords with them at all times." Helaman folded his arms. "The hatred of our Lamanite brethren is strong. They will do whatever they believe is necessary to win. If they think killing soldiers as they sleep is needed, they will do so." He rose from the table, stroking his rust-colored beard. Worry lines furrowed his forehead. "The Lord has revealed this same plan to me. I know it is what we must do. However, Gid will see this as cowardly. He shall have to adapt." Helaman paused, then said, "Please go on; it brings me great joy to know that the Lord's revelations will be read by many in the future."

I continued. "The Lamanites will try to kill us many times; but we will have to stay the course and not attack the city because, even though they will try to slay us, it will be their blood that will be spilled, not ours."

Helaman nodded, and a smile came to his lips, validating my words. He waited for me to proceed.

"Their provisions will arrive, and we'll take them."

"Yes." Helaman nodded. "Continue."

"The Lamanites will become weak and lose hope. They will virtually give the city to us without our losing a single man." I was glad to be finished and hoped Helaman would now reward me with the stone.

He sat down and leaned back against his chair. Placing his hands together in a steeple, he looked deep in thought. Ximon rested his snout on the prophet's leg.

I sat quietly, thinking about what I'd do when I returned home. After checking on Mom, I'd go see Gracie. I missed my little sister. I'd fix them something wonderful to eat; maybe some of Bella's stew and, of course, her cornbread. Mom would love it.

Helaman leaned his elbows on the table, looking me square in the eyes. "We shall need the Lord's help to convince Captain Gid that this is the strategy we must use."

"What?" Had he said *we?* A wave of disappointment washed over me as my hopes of seeing Mom or Gracie in the near future faded. Ximon came over and nuzzled my hand with his wet nose as if to console me.

"Go help Tarik prepare to leave." Helaman stood and started for the door. "Tell Lib your training sessions with him are finished and that he is to stay here with his mother. If I find him in Cumeni, I shall personally deal with him."

Helaman had kept a closer eye on me than I had thought. He knew I was training Tarik's little brother. If he knew all this, why didn't he know I needed to go home?

"What about the stone?"

Helaman walked toward the door. "The stone?"

"Yes, I thought that after I finished . . ." Tears clouded my vision. "I need to go home."

Helaman patted my shoulder. "Little One, the time has not yet come for you to leave us."

I sniffed and stepped away from him and the dog. But I knew as he said the words that he was right. I only wished I could get rid of the nagging worry that my life back home and the people I loved were slipping further and further away from me.

"I understand how you must feel." Helaman's voice was soft, mellow, calming. "But I know that it is for a mighty purpose; our Father in Heaven wants you here with me. He is taking care of your family. You are needed here. There is much more for you to do."

Looking into his coppery eyes filled with love and understanding, my worry melted and I knew deep in my soul he was right. "But . . . why me?"

"The Lord has sent you to me, and I do not question His wisdom. You must not either. You must have faith, Little One. You must lean on the Lord."

Oh, how I would lean. In fact, right now I felt as though the Lord would have to carry me.

⸸⸸⸸

"Uncle," I said as I tried to keep up with Gid as he strode toward Ima's tent. "It is good to see you."

A smile tugged at his mouth. "It is good to see you as well. Who is the sliver of a boy who has Helaman's ear?"

I knew Gid was not happy with the outcome of the meeting. He did not care for Syd's opinion. This saddened my heart. I wished I could tell my uncle the truth and soften his distrust, but Gid was a man driven by his passions. A confidence entrusted to him would not live long if he deemed it unimportant or if it came between him and victory.

"Syd came to us in Judea. He is a master fighter."

Gid looked at me as if I had swallowed too much balche and was now delusional.

"It is true, my uncle. He fights as I have never seen before." I needed to convince Gid. "He is teaching my warrior brothers."

At the mention of the warriors, my uncle's manner changed. He, like Helaman, worried about our safety. "Good. You boys were thrown into this fight without much training. I know it worries your mother." Gid glanced down the path to Ima's tent. "How is my sister?"

"Well." I started walking, hoping to keep his mind on my mother and not Syd. "It will gladden her heart to see you." I knew Gid would not soon forget Syd, nor would his suspicions of her be put to rest so easily. That was why I had suggested we should meet again once we were on Cumeni soil. If we were going to wait out the lamanites as Syd proposed, I would need to stay close to my uncle to make certain he took no action.

‡‡‡

When the disappointment of not getting the stone back had ebbed away, it was replaced by fear. Trepidation ran through me like a raging river. Even though I'd been training the warriors, I never really thought I would go to war.

But now it was here.

Now it was real.

As I neared camp, I saw the troops assembling in a mass of organized confusion, if that was possible. They were dressed for battle: spears, bows and arrows, daggers and such. Urgency was in their step, purpose in their intent. Some hefted packs filled with fruit onto llamas, some strapped Mariah's medicinal baskets to burros. I wondered where Mariah was. She had often visited me at Bella's, but I had not seen her for the last couple of days. Dust and voices filled the air. Tent doors flapped in the breeze as if waving good-bye.

I had to hurry. Many of the warriors had already headed to the city to meet Helaman and Gid at the stable. I still needed to talk with Lib before I left. The fact that Helaman had known all along that I'd been training the child was a bit disconcerting. Why didn't he stop me? I knew there had to be a reason. I hoped I would come to understand it later. Keeping the faith and believing everything had a reason for happening was hard work.

I hurried to Bella's tent. As I stepped in, I found Tarik with his mother and Lib with his ever-present Jukka. When the monkey saw

Ximon, it immediately headed over to play with its big friend. Ximon would have none of it.

Bella's round, usually happy face was now clouded with fear. Wanting to blend into the background, I began putting on the wrist and shin guards Tarik had given me. Out of the corner of my eye, I watched as Tarik hugged his plump mother to him. She hung on—a mother desperate to protect her child but knowing she must let go. I envied them and yearned for my own mother to hug me.

"Now," Bella said as she finally released him from her bear hug. "Take care of yourself. Keep faith close to your heart. And watch over Syd. I tried to fatten him up. He is as thin as a walking stick."

Tarik smiled down on his ima. "I shall."

He squatted so that he was eye level with Lib. "Take care of Ima." He hugged his little brother. "I am counting on you."

The monkey had returned to Lib's shoulder and now tried to climb on to Tarik, but he stood up, making Jukka grab hold of Lib's wayward hair, pulling it.

Lib yelped and patiently pulled the monkey down to his arms. I expected the boy to beg to go. Staying silent was not in his character; the boy was up to something. He might have fooled his big brother and mother, but he didn't fool me. I tried to shoot him a stern glance, but Lib didn't look my way.

"Ready, Syd?" Tarik asked.

I stood. Mom's purse strap was safely over my chest, the purse nestled on my hip. I shouldered my bow and leather quiver of arrows and slipped the deerskin shield on my arm. I nodded.

As Ximon and I followed Tarik out of the room, Bella hugged me to her the best she could despite my weaponry. This caught me off guard. Tears collected in my eyes. Deeply touched by Bella's spontaneous embrace, I quickly hugged her back. I glanced at her and saw in her gaze that she knew I missed my own mother. Again tears clouded my vision. I nodded at her and left with the dog by my side.

Tarik had waited for me. "You bring Ximon with you?"

"He's a good fighter." I patted my faithful companion's head. "And we may need him." What I didn't say was that at any time the Lord might reveal to Helaman that he needed to return the stone to me, and I was determined the dog and I would be ready.

Tarik nodded. "The animal does fight well." He rubbed his arm above his wrist guard in remembrance. "What did Helaman have to say?"

I suddenly realized Gid was supposed to be with Tarik. "Where is Gid?"

"He checked on Ima, took some of her bread, and left. He does not mean to be gruff," Tarik defended. "He merely wants this war to be over. My father works the land for both of them and this eats at my uncle. Though he knows he is being of great service to his people and our country, it is hard for him. His wife, my aunt Leah, is expecting a child. Her welfare weighs heavily on Uncle's mind."

"Now I understand why he's so anxious to storm the city," I replied, certain it would be extremely difficult to keep Gid from attacking while we waited for the enemy to surrender. I didn't say this to Tarik. I'd leave that up to Helaman.

We both heard someone coming down the path at the same time. Out of breath, Ozi came to stand in front of us. A spark of vitality shone in his ancient eyes. He was dressed for battle with helmet, spear, and sword. The helmet was too big for his gray head and his arm shook holding up the shield, but his spear hand was rock solid. "I am battle ready," he said to Tarik.

Tarik looked as surprised as I did. His mask of authority quickly slid into place. "Ozi, we need you to stay with the prisoners. As you know, most of the warriors leave today and the stockade will be low on guards. Helaman is counting on you to take charge here while we are away."

"But . . . I am Syd's guardian." Hope still framed Ozi's wrinkled face.

"I shall take care of Syd. You are not to concern yourself with his well-being." Tarik was all business and, I thought, a little too brusque.

The old man's face became somber; the spark in his eyes died away. He knew the unspoken truth. We thought he was too old to go to battle . . . too old to be my guardian.

Wanting to console him, I said, "Don't worry about me. With you here, we will know the prisoners are in good hands."

Ozi gave me a small smile. He looked at Tarik. "I shall do my duty, sir." He hugged me to him briefly and said, "Have no fear. The Lord dwells with the warriors." The old man quickly hurried away. I wondered if I would ever see him again. So much could happen.

Then I realized I didn't have the backpack. "I left something behind." I started running with Ximon tailing me. "Go ahead. I'll find you."

Tarik shrugged and continued on his way.

I decided to cut through the trees instead of keeping to the path, thinking I'd save time.

All at once, Ximon growled at the bushes. I heard a monkey and I knew I had just stumbled on Lib in the midst of his escape.

CHAPTER 24

PRESSING ON

"And where do you think you're going?" I asked, staring at the bush where Lib was hidden.

He crawled out with his spider monkey clinging to his neck. "With you," he declared. There was nothing apologetic in the boy's tone.

"No." I was determined he would listen to me. "This is not training. This is war. People are going to die."

"All the more reason for me to help." He stood tall and proud; determination shone in his glaring eyes. His entire eight-year-old frame stood tall with the intent to follow the warriors.

"Look," I tried to reason with him, "I know you think you can help, but what you'll do is sidetrack your brother and very likely get him killed. Do you want that to happen?"

His rigid shoulders slumped slightly. I knelt down in front of him. Ximon crowded against me, keeping his eyes on the energetic monkey. I pushed the dog away and focused on Lib. "I know you love your brother and want to be there for him. But he has an incredible responsibility to the troops and to Captain Helaman. He will not have time to watch over you."

"I can take care of myself." Though Lib's words were determined, his eyes betrayed his doubts.

"That may be, but Tarik will still worry about you." I took Lib's hand in mine. "Besides, if you come to battle, who will look after your mother? Tarik is counting on you to take care of her."

"Ima takes care of herself. I am going." He tugged his hand from mine. Fresh determination sparked in his eyes as he squared his shoulders. The spider monkey jumped from Lib to me. Ximon tried to playfully nip at the animal, but I saved Jukka in time and handed him back to Lib.

"What about Jukka?" Perhaps the animal might make the difference. "You can't take a monkey to war."

"You're taking Ximon." Lib glared at me.

"That's different."

"Jukka is little and will be less trouble."

"I don't think so," I defended. "All we need is a monkey squeaking to give us away."

"Or a dog to bark." Lib was good at arguing, but fortunately I was better.

"Well, you can't go because Helaman—the prophet—said so." I stood, folding my arms as I glared down on the little boy who so wanted to be a warrior. "In fact, the captain told me my training with you had to stop."

"You told him?" Lib's brows crinkled together at the thought that I'd betrayed him.

"No. He somehow knew. Did you tell him?" I queried.

"No! And if you don't let me go, I shall tell Helaman you are a girl." Lib was serious.

"Helaman already knows," I lied. It was the only way I could think to save the boy. I wondered how many white lies I had collected now in the hopes of doing the right thing. I pushed the disturbing thought aside as I returned Lib's serious stare.

He grew quiet as he tried to think of some comeback. Then he became reenergized. "I shall tell the troops."

Again I relied on the Helaman angle. "Helaman is depending on me to teach the warriors. If you tell them I'm a girl, he will not be happy."

Lib pulled his monkey into his arms. The boy grew somber, deep in reflection.

"Lib!" His mother called to him. "Lib!"

"Over here, Bella," I yelled. The boy's usually calculating face turned sad.

Bella stepped through the foliage. "I was certain I would have to borrow a horse to chase him down," she huffed. In her work-worn hands was my backpack. "Oh, you forgot this. I was uncertain whether you needed it."

Jukka latched onto the bag as Bella attempted to hand it to me. The monkey seemed quite pleased with himself. Many times I'd caught the animal sleeping inside it. I handed both the bag and the monkey to Lib. "Why don't you keep this for me until I return. Jukka can ride on your back inside the pack instead of pulling on your hair to stay on your shoulders."

Lib reluctantly took it; a glimmer of a smile brightened his eyes.

"Thanks, Bella," I said as I started down the path. "You and Lib stay safe."

"We shall." She put an arm about her son as Ximon and I walked away. As I looked back, I knew deep down that this would not be the last time I'd have to convince Lib not to fight.

‡‡‡

I hated leaving Syd behind. However, I had to hurry to the city. Uncle Gid was a determined man, and Helaman depended on me to do my duty and stay with him. I also hated leaving Ima alone with Lib. My brother had the determination of an ornery mountain mule. And Ima was not as tough on him as she should be. I would have to trust in the Lord and leave them in His care.

Walking to the stables, I saw that Baram and his men were organized and waiting. Baram had always been my nemesis, constantly trying to best me; of course, he never had. I knew that at its depth his rancor came from a jealousy of the relationship I had with my father. He had no relationship with his father, only a history of shame.

So why were Baram and his men gathered here before everyone else? He was planning something, but I had no intention of stopping to speak with him. He caught up with me.

"Gid asked me to be his second in command on our journey to Cumeni." Baram liked to boast about anything he knew would cause me grief. I knew he was most likely telling a falsehood.

"Then he shall have two," I replied. Baram's expression did not change, as if he had known I would challenge him. I went on. "Helaman will want me to go with my uncle, which makes me Gid's second."

"He may be your uncle, but Captain Gid knows whom to turn to when a job needs to be done." In his smug way, Baram could be as blind as a cave bat.

"Yes, he does, and he takes great stock in what his nephew has to say." I was not about to allow Baram to think himself superior to me, especially in my uncle's eyes.

"We shall see," Baram muttered.

Gid rode up then, leading my horse. "Tarik, at last. Helaman wants us to take the lead. Commander Baram and his squad are to leave with us also." Uncle handed me the reins.

There was no horse for Baram. He would walk with his men. I bit back a smile as I looked at the overanxious, too-willing-to-please commander and mounted my horse. We started on our way with Gid and me in front and Baram and his men behind. Baram's eyes were on my back, and I knew he had set his mind to be trouble on this trip.

†††

I ran to the stable, where everyone had assembled. Pushing through the crowd with Ximon by my side, I tried to catch sight of Tarik. Instead I ran into Dagan's broad back. Towering over me like a mountain, he turned around. Not only did he carry his spear and jawbone weaponry, but he had added a dagger as well. With his wide leather headband tied to his head, he reminded me of a cantankerous Harley rider. If I hadn't become his friend in training, I'd be more than a little intimidated.

"Have you seen Tarik?" I asked.

"Yes." He didn't go on, just looked at me.

"Well, where is he?"

"He went with Captain Gid." He snorted and wiped his cheek to his shoulder. "Rode out ahead with Baram and his squad."

"What?"

"Someone had to go first," he said matter-of-factly, as if I should have known. I had counted on walking with Tarik. The long march to Cumeni would be lonely without him.

Abraham joined Dagan and me. He, too, had added to his weapons. Not only did he shoulder his bow and arrows, but he had strapped on a scimitar and shield. "Syd, you may walk with us, if that is what has your concern." He gave me his friendly smile.

I nodded and tried to relax. Helaman rode out of the stable on his white stallion. His robes were gone, replaced by armor—a heavy breastplate and helmet. A warm feeling spread through me to see him all decked out. He was a warrior now, a captain in charge of an army. He was breathtaking, like the poster I had seen of him on Gracie's wall.

"I need to stay close to Helaman," Abraham said as he nudged both me and Dagan to move. "He will count on me as his second with Tarik gone."

I wondered why Abraham didn't have a horse like Tarik did if he was supposed to fill in for him. Maybe there weren't enough horses to go around. I fell into step but glanced behind to make sure Ximon followed. He was there, my ever-present friend. As I walked, I wondered why Tarik had gone with Gid. Even if Gid was his uncle, why would Tarik leave Helaman? As I walked, I began to realize that it made sense. He went to keep his uncle in check and to make him wait to act until we were all assembled in Cumeni.

"The city of Cumeni is farther inland than Antiparah," said Abraham as if he could hear my thoughts. "We will leave the coast and climb the foothills."

"Many dangers await us along the way," Dagan piped in. "Flesh-eating spiders, predatory snakes and, of course, jaguars that prowl the forests." His Harley face seemed to delight in sharing these tidbits with me, the novice to the area. I wondered why he wasn't with his squad. Maybe with Tarik gone, Helaman needed both the commanders near him.

I walked as if I weren't the least bit intimidated by Dagan's recounting of jungle dangers. I knew making our way through this region was bad enough during the day and that there was a high probability we would have to walk at night as well. We would be traveling on foot through a minefield laden with all sorts of creepy crawlers. And if we survived the jungle danger, the battle awaited.

I kept telling myself that everything would be all right. Ximon brushed up against me as if to comfort me with his presence. And he did help, a little.

We had walked for many miles when Abraham said, "Tell us about your home, Lake of Salt."

For a moment I wondered what he was talking about. Then I remembered what Tarik had told them.

"It's north of here. Mostly a desert. The mountains are close by, and they are beautiful. It's fall now, my favorite time of year. The holidays are coming—Halloween, Thanksgiving, and Christmas."

Dagan and Abraham stopped. I really needed to stop mentioning things these people knew nothing about. I motioned for them to keep walking as I continued. "They're celebration days. You have days you celebrate, don't you?" I looked ahead at Helaman on his horse and wondered if the prophet ever had time to relax, be happy, and celebrate.

"Of course we do." Dagan was eager to tell me this. "We most recently celebrated the day we became Anti-Nephi-Lehies. This is my favorite day of celebration." Dagan smiled as he told me this.

At first I didn't know what he meant by "the day we became Anti-Nephi-Lehies." Then I remembered. "That's right, you were called Anti-Nephi-Lehies before you took on the name of Ammonites."

"How do you know this?" Abraham looked at me suspiciously.

I'd tripped up. "Uh . . . your people's history is not a secret," I said as if it were a no-brainer.

He let it pass. To change the subject, I asked Dagan, "Why is this celebration day your favorite?"

Dagan's smile curled into a mischievous grin. "Well, it had not always been my favorite until Tarik and Abraham made it so."

"Do not tell him." Abraham was far from pleased with the direction our conversation had taken.

"Well, now you have to tell," I teased.

Abraham set his jaw, his smile as well as his sense of humor gone, if he truly had one. He glared at his friend.

Dagan wasn't the least bit intimidated. "A couple of years ago on this day, Abraham and Tarik decided to try to find the place where our forefathers buried their weapons."

"Dagan, I will not warn you again." Though Abraham's voice was stern, I could see he fought a smile. "It happened more than five years ago. Tarik and I were only ten and one years old."

"It is still a good story." Dagan looked around, making certain that I was the only one to hear besides Abraham. "For two weeks, every night they would sneak out to dig in the foothills of Jershon until one night they did not return."

"Why?" Now the story was becoming interesting.

"Wait and you shall know. Tarik's father organized a search party. They found Abraham and Tarik up a tree being guarded by an old, toothless jaguar, who was content to wait until they climbed down."

I could imagine a young Tarik and Abraham being obsessed with the idea of finding weapons and then being scared out of their minds by the large cat. "Oh, this is good. I'm going to tease Tarik."

"I have not told you the best part," Dagan looked at Abraham as if to gain permission to continue the tale.

Abraham huffed and then shrugged his shoulders. "I suppose Syd would find out eventually."

"They went through all that humiliation only to learn that the weapons of our forefathers were buried somewhere in the land of Midian, far away from Jershon." Dagan laughed, and Abraham chuckled a little.

"I merely followed Tarik," Abraham defended.

"And I'm sure he would say he followed you," I teased. I envied these two boys and their friendship. I didn't have a close friend like that. I supposed I had Colin, but that wasn't the same. But I did have Gracie and Mom. So I was covered when it came to having people around me who cared, but having a friend to get into trouble with was something foreign to me. I was always the tomboy, the odd girl out. Yet deep down I yearned for a girlfriend who I could giggle with over stupid things like makeup and dating.

It was funny; I hadn't really missed having a bosom buddy until moments like this. I looked at the two guys walking beside me. By sharing this little childhood memory, Abraham and Dagan had treated me like one of them, a guy. Despite wanting a friend of my own gender, I was glad to have taken a step closer to being accepted by these young men. And that would do for now. We walked on in silence, comfortable enough with each other that there was no need to continue talking.

Night was fast approaching by the time we'd reached the foothills. The path climbed steadily upward. The distance between us and

Helaman grew farther apart. Dagan struggled to keep up. His breaths were short and heavy. Abraham stayed close by his friend.

"Would you tell Helaman to slow down?" I asked Abraham.

He looked at me as if I were insane.

"Oh, for the love of male pride." I raced ahead, catching up with the white stallion.

"Helaman," I gasped, trying to gain my breath. "I think the men need to rest."

He pulled up on the reins. "Forgive me. My thoughts have been elsewhere." He glanced about. We were amid a grouping of giant boulders. "I know of a place not far from here where we may rest," he said. "We'll stop there for the night."

I hurried back to Abraham, who looked at me as if I'd committed a grave sin. I shrugged it off and turned to Dagan. "Helaman said we will make camp in a little bit."

"He should not be stopping for me. I could walk all night," Dagan wheezed.

I rolled my eyes toward heaven.

We ended up camping along the road in a small glade. I carefully looked for spiders and snakes, settled down on a patch of soft moss, and promptly fell asleep.

All too quickly, Ximon was licking my face, waking me up to the metal-gray light of predawn. Everyone was preparing to leave. We traveled through the day, eating what food we carried or scavenged from along the way. My feet ached. I'd never walked so much for so long in my entire life.

I had thought I was pretty fit, being a black belt, but this was too much. I plodded on, keeping my gaze on Helaman and his horse. Sometimes he dismounted and walked with the troops, encouraging us, keeping up our spirits. Toward nightfall he rode ahead. Still we marched. Finally, he returned.

"We have been on Cumeni soil for some time now. The city is not far. I can see Captain Gid's camp over the rise."

As we neared the camp, Tarik ran out to greet us. He looked troubled and went straight to Helaman.

Abraham, Dagan, and I rushed up to hear what he had to say.

"I could not stop him, Father." Tarik inhaled deeply as if reluctant to deliver the bad news. "My uncle and his men go to attack the city as we speak."

CHAPTER 25
THE MEETING

Cumeni could not to be taken this way—this was not what was supposed to happen according to the Book of Mormon. If the outcome of its capture changed, other things could change as well. Had it concerned Gid enough that Helaman had appeared to consider my suggestion that he'd gone ahead with his original plan without us? Was it my fault for making the suggestion? Something had to be done, and fast.

I looked up at Helaman, who towered over me atop his white stallion. Our gazes locked, and I knew he too felt the urgency of the situation. He nodded at me as if he had read my mind. Then he turned to Tarik. "Keep everyone in camp!"

He kneed his horse and yelled, "Ximon, come!"

My Great Dane took off chasing after Helaman as if a T-bone steak were tied to the horse. Why would Helaman want Ximon with him? What good would the dog be? And why had the animal immediately responded to his command?

I remembered several days ago, when Ximon and I had been in Helaman's office, how the animal had warmed to him. I hadn't ever seen the dog act like that before except . . . with Steve Smith. I thought about this. The dog, the stone, and the backpack had all been Steve's. And, what about his two friends? What were their names? . . . John and Bob. I wondered what was going on here. Something was not right.

A movement out of the corner of my eye brought me back to the present. Everyone had started running through the empty campsite. Leaving my perplexed thoughts behind and making a mental note to have a serious talk with Helaman, I too ran and became caught up in what was taking place with Captain Gid and his troops.

We all followed Tarik to the ridge which overlooked the valley and the city of Cumeni beyond. I noticed a dry moat, not unlike Judea's, surrounding the town, with a wall of timbers built on top of an earthen mound. In the towers overlooking the palisades, Lamanite soldiers anxiously awaited for the imminent attack.

Gid's army was an awesome force of over six thousand. They moved across the valley floor like a great armada. How in the world would Helaman stop them?

I searched the valley, looking for a lone rider and a dog. "Where's Helaman?" I asked Tarik as I found myself standing beside him.

"There." He pointed north, and I saw Helaman galloping on his stallion with Ximon chasing close behind.

"Let's go!" yelled Abraham, motioning for everyone to follow.

"No!" yelled Tarik, stopping the mighty surge of soldiers that was about to swarm down the valley to come to their leader's aid. Tarik stepped in front for all to see him. "Helaman said to stay in camp, and we will do just that."

A strange quiet settled over the stripling warriors. We were mesmerized by the scene taking place before us.

Captain Gid, and probably Baram with his squad of one hundred warriors, were in front of the mass of soliders. Helaman had made his way to them. He yanked back on the reins, halting his steed in a cloud of dust.

Helaman leaped from his horse and hurried to Gid. Gid held up his arm, signaling for everyone behind him to halt. Slowly, he climbed off of his mare.

The mighty captains stood face-to-face, and I wished I could hear what they were saying.

Gid made sweeping gestures with his hands, and I could imagine he was pretty worked up. Finally, he turned on his heel and started walking back to his horse as if to resume his attack on the city.

Helaman motioned to Ximon. My mouth hung open as I watched the Great Dane shoot after Gid, knocking the captain over with his paws. The dog had done the same thing to Tarik on the night Helaman had me thrown in the stockade. Baram immediately started after Ximon with his wooden club.

I gasped; Baram meant to kill my dog. I grabbed hold of Tarik's arm.

Helaman stopped Baram, holding up a hand and then pulling Ximon away from Gid. Helaman then helped the captain up. Then the two captains walked away from everyone, either talking or arguing, I couldn't tell. But Gid no longer made sweeping gestures with his arms, and he seemed to have calmed down.

I would have thought that having Ximon bowl Gid over would have enraged him, but the animal's actions seemed to have had the opposite effect. Or maybe Helaman had been the calming balm for the overexcited captain.

Gid placed his fist over his heart in what appeared to be a salute to Helaman. The chief captain returned the sign. Then they turned, mounted their horses, and headed our way. Gid's army stayed where it was.

I remembered I had grabbed hold of Tarik. I looked at him. He smiled. I let go and scanned the crowd, worried that someone had seen me latch on to his arm. It seemed no one had noticed.

I tried to see Ximon, hopeful he would not be left behind. He trotted next to Helaman's stallion. The horse and dog made a handsome pair, fitting for a chief captain.

✠✠✠

Twilight had fallen by the time we returned to the deserted campsite the warriors would be sharing with Gid's men. For supper we chewed the dried meat Bella had sent with us. I busied myself with starting a fire. Tarik helped, and so did Dagan and Abraham. I stood close to the crackling fire as Abraham and Tarik swapped stories of their journeys here.

Tarik told us that as they had traveled, Baram had pressured Captain Gid to move forward with an attack, saying that the battle would be over before Helaman and the troops arrived. Tarik, of course, took Helaman's side and begged his uncle to wait.

I wondered why Baram was so anxious to fight. Why would he want to forge ahead without his leader and the rest of us? I thought back to how he had attacked me while I was trying to teach the commander. It seemed Baram had some issues.

"What's Baram's story?" I asked. Tarik scooted over so I could sit between him and Abraham. I settled into the vacant spot.

"He has always questioned authority," Abraham said. I remembered the night before I'd come here, when I'd told the stripling warrior story to Gracie; I thought of how I had studied the picture of them and wondered if there weren't one rebel among their ranks. Maybe Baram was that rebel.

"Long ago, his father betrayed our people and joined the Lamanites. I think Baram is ashamed of his father and is trying to show Captain Gid he is a dedicated fighter." Tarik gazed at the fire. "He would do anything to be Gid's second."

"Also, he is jealous of Tarik and you, Syd." Abraham nodded. "Baram wants some of the glory."

Dagan joined us. He'd been gathering firewood and dropped his bundle. "What are we talking about?"

"Baram," I answered.

"I see. Tarik, you should tell Syd about the time—" I didn't hear the rest of what was surely another embarrassing story, for at that moment Ximon jumped between Tarik and me, bathing my face with his tongue.

I hugged his neck and stroked his back. The Great Dane was obviously tickled to see me; his hind end wobbled in giant puppy wags.

"Syd." Helaman's voice came from behind us. I immediately stood and turned to face him. "Please come with me. Tarik, you as well."

I glanced at the others who had witnessed my being singled out with Tarik. A little embarrassed, I shrugged and followed, but I felt every pair of eyes on me as we disappeared into the darkness.

⸸⸸⸸

Helaman had asked several others to join his meeting with Syd and me. A couple of Gid's men were with him . . . and Baram. I shot my rival a suspicious look. He was a constant thorn in my side. I remembered his attack on Syd and felt a hot wave of anger. If he had hurt her, I would have used his own dagger on him. And now Baram had stirred up trouble between Helaman and Gid, nearly setting off a battle. Why was Baram campaigning for war? I was certain his motives had to do with his father joining the Lamanites. Still, why would this encourage him to push for battle? Why seek bloodshed? If Baram wanted to show his leaders loyalty, why not merely follow their counsel?

The two men from Gid's army were burly Nephites, regular soldiers who had been fighting against our Lamanite brothers for many years. Gid, his two soldiers, and Baram stood to one side of the campfire. Helaman, Syd, and I stood on the other. We were outnumbered. But the truth was, we were all on the same side.

"If we are patient, we may avoid many casualties," Helaman said. "Since our forces are few compared to the Lamanites, I strongly feel we should do as Syd advised in Antiparah and wait out our Lamanite brethren." Helaman folded his strong arms. His intense stare at my uncle demanded a reply.

Why had Helaman singled out Syd? This would only add fuel to Uncle's distrust of the plan. Gid saw Syd as an intruder, and a puny one at that, which irritated him even more.

"Again with the waiting." Gid paced. "Did Nephi hold back his sword from Laban? Did Abinadi cower before King Noah? The Lord is on our side. We must strike now." He pounded his fist in his hand. Whenever Uncle talked about our forefathers, I knew he was worked up.

Helaman was silent, wisely letting the seasoned officer rant and rave for a while. Standing beside my chief captain, I was silent as well. I glanced at Syd, whose doelike eyes took in everything.

"You take the word of this boy—" Gid pointed at Syd, who stood there in the black clothes that hid her gender, "who has not the courage or strength of a mouse, and who looks as though he could not kill even a rabbit—over my word?" Uncle spit into the fire. The embers sputtered, smoked, and died.

Syd looked as though she wanted to vanish into the campfire smoke. Helaman needed to counter this mistaken idea and squash it before it grew through rumor. But he said nothing.

"Uncle." I broke the spell. "Syd is a strong, seasoned fighter. He has trained our warriors in defensive fighting. He could easily kill a rabbit—and a Lamanite as well."

Gid cleared his throat and paced. Every once in a while he glared at Syd from across the flames as he contemplated my words. Syd stood tall, though she was a head shorter than the soldiers around her. I knew she would hold on to her dignity.

Finally, Gid uttered, "To wait like cowards goes against my every instinct."

"It will be difficult, yes, but better to wait than bury those young boys whose lives have been entrusted to me." Helaman was now appealing to Uncle's fatherly side.

"You have given this much thought," Gid said as he relaxed a bit and settled down on a log. Helaman followed his example and sat. We all sat except Baram. He remained on his feet, glaring at me. When he realized he was the only one standing, he finally sat.

"Tonight our forces must join together and surround the city." Helaman had everyone's undivided attention. "No one goes in, and no one comes out of Cumeni. Our men need to be watchful and wary. The Lamanites are not fools. They will try to kill us, but instead they shall be surprised by how prepared we are. Our men must sleep on their swords."

"Good!" Uncle nodded in agreement.

"We shall seize the Lamanites' provisions as they arrive," Helaman continued.

Gid grumbled an agreement, but I had my doubts about how compliant Uncle would be if battle did not come soon.

‡‡‡

After day three, cracks in Gid's commitment appeared. Several of his men had been attacked during the night as the Lamanites sneaked out, trying to escape the city. I would have thought this little bit of action would have made the mighty warrior content, but it only seemed to aggravate him more. Helaman was able to calm him down, but I feared what day four would bring, especially if the expected Lamanite provisions did not arrive.

I spent much of those three days with Tarik. We worked together as equals. The other commanders would periodically report to him, and then he and I would report to Helaman. I would also go with Tarik to check the troops. Our food supplies were low; however, most of the warriors were optimistic or at least put on a good face. Many times Tarik and I would temporarily take over for a weary commander and let him take a much needed break.

For me, moments alone were few and far between. I also saw less of Ximon. Lately he divided his time between me and Helaman. I didn't mind. If I had to share the dog, I was glad it was with the prophet.

Several times I tried to find the right moment to speak with Helaman about Steve Smith, but there never was a right time. My questions would have to wait until after Cumeni was taken.

On the fourth day of our stakeout, tempers were stretched, nerves were frayed. I made my way back to my post that night, feeling weary in both body and spirit. Every muscle in my body ached from sleeping on the ground. And I wasn't smelling so fresh these days. I needed a bath in the worst way. All the warriors needed baths. I had never heard anyone talk about the smell of war, but it was rank. And I was one of the rankest.

Suddenly I caught sight of a large Lamanite covered with black war paint ahead of me, sneaking through the brush. His attention was focused on the other warriors, not on me.

I quickly scanned the foliage, but the Lamanite seemed to be alone. Then I heard someone approaching from our camp. I ducked behind a tree. After a moment, I peeked to see who it was.

Baram crawled through the brush, heading toward the Lamanite. I placed an arrow in my bow, prepared to defend him. I aimed at the sneaking Lamanite and was about to let the arrow fly when the Lamanite stood. Surprised by the enemy's sudden change of position, I quickly glanced toward Baram.

He, too, no longer crept through the brush but had risen to his feet. Baram approached the Lamanite.

And then they began to talk.

CHAPTER 26

SECRETS AND LIES

I crept closer, using the brush as cover. Every nerve in my body tingled as I tried to understand what was happening. Baram was meeting with the enemy, of that I was certain. But why? I had to get closer to hear what they were saying. A twig snapped under my foot. I froze, staring at the Lamanite and Baram, praying I hadn't given myself away. No one turned around.

"Gid would have stormed the city," Baram sneered, "but Helaman was swayed by the cooing of Dove-boy." His lip curled with disdain.

Dove-boy? I rolled my eyes. He must have meant me. I mulled over the situation as I watched the shadowy figures interact. If Baram's father had joined the Lamanites, why not Baram? This was bad. Whatever they were up to, I needed to know.

"Push Gid more," the Lamanite demanded. "If you attack tonight we can end this standoff by morning. And your father will be safe."

"Gid is on patrol. When he returns, I will do what I can," Baram replied.

The Lamanite nodded curtly. "So far, I have protected your father. As each day grows longer with no supplies, they blame him as well as your people."

Baram was being blackmailed to help the Lamanites. No wonder he had tried to force a battle.

"I shall see that it happens tonight," Baram promised the heavily built Lamanite who must have been satisfied with this answer because he turned and headed back the way he had come.

Baram returned to camp.

I stood there, dumbfounded. I wanted to chase after Baram and demand he tell Helaman what was going on. But as I thought about what I'd heard, I realized the Lamanites would likely kill Baram's father if he said anything.

Still, Helaman needed to know. And I was the only one who knew what was going on—besides Baram. Maybe this was why I had been sent here.

As soon as I returned to camp, I headed for Helaman's tent. His white stallion was staked outside, so I knew he was there. Dagan stood guard. I found him drinking water from a teardrop-shaped gourd. "Looking for Tarik?" he asked as water dribbled down his thick chin.

"Helaman, actually."

Dagan pointed to Helaman's tent with the gourd. "Tarik's been in there with the captain for a while. It can't be good that he's been in there so long."

"Why?" I asked.

"Means change."

"Change is good." I tried to be cheerful. "Aren't you tired of waiting?"

"Maybe so." He hung the gourd above the water barrel. "There is a girl back in Jershon. I wonder what she would do if something happened to me." True concern was woven through his words. I was surprised that this brawny guy had a soft side, and I couldn't think of a reply.

Without warning one of Gid's soldiers rode up, leaped off his horse, and while trying to catch his breath and speak at the same time, uttered, "Provisions!"

For a second, I struggled to understand what he was talking about, then understanding came. "You've seen the Lamanite provisions coming?"

He shook his head, drew a deep breath, and said, "Captain Gid captured them."

Dagan quickly escorted the rider inside the tent and immediately returned. The two of us then waited in tense silence. I wanted to ask the rotund Ammonite more about the girlfriend he had seemed so worried about before the soldier arrived, but I also wanted to overhear what was being said inside the tent, so I kept my silence.

Finally, Helaman and Tarik emerged with Gid's soldier beside them. Helaman wore his armor and looked ready to leave.

I expected smiles to be on their faces, but they were grim-faced. Helaman stared at me for a moment, and it seemed as though he wanted to say something but didn't have the time, or couldn't. I wanted to tell him about Baram, but with these new developments, I doubted it would be high on Helaman's list of concerns. Still, he needed to know. "Helaman," I began.

"We will speak later, Little One," Helaman said quickly. Then he abruptly turned away, and he and the rider mounted their horses and rode off.

Dagan, Tarik, and I stood like a row of birds as we watched them disappear into the night. Ximon ambled from the tent and nuzzled my hand, wanting to be stroked. I patted the animal and looked over at Tarik. Maybe I could tell him about Baram. Tarik would know what to do, and he was Helaman's second in command. I decided it would be best to wait until Dagan left.

Tarik's forehead was furrowed as he turned away.

"What's wrong?" I asked.

"Gid's man just told us that King Ammoron sent many troops with the provisions." Tarik bit his lower lip, lost in thought, and then said, "We expected only a few more Lamanite troops, but the rider told us there are thousands. That Gid was able to capture them with so few forces was a miracle."

"What will Helaman do?" I asked.

"The women and children of Judea need provisions. They are starving. We shall send the supplies we have captured to them." Tarik sighed.

Dagan chewed at his fingernail. "If you send all the provisions away, what will we eat?" His stomach growled as if on cue. Dagan had lost weight since we'd left Antiparah. And I knew he was more concerned over his squad than himself. Those young boys needed more than jerky to live on. Our supplies were desperately low.

"Helaman says the Lord will provide." Tarik shrugged. "He has sent for Ima and the other cooks. Mariah as well." He glanced at me, and from his look I knew that Mariah's coming meant more fighting was on our horizon. He added, "They should be here in three days."

Dagan's face brightened with relief. Tarik patted his friend on the back. "Tell the others about the capture. It will cheer the troops. Have the commanders assemble here as soon as possible. We need to make plans."

Dagan nodded and lumbered off.

I was glad to know that I would see Bella soon. However, I felt nervous about having Lib so close to the battlefield. The boy was bound and determined to fight, and close proximity would give him more opportunity, especially since I had trained him. Lib was not a stripling warrior; he was just a kid. Would his faith be strong enough to shield him?

I turned my thoughts back to the capture of the Lamanites and their supplies. I suddenly felt a sinking feeling in the pit of my stomach. I asked Tarik, "What about the prisoners?"

"They are a problem." Tarik swiped his hand over his forehead and began walking toward the campfire.

"Why?" I asked, hoping my recollection of what was going to happen next was wrong.

"When the city of Cumeni surrenders, we will have so many prisoners we will not be able to feed them all, even with Ima and her many cooks."

"What does Helaman plan to do?"

"I am not certain. We were talking about our provisions when the rider arrived."

Pressing past my foggy memory, I recalled that the prisoners had been a problem during the siege on Cumeni. I had faith, however, the Lord had already revealed to the prophet what would happen here and what needed to be done.

"We need to send the prisoners to Zarahemla," said Tarik. "There are so many, and we have few men to spare. We must march toward the city of Manti as soon as Cumeni is ours." Tarik shook his head as if he could erase his worries from his mind.

Then I remembered why I had initially sought out Helaman. "We have another problem as well."

Tarik looked at me with a pained expression, as if he'd already been served his limit of bad news.

"I think Baram's father is being held captive in Cumeni."

"What?" Tarik stared at me.

I explained what I'd seen. Tarik remained quiet. Finally he said, "No one knows who Baram's father is or where he resides, but I do not believe he is in Cumeni. Perhaps Baram knew you were listening and is playing you for a fool. Did you have a good look at the Lamanite?"

I thought about the Lamanite I had seen sneaking in the bushes. "Kind of. He was big and covered in black war paint."

"Black paint? The Lamanites of this area use red." Tarik thought for a moment. "Besides, not one of them could have left the city without our knowledge. I am certain Baram is up to mischief. His thirst for glory may be his downfall."

"Why would he target me?"

"I do not know. However, we shall find out." Tarik started off in the direction of Baram's campsite.

"But . . ." Syd tried to stop me. "Shouldn't we talk this over with Helaman?" Her question did not deter me. Quickly walking up the path leading to Baram's camp, I became even more determined to have it out with him. Still, I first needed to learn what he was up to.

"Tarik," Syd yelled after me. We had entered a dense forest. The trees made a canopy overhead. The air was thick and humid beneath the mighty tree boughs.

I took hold of Syd's arm. "Quiet! It is hard to sneak with you yelling."

"We're sneaking?" Syd asked.

I wished I could see her expression. The shadowy protection of the trees made seeing her facial features impossible. I knew that her bright eyes would be wide with questions.

"Should we? Sneak, that is?" she asked.

Releasing her, I said, "Yes. I must be certain of his motives before calling him out in front of Helaman."

"Call him out?"

There was no time to explain. We had already spent too much time at Helaman's camp, giving Baram time to do whatever he planned. I took off. Ximon and Syd followed.

Stopping at the edge of the tree line, I looked down into Baram's camp. Amos, one of Baram's loyal squad members, was scrubbing black paint from his face with wide-leafed ferns.

"That's him," Syd said softly.

Crouching down, we moved behind the protection of the brush surrounding the camp. Once we were within hearing distance, we stopped.

Baram and two of his men had joined Amos, helping him peel off his disguise.

"You should have seen it!" That was Baram. "Amos makes a good lamanite."

I heard laughter.

"Dove-boy went straight to Helaman with our story. He will look a fool when I claim to know nothing about meeting with a lamanite." Baram was quite proud of himself.

"It is high time you gained Helaman's favor over the stranger," someone piped up. I could not see his face; however, the voice was familiar.

"Yes." Baram gloried in the idea. "The mouse will be lucky to stand in the presence of Helaman's horse when I am through with him. And Tarik . . . he will be the next to fall from grace."

More laughter.

Baram wanted my position of favor with Helaman, this I knew. But to hear him say it out loud and for him to recruit his squad in his deceptions boiled my blood.

"What if Syd . . ." Amos stopped. "I mean, Dove-boy, recognized me as a member of your squad?" he finished. Regret and trepidation filled his voice. Amos had a gentle nature, and participating in such a deception did not seem to be to his liking.

"That is why, Jawbone, you were covered in black paint." Baram seemed to have an answer for everything. That he would demean even one of his own men rankled me.

"But . . ." Amos began to object.

"Stop!" Baram commanded. "Everything will work out. Trust me."

Another soldier, whose face I could not see, said, "We will protect you. Have no fear, Amos."

At that point, Dagan entered their camp. "Tarik asked me to tell all the squad leaders that Captain Gid has captured the lamanite supply wagons and troops," he told Baram.

Silence reigned over the small group.

Dagan seemed surprised at their lack of response to what was supposed to be good news, but he continued, "Baram, Tarik wants you to meet him at Helaman's campsite."

Baram remained silent. Shrugging, Dagan turned and left.

I motioned for Syd to follow me. We returned the way we had come through the dark forest, not stopping until we were past the canopy of trees and heading toward Helaman's camp. The moon shone down on the tent in a silvery glow. The welcoming flames of Helaman's campfire beckoned to us. Just before we got there, I pulled Syd aside.

"You must remember, Baram is not your friend." I looked down on her. Moonlight kissed her innocent face.

"What was your first clue?" Syd chuckled a little.

I took her by the shoulders. She could not take Baram's threat lightly. "When we go to battle, I will not be able to watch over you. Be on guard against Baram and his men."

"Sure." Now Syd sounded scared.

I did not release her but studied her gentle features. My mouth went dry. My stomach felt as though my horse had kicked me. If something were to happen to Syd, I did not know what I would do.

"Don't forget," she said, "I know how to defend myself."

I leaned closer. "If something were to happen to you . . ." Syd stood so close that I felt warmth from her body. Her lips were but a hair's breadth away from mine. I wanted to pull her into my arms and keep her safe from this war, from Baram, from everything. Instead I stood there saying nothing, doing nothing. I hardly dared breathe.

"Tarik," someone called my name.

We stepped away from each other.

"Over here," I replied.

Abraham traipsed through the brush to us. "I thought I saw you out here. Good news, about Gid capturing the supplies." He looked at Syd and then at me. "Are . . . we meeting?"

"Yes." Turning away from Syd, I started for camp, hoping Abraham had not seen how closely I had been standing next to her. I kept my *face turned away from Abraham, fearing that if he looked upon it, he would be able to see the emotions churning within me.*

My heart hammered within my chest as I thought about Syd, about Baram's disloyalty, about Cumeni. As I glanced behind me, my eyes caught Syd's. And those brown eyes made me believe that all would yet be well.

CHAPTER 27
The Nephite Way

Because Captain Gid had captured the provisions and Lamanite troops, Baram's plan to make a fool of me never came to Helaman's attention. Tarik thought it best not to burden Helaman with news of the malicious prank; however, he did assign Baram and his men the main responsibility of guarding the new prisoners, which kept them plenty busy and away from me.

The next two days dragged by. As I had more time to myself, my worries over my mom and Gracie found me again. I knew the Lord would keep them safe, but still I agonized about Mom's health and Gracie's well-being. Many times I'd catch Helaman watching me, then he'd give me a fatherly smile that said all would be well. I was puzzled, though, as to why he still kept the stone from me.

At last, after what felt like an eternity, the Lamanites who held the city of Cumeni surrendered without a fight. And our prison population exploded. Their needs far exceeded those of our own troops. Baram's squad could no longer contain them, so guarding the prisoners became a chore for everyone.

The day after Cumeni had fallen, Bella, Lib, the other cooks, Mariah, and the nursemaids arrived. It was a relief to have other women in camp. Even though everyone—except Tarik and Lib—thought I was a boy and treated me as such, there was comfort in having those of my own gender close.

Ozi had come as well. I was saddened to see that the elderly man's health had deteriorated. His face and body sagged like a boiled prune. Tarik ordered Ozi to bed rest. With Bella's permission, I had the old man take my space in her tent. He seemed to relax and slept for a couple of days, with Mariah, Bella, and me giving him nourishment as often as he would take it.

One afternoon, Lib cornered me. "I have a new weapon."

I couldn't imagine what he was talking about, and he refused to tell me, so I followed him away from camp where we would be alone. That is, as alone as the Great Dane and monkey would allow. The two animals acted like long lost friends, tumbling and falling all over each other.

Once Lib felt we were a safe distance from camp, he pulled leather straps from his tunic. Tied to the end of the straps was a bigger piece of leather . . . a crudely crafted slingshot.

"Where did you find this?" I asked.

"It is mine." He became defensive and put it back in his tunic. "Do not tell."

"I have no intention of telling anyone." And I didn't. "In fact, a slingshot is a good thing. With this weapon you can be like David, who killed Goliath. Do you know this story?" I tried to recall how long ago the prophet Lehi had fled Jerusalem. David's time was about a thousand years before Christ. And Lehi had lived around 600 B.C. I was sure that many Bible stories had been handed down to the Nephites.

"I know David was a mighty king." Lib seemed genuinely interested.

"Before he was king, he was a young man who tended sheep." I sat on a large rock. Lib sat beside me, eager to hear more. "His people were in a battle with the Philistines."

"Like we are with the Lamanites," he piped up.

"Yes. But the Philistines had Goliath of Gath on their side. He was a giant among men, and his armor was made of brass. His spear was made of iron, which was very heavy, and no one wanted to fight him."

"Except David, right?" Lib clutched his slingshot.

"Yes, David was a young boy, but he knew how to use a sling. When Goliath saw David, he made fun of him. So do you know what David did?"

Lib shook his head, his Hershey-colored eyes wide and shining.

"He slung a stone, hit Goliath in the forehead, and killed him."

Lib's mouth dropped open.

"It's true." I hoped this helped him understand how dangerous the slingshot could be. "If a slingshot could kill a giant, it could kill an ordinary man, too."

I knew that by telling Lib this story, it was possible I might embolden him, might give him ideas that would get him killed. But I knew Lib was determined to fight, and it was better he fought with a slingshot than in hand-to-hand combat. At least with a slingshot he'd have a chance to distract someone long enough for him to run away. Maybe.

"I can hit a mark, like David." Lib picked up a stone. "Watch." He flung the stone and missed the tree branch he'd aimed at. His face creased into a frown.

"Practice," I said getting up. "All it takes is practice." I glanced around. We were too far from camp, and I didn't want Lib to come back to this place alone. It could be dangerous. "Only practice closer to camp."

He smiled. We shared another secret, but at least this one had the potential to save his life.

‡‡‡

As the days passed, Ima and the other cooks found it increasingly impossible to provide for everyone. Ima's famous soup became mere liquid with spare pieces of squash and corn floating in it. Her cornbread turned into very thin corn wafers.We had run out of dried meat, and because of our troops' presence, most wild animals had long ago left the region, making hunting pointless.

The prisoners were starving.

My troops shared their own meager rations—bits of roasted tuber, a few spoonfuls of watery soup—with the captives. Our plight only grew worse with time. And still Helaman received no word from Captain Moroni or Zarahemla.

One night while I was on guard duty, as I waited for my replacement, a desperate lamanite broke through the wooden barriers we had hastily constructed. The man's eyes were wide and frantic until he saw me. Then he took on a look of focused rage. He raced toward me, no weapon in his hands, yet he charged as though he held a dagger. I easily dodged him, but he turned and leaped at me, his eyes lit with madness. I reflexively drew my sword.

He stopped, smiled, and before I could move, lunged at my blade. The steel ran through his midsection, and he toppled to the ground. I stood *over him solemnly. The man's ribs showed through his skin, yet his belly was bloated. I recognized the signs of starvation. Within Cumeni, the lamanites had been without supplies long before we had arrived. The man had deliberately killed himself. It was becoming a pattern; other lamanite prisoners had tried to escape and had been killed in like manner. I felt sorrow as I looked at the man who, though my enemy, was also my brother.*

Many times I had thought to ask Syd what her Book of Mormon said about us and what we could do to stop this. However, something inside me warned me not to ask, so I determined to not ask her. Instead, I performed my duty and waited for Helaman's command.

‡‡‡

Desperate to alleviate the suffering of prisoners and troops alike, Helaman called a council. In attendance were Tarik, Abraham, Baram, Dagan, Captain Gid, and me. We stood around a makeshift table inside Helaman's tent, gazing at a crude map.

"Soon we must rally the troops and march to Manti." Helaman pointed on the map to a city atop the mountains. "Our people there suffer under the hands of Ammoron; but we must see to our immediate problem of low supplies and prisoners before we can go to their aid." Helaman's somber tone scared me. I'd never heard him sound so grave.

"Kill the prisoners," Baram piped up as if the answer were obvious. "They have not hesitated to slaughter our people when captured. I say blood for blood."

"This is not an option," Helaman replied. "They are our brethren. We only kill to defend."

Baram's face reddened with sheepish embarrassment and a trace of anger.

"If they keep escaping and attacking us, before too long they will all be dead anyway." Captain Gid cleared his throat. "Perhaps this is the solution to our problem." I was surprised that Gid was agreeing with Baram.

"That is not the Nephite way." Helaman shook his head. "We are merciful and forgiving."

Forgiving. I'd always struggled with the notion of forgiving my enemies. I had never understood how I could forgive someone who deliberately wanted to hurt me or my family. I began to understand a little, however, as I listened to the conversation. It seemed that in this situation, forgiveness meant the difference between life and death for the Lamanites.

My thoughts turned to my father. His absence throughout the years had hurt me. He had hurt Mom. And Gracie? My little sister didn't understand, but she had been hurt nevertheless. I realized that, in a way, I had been acting just like Baram and Gid, who wanted to kill the prisoners and be done with it. I'd never said that I wanted my father to die, but I had said I never wanted to see him again. I wanted to see him pay for the years of neglect—for not being there. Were my thoughts the Nephite way? I didn't think so. But I struggled to find the desire to change my heart.

I brought my thoughts back to the issue at hand. I knew the Lord had revealed to Helaman what he needed to do, but I also felt strongly that I was here to give Helaman comfort and perhaps shoulder some of the fallout over what had to take place. I turned to Helaman and said, "You mentioned earlier that you were going to send the prisoners to Zarahemla and that the leaders there would be able to feed the prisoners and put them to work restoring all the cities in need of such help."

Helaman nodded at me knowingly. Captain Gid gave me a look, and Baram glared. Tarik said nothing. Abraham rubbed his temple as if the entire situation gave him a headache. Dagan stared blankly at the map.

Tarik finally spoke up. "This would be a solution; however, we lack the manpower to escort the prisoners to Zarahemla. It is only a matter of time before the Lamanites send troops to fight us, and if our troops have been divided, we will not be able to hold the city. Besides, managing all the prisoners over so many miles would be an impossible task."

"Horsefodder!" Captain Gid slammed his hand down on the table. "My troops are strong. They can manage the Lamanites." He sucked air between his teeth, as though giving what he was about to say a lot of thought. "My army will take them to Zarahemla. There are no delicate flowers among my men."

Helaman's eyebrows raised, but I saw in the glint of his gaze that Gid had said exactly what the chief captain wanted him to. "Captain Gid, we shall wait here until you and your men return. At that time, we shall take some men and journey to Manti as soon as possible."

Gid nodded, indicating that returning quickly would be no problem.

Helaman looked at me, and in his gaze I knew he appreciated my help in encouraging Gid to step forward. My eyes held the prophet's. Had the Lord revealed to him what would happen next? Surely He had. I wondered how the prophet received revelation. Was it moment by moment or a day or week ahead? I had no idea. All I knew was that Helaman had contact with the Lord. He would be told and warned when he was supposed to be told and warned. My job was to support this leader. I had come to realize in the past days and weeks that history had already been written and that the Lord's purposes would not be frustrated. And even though I knew Gid's taking the prisoners to Zarahemla would fail, I knew in my heart that I didn't need to say anything.

⁂

After the council broke up, Baram tried to convince Helaman that he and his squad should go with Gid, but Helaman stood firm. He looked over Baram's head at me with a knowing sadness in his eyes, his expression speaking volumes. Helaman could not spare Baram, and he knew what lay in store for Gid and his men. I was consoled knowing that the prophet received constant guidance from God. I wished with all my heart that Helaman would be directed to return the stone to me so I could go home before the horrible events unfolded.

I left and headed to Bella's tent to retrieve my bow and arrows. I decided some target practice might help relieve my anxiety.

"You surprised me by agreeing that Gid should take all of the prisoners." Tarik fell into step beside me.

"I don't know what you mean," I said slowly.

"I think you are withholding information." Tarik glanced at me as we walked. "Are you?"

"Helaman knows what's best for everyone." I stopped walking.

"His mind is weighted with many matters." As we began walking again, Tarik said, "Something very bad is going to happen. You know this."

I pressed my lips together, wishing he would change the subject. Then I replied, "Helaman knows what he is doing. He looks to the Lord for counsel."

Tarik thought a moment, then said, "Your Book of Mormon tells what will happen, does it not?" He was right on the mark.

"Yes, it does."

"And what does it say will happen?" Tarik implored; he seemed torn in asking me, as if he knew he shouldn't.

"Things have to unfold the way they are meant to," I said as gently as I could. "Please don't ask any more." I searched his face, hoping he'd understand. His brows slanted as if he were trying. I thought of the story of the battle at Cumeni and added, "You're right though; we must prepare for the worst."

His shoulders slumped as he took in what I had said. Then, inhaling a deep breath, he started away. His pace quickened. "Gid leaves with the prisoners in the morning," he said over his shoulder. "My brothers will be left alone to guard the city." He stopped and looked at me.

"We must be prepared." He turned and walked away.

I prayed that I had not said too much. Or enough. I knew in the next few days the fighting would be bloodier than any battle the stripling warriors had ever seen.

I wished with all my heart that it did not have to be so—but it was not my place to change history. I knew that I was in the midst of the unfolding of events that I did not truly understand and that had been set in place long before I had arrived.

I took comfort in knowing that the warriors' faith would shield them. I prayed with all my might that I'd said the right things and made the right choices . . . and that my presence would harm no one.

CHAPTER 28
FRESH RECRUITS

The next day started out well enough, but it ended in disaster.

Bella and the other cooks seemed ashamed to offer us the meager portions of what seemed to be the last of the corn wafers. Mariah stood in line with me.

"It is good to see you," Mariah said to me as Bella gave me a single wafer.

"Good to see you, too." I took the wafer. Bella smiled, but I noticed her cheeks were no longer cheery and red, and she appeared tired. She had lost weight. We all had, but Bella in particular. I wondered if she had eaten at all, knowing that so many were going without. I wanted to ask for another wafer for Ozi, but I knew there were none.

Mariah and I left the tent together. She tucked her wafer in her apron, and I knew she was probably taking it to a hungry soldier. I saved mine inside my *gi.*

I looked up at Mariah, and when our eyes met, I could tell that she knew I had hidden mine for Ozi.

"How is Ozi this new day?" she asked as we made our way down the trail.

"He was asleep when I left." I smiled.

"Ozi astonishes me. He is from Ablom, you know."

"He told me." I nodded.

"Those people are sturdy stock. Ozi has seen much war." She stopped once we were a away from the cooking tent. "I worry for Helaman and his boys."

I didn't know what to say; I was worried too.

"You have taught them your way of fighting." Her sisterly smile made me feel as though we'd known each other forever. "You have prepared them well?"

"I have done my best." I knew she wanted me to say something comforting, something to alleviate her worry. "They learn fast." I tried to think of something else. "And they're very strong."

"So are the Lamanites," she said, discouraged and concerned.

I wanted to encourage her, to say what she needed to hear. Soon she would be busier than ever tending the wounded, but right now she needed something uplifting, something to see her through.

"Mariah, remember the night I first met you?"

"Yes. You flipped Tarik to the ground." Mariah smiled as she remembered.

"Yeah, that was fun." I paused, remembering for a moment, then continued with my main point. "But that night I overhead Helaman talking with you in the medicine tent."

"Go on." She pulled the scarf off her head, letting her curly hair escape. Wrapping the scarf anew, she tied it around her unruly locks.

"He told you his sons were spared because of their faith."

She nodded.

"I know that this is true. And we must also have faith, Mariah." I could hardly believe I was giving the talk Helaman had given to me not long ago. Saying these words to Mariah reinforced the testimony within my own heart.

Mariah patted my shoulder. "I hope it is enough. Faith or not, I fear my medicine baskets are sadly lacking for what lies in store for the warriors."

Not knowing what else to say to soothe her worry, I said, "I need to take this food to Ozi before he withers up."

She gave me a quick hug, and I left.

Tromping down the path, I caught sight of Captain Gid. He was guiding his spare troops, who held their swords at the ready. They walked beside the turbulent sea of prisoners. The mission the captain had taken on was both cumbersome and doomed. I prayed the Lord would spare Gid and his men from many injuries.

Unable to watch them travel farther, I turned away from the

sight. As I drew near Bella's tent, I found Ozi waiting for me, sitting outside on a stump. "I am fit to fight," he said.

Ozi knew of our dire circumstances, and it was apparent that he wanted to help. However, he was as weak and wobbly as a three-year-old karate student. His determination inspired me. I gazed into his bloodshot eyes underscored with pouchy skin no amount of sleep would take away. He was dead serious about fighting. And I knew I needed to treat him with respect. Handing him the wafer, I said, "Good. We'll need you."

He smiled and gummed the morsel.

Lib dashed out of the tent at that moment, nearly colliding with me. A chattering Jukka rode in the backpack strapped to Lib's shoulders.

"Where are you off to?" I didn't want him practicing with his slingshot; not today. There was too much upheaval, too many people about.

"Around," he muttered.

"Stay close," I warned.

"I shall follow him." Ozi started after the boy, chewing on the wafer. And though I was concerned over Ozi's strength, I decided that Lib probably would be more contained knowing Ozi was with him. I watched as they walked away, Lib and monkey in the front and Ozi bringing up the rear. I smiled at the sight, then turned my attention back to the morning's responsibilities.

Tarik had wanted me to exercise the commanders while Helaman was busy with Gid. I was late, so I hurried to the designated meeting spot in a glade not far from camp; however, upon my arrival I found no one there. I sighed. One of the most important battles in Book of Mormon history loomed before them, and not one commander had showed up to spar.

Finding myself with nothing to do for the time being, I decided to hone my archery skills. I had taken up the habit of carrying my weapons with me, like the other warriors.

I picked out a large tree stump, brought my wooden bow to the ready, and rested the long arrow with the sharp obsidian tip on my left fist while drawing back the sinew bowstring. Gazing down at my target, I let the arrow fly. It slid through the air and stuck solidly in the wood.

"Not bad." Tarik said from behind me.

I whirled about, chiding myself for not realizing someone was approaching. "Abraham has taught you well. Did he also teach you how to use a dagger?" Tarik asked.

"He didn't need to," I replied. "I have a black belt, remember."

"So you have told me." Then, grinning wickedly, Tarik quickly swung around while drawing his dagger from its sheath and grabbed me. With the knife in front of my face, he said, "If you allowed your enemy to do this, you would be dead. No black belt would stop him."

I elbowed Tarik in the stomach, grabbed his arm, and flipped him over my head. Glaring at him, I said, "I don't expect a friend to pull a knife on me. I would expect it from a Lamanite."

Tarik shook off the leaves and dirt that clung to him as he stood. "You should expect it from anyone." He slid his dagger into its sheath.

"Not you." I smiled. He smiled back and stepped toward me as if to touch my face, but I moved away. I could not handle gentleness now. I had to remain strong, focused.

"So, where are the commanders?" I asked, picking up my bow and arrows.

"Change of plans." Tarik's face turned grim as he remembered the plight we found ourselves in. "Helaman wants to meet with you and me."

I was ready to leave when something made me think of Ozi and Lib. I knew I should check on them. "I need to speak with Ozi first."

"Why?" Tarik looked at me, confused.

"He followed Lib into the forest to keep an eye on him. I need to check on them."

Tarik rested his hand on his sheathed dagger. "I am fond of the old man, but there are times I wish he had stayed home." He started walking. "I will tell Helaman you are on your way." And with that, he charged off.

Hurrying down the path I had watched Ozi and Lib take, I realized they had gone deep into the forest of canopied trees. Hadn't I told Lib not to go far? And what had Ozi been thinking to let him? Still, how could I expect a feeble old man to stop a precocious eight-year-old child? As I neared the trees, a feeling of unease came over me. Every since the night Tarik and I had spied on Baram, I had avoided this area. I decided that the place would make the perfect setting for a horror movie.

As I walked, goosebumps crawled across my skin, and paranoia chased after them. I walked farther into darkness and inhaled the scents of moss, dirt, and wood. I couldn't hear Lib or Ozi. Even Jukka's monkey chatter was not to be heard. I wished Ximon were with me, but the dog was with Helaman.

I slowly proceeded, intensely aware of my surroundings. The path came to a fork. Tarik and I had turned left here, so I did the same, thinking that perhaps Lib and Ozi had gone toward Baram's side of camp.

At the edge of the tree line, I stopped and looked down at Baram's camp. No one was around, and there was no sign of Lib or Ozi. The two must have turned right at the fork.

I retraced my steps, quietly going back the way I had come, straining to hear some type of sound—a bird, a monkey, anything—but only eerie silence cloaked the shadows.

A breeze rustled the leaves. With nerves stretched as tight as my bowstring, I brought an arrow to the ready and started down the path's right fork.

A chill coursed down my spine. As I passed a large moss-covered tree trunk, I gasped. Lying in front of me was a body, facedown on the ground.

Ozi!

I fell to my knees, quickly setting my bow and arrow aside, and turned Ozi over. There was a bump the size of a mango on the side of his head. I quickly felt his neck for a pulse. A strong beat relieved some of my worry.

What had happened?

And where was Lib?

I needed to take Ozi to Mariah, but first I needed to find the boy. Gathering up my bow and arrow, I once again headed down the path.

Scanning my surroundings, I walked on as quickly and quietly as I could. I had only walked a hundred yards when I stepped on something soft. Glancing down, I saw Jukka. He lay dead at my feet, a tiny dart shaft protruding from his back.

Panic washed over me like a tsunami. This had been a deliberate, evil act. And whoever was responsible had Lib. Forgetting my own safety, I raced ahead, searching frantically. As I ran through the silent jungle, which seemed to be holding its breath, the only noise was the swish of vine-draped tree limbs. As I moved farther into the jungle, hesitation began to creep over me; I knew I couldn't do this alone. Should I run back to find Tarik? Precious time would be lost, and what would become of Lib in the meantime?

I knew that I might already be too late.

I made a quick decision and whipped around to retrace my steps. As I turned, I ran right into Amos, Baram's cohort. Tempted to release the arrow strung in my bow, I hesitated. And at that moment, Amos motioned for me to follow him.

I didn't know what to do. Was Amos acting on Baram's orders? What if Amos had attacked Ozi and killed Jukka? Was Baram so bent on making a fool of me that he would risk having one of his men hurt Ozi and Lib? And if so, what would stop Amos from hurting me?

Amos was as tall as the Lamanite that had fought me in the stockade but not as hefty. I knew that I could take him if necessary. I decided to follow. I clung to the fact that Amos was a stripling warrior, and I prayed he was more loyal to God than to Baram. In my heart I did not believe that he had hurt Lib or Ozi or that he would hurt me now.

We ran through the brush as quickly and quietly as deer. I did my best to keep up with the big man; he ran with incredible speed. Amos finally stopped and put his arm out so I wouldn't pass him. Peering around him, I saw the backs of four Lamanite warriors scurrying away. Red paint had been splattered over their bodies. One man carried a figure slung over his shoulder . . . Lib. Was he dead? If Lib were dead, surely they would have left him. He must be alive.

Amos pointed to what I hoped was a shortcut to wherever the Lamanites were headed. We raced through the trees and over brush and rocks until at last we came to a stop at the south end of the forest.

My breath caught in my throat as I looked down at the valley in front of us. Thousands of Lamanites, fresh recruits from Ammoron, milled about, preparing to destroy Helaman and his stripling warriors.

CHAPTER 29
Two Best Fighters

As we looked across the valley, I saw that the four Lamanites had reached their comrades before we could intercept them. I realized that the group must have been a scouting party that had stumbled upon Lib and Ozi.

Lib's little body, draped over the Lamanite's shoulder, looked so lifeless. As the group of Lamanites walked across the valley, the leader of the four turned about and gazed in our direction. Amos and I ducked, but I felt certain he'd seen us.

Amos looked down at me with hound-dog eyes. The distrust I had felt for him earlier was gone. I was sure that he had risked his life to bring me here. We both knew without speaking that we could not go after the boy. We had to return to camp. We had to warn the others.

"Ozi is farther down the path," I told Amos. "Help me take him to Mariah."

Amos nodded and followed. As we passed Jukka's body, I stopped. I couldn't leave him there. Amos gently picked the monkey up and hid it in his bundle.

"I shall bury him once we have seen to Ozi." Amos's deep, baritone voice was soft. His black eyes had become cloudy with tears. I wiped away the moisture on my own cheeks. I was sure now that Amos had not been a willing accomplice to Baram; this warrior had a tender heart. I knew I could trust him. Giving Amos a grateful pat on the shoulder, I nodded in agreement.

We hurried on toward Ozi. The elderly warrior badly needed help, and I needed to tell Helaman what we'd seen as soon as possible.

As we approached the spot where I'd come upon Ozi, I looked around in confusion. He was gone.

"He was here," I told Amos, and a sick feeling washed over me. Amos immediately began searching the surrounding brush. Panicking, I raced down the path. Near the fork, I finally spied him. Somehow Ozi had made it that far before collapsing again.

"Over here," I yelled to Amos. Thin and frail, Ozi looked like a skeleton with clothes draped over him. White wisps of his thistle-down hair fanned his gaunt face.

I shouldered my bow and knelt down, again feeling his neck for a pulse. "He's still alive."

Amos carefully lifted the old man over his shoulder as though he were as fragile as a newborn fawn. Quickly, we resumed our trek to camp.

We passed by several tents, and I motioned for Amos to take Ozi over to Mariah's medicine pavilion. Though I was worried about Ozi, I did not follow Amos; it was critical to everyone's safety that I inform Helaman of what I'd seen and tell Tarik about Lib. Amos and Mariah would care for Ozi.

I headed for Helaman's tent. The campsites were crowded as the troops prepared to fortify the city, which had been left in their charge.

With the new threat at our doorstep, I wanted to yell for the troops to hurry, but I would not incite panic yet. Helaman was our commander; he would decide our course of action. His tent finally came into view.

The commanders had assembled in front of the tent. Helaman, clad in full armor—helmet, breastplate, and wrist and shin guards—was addressing them. Ximon stood regally beside the captain. Was Helaman dressed in battle armor because he already knew the Lamanites were ready to attack? I could not afford to assume. I had to say something.

"They're here," I interrupted, trying to catch my breath. Ximon crossed over to me and licked my hand. Quickly patting him, I nervously looked about and noticed that the troops I'd seen on my way had followed me. They must have sensed that something was wrong. The entire area was filled with the sons of Helaman, eager to hear what was happening.

Helaman stopped his address and immediately came to me. "Who is here?" he asked.

"The Lamanites." I gulped. "There must be more than six thousand."

Tarik had come to stand beside me as well. "How do you know this?" he asked. Tarik's concern knitted his forehead. He, too, was ready for battle: his sheathed sword and dagger hung from his sheep-skin waistband, and he held a spear tightly in his fist.

"I saw them," I squeaked out.

"Where?" Helaman's tone was stern.

"The valley floor, on the south side of the forest." I turned to Tarik; I had to tell him about Lib, and yet I hesitated to disclose the most dreadful news at this critical moment. Instead I said, "Amos was with me."

Tarik shot me a confused look, as if he knew there was more to my story but didn't want to question me further in front of everyone else.

"What do we do, sir?" Abraham asked Helaman. I suddenly became aware that the commanders had surrounded us. The Ammonite faces around me had paled with fear, yet they stood at the ready for their chief captain. Even Baram was with them. And behind them was a throng of young warriors equally anxious to hear what we were to do.

Helaman pulled off his helmet, placing it under his arm. He relaxed his stance. "We must remain calm," his voice boomed out for all to hear. "Fear is our enemy. Take courage in your skills." He put his hand on my shoulder. "Remember what this young man has taught you." I felt a little queasy. Had I taught them enough? Then Helaman said, "But most important of all, take courage knowing that we are in the hands of Almighty God. Hold fast to your faith."

"Sir," Dagan piped up, "maybe we can send for Captain Gid and his forces." Dagan's voice held a thread of uncertainty, yet his face was hopeful. "They just left. They cannot be far away. I can ride out and ask Gid to turn back within the day."

"No." Helaman stopped the idea. "What would become of the prisoners?"

Dagan gave no answer, his hopeful face turning somber.

Helaman continued. "Captain Gid and his troops are doing us a great service by taking the prisoners with them. They cannot return."

"But there are only sixty and two thousand of us." The once eager Baram now appeared reluctant to fight. "How can we possibly win?"

It seemed that Baram had no qualms about making a fool out of me or fighting as long as we outnumbered the enemy. But training was over now. We were on the verge of fighting to the death, and I was pretty sure he was scared out of his sandals.

Helaman handed his helmet to me and, in a fatherly gesture, put his arm about Baram's shoulders. Looking at each one of his courageous leaders, he said, "We have fought them before, in Judea." He left Baram and the leaders and walked out among the troops, looking at them with pride and hope. "We won the battle for Judea. We can win again."

"But, sir." A boy no older than thirteen piped up. "Antipus helped us. And he is dead, killed by the sword of a Lamanite."

My heart stopped. What could Helaman say to this? The boy was right. Antipus's troops had helped to win the battle. The battle for Judea, while fierce, would be nothing compared to what these boys were about to face alone, without the help of a seasoned army.

And though I had read about the coming battle and how it would end, I still felt a knot of dread tighten in my stomach. I had read the story to Gracie in the comfort of my home, before I'd cut across time, before I'd wrinkled history with my presence, before I had come to know so many of these warriors individually and stood with them shoulder to shoulder. I knew that all of this should have made my belief stronger, but somehow it made me worry even more. It was one thing to read of faith; it was quite another to depend on it.

I knew from the scriptures that these young men would be saved because they were spiritually prepared for what lay ahead. Their faith would guide them, empower them, and shield them. Still, a nagging little doubt sat on my shoulder, whispering in my ear.

What if, instead of relying on their faith and their swords, the warriors tried to use karate moves they had not quite mastered and were cut to shreds? Fear ballooned inside me. I searched within me for my own faith. *Believe,* I told myself as I looked across the sea of faces surrounding me.

I looked up and saw that Helaman was still standing before the young man who had asked him a question. At last, he said, "What you say is true. Antipus is dead. But have you forgotten that we came to his troops' rescue? Without us, Judea would have been captured by the Lamanites. Without us, their women and children would be slaves."

Helaman paused a moment, letting what he had said sink in. And then he looked across the crowd and added, "What did your mothers teach you?" I immediately thought of my own mother; she had also taught Gracie and me to have faith.

Helaman's gaze roved around the crowd and stopped on Baram, who seemed humbled. The captain stood still, patiently waiting for a reply.

"To have faith," Tarik interjected, taking his place at Helaman's side.

"Indeed, my warrior sons. As I have watched you, not only in battle, but as you have trained, I have seen how powerful your faith has become."

Standing in front of his boys, Helaman truly spoke like their father. He said, "It is true we shall face a great force." He stopped for a moment as if searching for the right way to say something. "The Lamanites are determined to spill our blood. They are strong and full of hate, for we are descendents of Father Lehi, and we have chosen a different path." Helaman clenched his teeth. His eyes became determined. "They have no pity and will show us no mercy." He pointed to Tarik. "You, Tarik." Then he pointed to Abraham. "And you, and all of you. We are different in this respect. We have mercy in our hearts." His fist rested on the breastplate of his armor, over his heart, as he scanned the young men before him. "We hate violence, but when our people—our loved ones, our babies—are threatened, *we shall fight.*" He then grew quiet, his gaze purposeful. Drawing a deep breath, he continued. "We shall even kill to stand up for what we believe and for what we hold dear.

"You are boys and yet you are men. You are warriors, and God will shield you because of your faith. *He* will sustain you. *He* will bless you with fearlessness and strength. You will be tireless and filled with the spirit of the Lord, who will keep you.

"There shall be a record of this day, of this battle." He paused. The Spirit shone in his gaze as he looked at me. Tears sprang to my eyes as I humbly stared back at him. He turned to the warriors again. "It shall be written that you were firm in your conviction, undaunted in your valor. Millions of our brethren will read the record of what we do this day; they will read that because of the faith your mothers instilled in you, *we did succeed!*"

A glorious shout erupted from the warriors. I stood frozen to the spot, overwhelmed by their presence, by the power of the man who led them, and by the Spirit that burned within me.

"Prepare for battle," said Helaman. And with that, he turned from the troops and motioned for the commanders to follow him inside his tent.

We crowded around the table by the map. I set Helaman's helmet on a chair and stayed by Tarik, wondering when I would have a moment to tell him about Lib.

"Syd, show us where the Lamanites are." Helaman said.

I looked at Tarik and wished he could read my mind. I would have to wait to talk to him until the strategy session ended. I studied the drawing before me and pointed to the area where Amos and I had seen the Lamanites.

"Shall we attack, sir?" asked Tarik. "They do not know we have sighted them. Let us take them by surprise."

"No," I answered. Everyone looked at me. "I mean, I don't think we can count on taking them by surprise."

"Why?" Helaman asked with concern.

"I went to the forest to find Ozi." I avoided Tarik's eyes; I couldn't bring myself to say Lib's name. I pressed on with the story. "Ozi must have surprised their scouts, because I found him knocked unconscious." I knew Tarik would remember that Lib had gone with the old man.

"And what of my brother?" Tarik asked.

I swallowed hard. "They have him." I bit my bottom lip.

"Why did you not fight!" Tarik demanded.

"Syd will explain, Tarik." Helaman looked at me, encouraging me to continue. Tarik frowned, then paced as I told them everything—how I had found Jukka dead, how Amos had helped me, and how the

Lamanites might have seen us. Once I had finished, Tarik stood beside Helaman, waiting to hear what we would do.

All was quiet.

Finally Helaman broke the silence. "Because we have won many battles, King Ammoron almost certainly sent Chief Captain Nelek and his troops." For some reason Helaman looked straight at Baram. Baram turned from his gaze. Helaman continued. "Nelek is cunning and leaves no prisoners, but he has his weaknesses."

"What weaknesses?" Abraham asked.

"He prefers to attack at dawn when his troops are well rested. So we shall strike in the hours before dawn, while it is still dark. We will use Cumeni as protection." He pointed on the map to the city. "We shall attack them on their weak left flank. Our right wing will be protected by the archers and cavalry. Tell your men we leave at twilight. We need to find our positions."

The leaders started out and Helaman said, "Tarik and Syd, wait." The others filed out.

Ximon had been at Helaman's side throughout the meeting and now sat down obediently at his feet.

Helaman stood silent a moment, gazing at Tarik, then at me, with a compassion that pierced my very soul. "The two of you are my best fighters." He rested his hand on Ximon's great head, the touch as graceful as a blessing. "Take Ximon with you. You will need him."

I heard the slight intake of Tarik's breath and sensed him straightening, a soldier ready for his orders.

Helaman looked at me, then fixed Tarik with an unwavering gaze. "Go to the Lamanite camp. Find your brother."

CHAPTER 30

UNDAUNTED AND TRUSTING

With Ximon at our side, Syd and I walked in silence amidst a camp full of frenzied activity. Some warriors were sparring, others were target practicing with bows and arrows and spears. They looked to me with concerned faces. Each warrior had a prayer on his lips. We stopped by Ima's tent. Syd waited outside while I told my mother the grave news.

As we walked toward the jungle, Syd asked, "Is your mother all right?"

"No, she is not," I replied curtly. Ima's crestfallen face filled my vision. Lib had always been a handful and my mother counted on me to help her. I had let her down, although she would never say so. She would never lay the blame of Lib's capture at my feet, though it belonged there. If I had not been so preoccupied with other matters, I would have watched over my little brother more closely.

We reached the jungle; the trees were so thick and their branches woven so tightly together that they squeezed out the light from above. Stepping beneath the heavy, vine-covered boughs, I felt as though I had stepped into a crypt. In the darkness, a sense of foreboding engulfed me like the dark mists of Lehi's dream.

When we came to the fork in the path, we turned right, heading for the Lamanite camp. Passing the spot where Syd said Ozi had lain and the place where Jukka had died, we quickened our pace; I was overwhelmed by the urgency to save my brother.

We continued in silence. Many times Syd looked as though she wanted to say something, but her words could not soothe my anxiety. Shame and guilt filled me. Syd had done nothing to deserve the bitterness I carried. The bitterness was mine. Mine alone.

Reaching the bluff overlooking the lamanite encampment, we crawled on our hands and knees and climbed to the top. Without prompting, Ximon crawled on his belly between us.

"They have not advanced," Syd said in amazement.

The enormous lamanite army had set up tents. Many campfires glowed throughout their encampment. They were bedding down for the night. Helaman had been right. "It seems they did not see you after all." I tried to look at Syd, but the dog was in the way.

"I was sure they looked right at me; and if they didn't see me, they most likely saw Amos; he's about two feet taller than I am." Syd seemed certain.

"They are puffed up with pride, thinking themselves mightier than our army." I pushed the dog back and continued. "If Helaman is right and Captain Nelek is down there, you should know he is a vain man and one of King Ammoron's most bloodthirsty leaders."

"Captain Nelek doesn't scare me. Lib is down there. And if they've hurt one hair on his little head, I'm going to make them wish they'd never been born," Syd said, her big brown eyes lit with the fierceness of a warrior. Somehow between training the troops and worrying over her own family, she had come to care for my brother as I did.

My bitterness melted away, and I told her my plan.

⁂

Twilight was upon us as we crouched low and moved toward the Lamanites. We made our way down the hill, hiding behind boulders and trees. Once we were on the valley floor, we found the creek I had seen from the small bluff. The deep stream meandered through the Lamanite camp.

Crouching down and using the long grasses of the creek bed as cover, we sloshed through waist-deep water as quickly and quietly as possible, following the water's flow. Gnats and river flies swarmed us. Mud sucked at our sandals. And when there wasn't mud beneath our feet, slippery, moss-covered rocks threatened to make us fall. Ximon managed to follow unfazed. All the while I kept thinking about how Helaman and the troops planned to attack the Lamanites in a few hours. We had to get in and out in a hurry.

We stopped about thirty feet from the nearest tent. The shadows of night closed in around us. "We need to float in. The current is shallow, but deep enough to hide us," Tarik said as he lay down in the stream.

I did the same. The cool water swallowed me up to my neck.

Ximon dog-paddled up to me. He was a most extraordinary animal. Sometimes unpredictable, but my faithful companion nevertheless. He was intent on being part of our covert operation. And I hoped we could count on him.

As we neared the Lamanite camp, voices drifted toward us.

"You break wind loud as a curelom," said someone. Many male voices chuckled.

I made a face. I thought only the football cronies at Suncrest High had conversations of that sort. But it seemed that guys were guys no matter the era.

"Your wind smells like a Nephite," came the reply. More laughter followed.

I looked over at Tarik, who didn't seem to hear any of this but kept his attention focused on moving forward. We continued quietly swimming farther into camp. I could not believe we were so close. Evidently, the guards only worried about an attack by land.

All at once, Tarik stopped, grabbed me, and pulled me close to shore. Only ten feet in front of us was a man watering horses. Ximon crawled up on the bank and shook. The horses reared and whinnied, sensing the dog's presence.

I felt a wave of adrenaline course through me as I prepared to be discovered. Why had Helaman told us to bring the dog?

"Whoa!" The man coaxed the animals to calm down all the while peering into the shadows, trying to find what had riled his horses. "Who goes there?"

Ximon sat on the bank and didn't move. The grasses hid most of him; only his pointy Great Dane ears peeked above.

Fortunately the man didn't notice. After a few moments the horses calmed down enough to finish drinking, and their handler led them away.

"Close call," I whispered to Tarik as I relaxed a bit.

Tarik seemed more edgy than ever. We pressed on.

Passing the watering hole, I looked to see where Ximon had gone. He seemed to have disappeared.

Then, out of nowhere, chaos broke loose. Several men jumped out of hiding and ran toward us full tilt. Water splashed as we frantically scrambled to meet them. My karate reflexes sprang into action as I whirled around to give one of my attackers a sweep kick. However, my anchor foot slipped on the slick creek rocks. Before I knew what was happening, strong arms banded about my neck, choking me. I twisted and turned, flailing as I tried to land a punch and claw at the steel bands that had been placed around my throat, but my assailant, a Goliath of a man, cuffed me one, stunning me. Jerking my bow and arrows away from me and stripping me of my dagger, he threw me over his shoulder.

Dazed, I blinked hard and looked around, trying to see what had happened to Tarik. Several Lamanites grouped together. They had him. It seemed that Tarik had been knocked unconscious. I prayed he was alive.

CHAPTER 31
CAPTAIN NELEK

I decided the smartest move would be to feign unconsciousness. I hoped that this way I would learn where they were taking Tarik and maybe even discover their plans.

A crowd gathered around as the Lamanites who had captured us traipsed through camp. Soldiers poked at me, some spat on me, and most of them called me names. Out of the corner of my eye, I tried to see where we were heading. We were on a path that led to a large domelike tent in the middle of camp. This place had to be Captain Nelek's headquarters.

As we approached the tent, I felt my courage quickly draining away. When we reached the entrance, a guard jerked opened the flap, and the men carrying Tarik and me on their shoulders walked in as if they'd conquered a mighty army. A fire crackled in the center of the tent. The area swam in a yellow glow. Upon our entrance, a group huddling near the fire scattered like guilty children.

"Where is Captain Nelek?" the man carrying me barked.

"I am here." A small, squat man strode toward us. His dirty, black hair hung in long dreadlocks; it looked like a place where crawly things would nest. A thick, dark eyebrow covered both of his black, vacant eyes. Jowls hung past his neck, resting on his collar bones. He had only one arm. The other had been cut off just below the shoulder.

"What have we here?" He walked to the man holding Tarik, grabbed a hunk of Tarik's hair, and pulled his head back. Tarik's eyes were closed, but I saw them flutter as the squat man released him.

Nelek looked at me before I could shut my eyes. "This one is awake." He sauntered over.

Horrified, I tried to think of what to do. The hulk holding me dropped me to the ground. Fortunately deerskin pelts covered the area. Still, I landed on my bottom with a thud, biting my tongue. The metallic taste of blood came into my mouth. The Lamanites dumped the unconscious Tarik beside me.

Offering a silent prayer, I quickly sized up my situation. Captain Nelek was directly in front of me. A group of five men stood behind him, blocking my path to the door. Several stray Lamanites were scattered around the tent. This was about as bad as it got. Time to pull out the charm.

"Your majesty, King Ammoron," I said as I gave a short bow to Nelek.

He smiled a yellow, toothy grin. Perspiration beaded across his forehead and upper lip. "Do not presume flattery will help you." He glowered down at me. "I should kill you for calling me king."

"Forgive me," I said. "I meant no insult. I simply mistook you for the great king Ammoron."

With no warning, he gave me a quick kick in the gut. Razor-sharp pain stabbed through my middle and took my breath away. He grabbed a fistful of my short hair near the scalp and jerked me back so he could clearly see my face. Evil intent lit his black eyes.

"Ammonite scum!" he hissed. "You are a traitor to your people. I especially enjoy killing traitors."

His words filled me with hot rage. Fueling my anger into strength, I yelled, "Hai!"

My scream took Nelek by surprise, and he loosened his hold. I punched him in the gut, reached up, and grabbed his hand. Twisting his arm as I stood, I pulled him into a joint lock, using my other hand to press against his elbow.

His men awoke to my attack, coming at me from all directions. I pulled on Nelek's arm, shouting, "Back off or I'll break the only arm he has."

The vultures circled around us. I had a hard time keeping my eyes on all of them while trying to maintain my hold on the captain. I stumbled and saw someone leap toward me. Jumping to the side, I pushed the captain into my place as I released my hold. Someone else jumped on my back, knocking me to the ground.

Then suddenly my attacker was gone. Scrambling to my feet, I found Tarik by my side. He winked, and for a small moment I really thought we could take them.

And then the bubble burst as we were tackled by a horde of Lamanites.

My strength was gone; I had no more fight left. The Lamanites quickly tied me to a tent pole. It seemed that Tarik's strength had been short-lived as well, as soon he was tied up next to me.

The Lamanites huddled around Nelek. It looked like in the scuffle the captain had become injured. They hurried away with their leader, leaving a guard behind to watch Tarik and me.

I strained against the ropes. Resting now and again, I tried over and over to slide my hands free. My fingers became swollen and my wrists were rubbed raw. Tarik, too, struggled against the bands that held him. We both felt the urgency to get out of there. A couple of hours before dawn, Helaman and the warriors were supposed to attack. Tarik and I had planned to rescue Lib and return long before the fighting began. Getting captured wasn't on the agenda. The minutes continued to tick by and we became more and more frustrated.

It had been at least two hours before the Lamanites returned en masse. Nelek was in the middle of them. He came toward me, an obsidian knife in his one hand. His eyes lit with glee. He fully intended to cut me apart like a side of beef.

"Coward!" yelled Tarik. "Let him go and fight me!" One of Nelek's soldiers punched Tarik in the stomach. He gasped deeply. I winced.

Nelek wiped his mouth with the back of his grubby hand. Licking his lips, he drew close. He raised the dagger high above my head.

I closed my eyes, waiting for the inevitable and praying death would be quick.

"Captain, we are being attacked!" came an urgent cry.

I opened my eyes and saw that a battered soldier had stormed into the tent. Blood dripped from a gash on his forehead; his shocked face was pale with fright.

A bewildered Captain Nelek swung about.

The winded soldier continued. "They fight as though possessed, arms and legs everywhere."

Captain Nelek forgot Tarik and me and left the tent with his men trailing after him.

The battle had started.

For a split second, pride surged through me as I recalled what the messenger had said: *arms and legs everywhere*. The warriors were using the skills I'd taught them! Maybe their training had paid off.

I glanced over at Tarik. He looked at me. Unbelievably, the Lamanites had left us alone. Breaking the silence, I said, "We've got to get out of here."

Again we struggled against the ropes that bound us, but this time with fevered hope and determination. The cords seemed to tighten with each jerk and pull. "It's no use," I cried.

"Keep trying." Tarik frantically worked at his bonds. Finally, miraculously, his hands pulled free. Without pausing, he quickly untied his feet and came immediately over to help me. In no time, he untied my ropes. I fell into his arms, hugging him as tightly as I could. Tarik hugged me back. We were safe, we were together. Reality slowly crept back as we took in our surroundings. We were in a bad situation, and we still had a mission.

"Where did they put our weapons?" Tarik began searching through the tent, pulling up pelts, checking every possible place. I found them near the fire. We quickly sheathed our daggers, Tarik grabbed his spear, and I shouldered my bow and quiver.

Peeking out the door flap, I saw a camp in chaos. Frantic Lamanite soldiers with bloodlust on their faces ran toward the battlefield carrying swords, clubs, and spears. They yelled and shrieked as if they could gain strength from their own ragged voices. It seemed that going out into the melee would be suicide, but I knew we had to do it. I looked up at Tarik and asked, "Where do you suppose they have Lib?"

"The Lord will help us find him." He stepped past me into the night. I knew that he was right. I followed with a prayer in my heart.

We kept out of the way as best we could, melting into the background, staying close to the tents, letting soldiers dart by as they scurried on their way. Surprisingly, no one stopped us. We checked one tent after another, searching in the shadows and down near the stream.

No Lib.

The scent of heavy smoke coiled through the air. Glancing behind us, I saw that the forest was on fire. When we found Lib, we'd have to find a new route to our camp. In the distance, I heard faint tortured wails and the clang of swords. Death had found the night. And through it all, I heard a bark.

A Ximon bark.

I spun around. There stood the Great Dane near the cooking tents. He was standing next to some crates. Tarik saw him at the same time I did. We dashed to the dog. The animal didn't wait but led us between crates loaded with different animals—mostly pigs and wild turkeys.

Finally, when he came to the very last crate, Ximon stopped. The crate held a frightened Lib, who was huddled up in a ball as if he'd been beaten, beaten so badly he'd curled up into himself.

"Lib!" Tarik cried as he shook the wooden bars. There was no movement from inside.

I pressed my face to the small poles, trying to see Lib's features in the dark. Lib looked up. And through the threads of the dark night, I saw that his lip and one eye were badly swollen. He stared at us in disbelief.

Lib uncurled his legs and arms. Desperation and fear over took his body as he cried, "They killed Ozi! They killed Jukka!"

Tarik frantically worked with the lock, trying to pry it open with his dagger. Flustered, he grabbed a large rock and beat the chains apart. Flinging the door open, Tarik scooped his little brother into his arms. The boy clung to Tarik, sobbing into his bare shoulder.

I smoothed Lib's hair away from his bruised face. "Ozi is still alive," I said, hoping a bit of good news might cheer him. I hoped that I was telling the truth.

"Come on." Tarik made his way past the cages. I noticed many did not have a lock as Lib's had. So I released the turkeys and pigs as I passed. Ximon chased after them, shooing them farther away.

Now all we had to do was get out of the Lamanite camp, slip by the raging battle, find a way through the burning jungle, and take Lib to Bella. No sweat.

CHAPTER 32
WHAT ABOUT LIB?

We stayed close to the creek, slowly making our way through the grasses and muddy bogs. Tarik carried his little brother, the boy clung tightly to him. Snakes slithered between our legs, and gnats and mosquitoes clouded our vision. The night was filled with battle cries, the flicker of fire in the distance, and the all-consuming feeling of dread. We were on the very edge of destruction.

As I followed Tarik, I realized that we were on a straight course to end up right in the middle of the battle, and as much as I wanted to steer clear, I knew the stripling warriors needed all the help they could get.

But what about Lib?

Tarik stopped, waiting for me to catch up. As I stepped up beside him, he said, "I must go." He looked down at me. "I must fight beside my brothers."

"I know." I wanted to go as well. "But we need to take your little brother to camp."

"You must go on alone." Tarik handed Lib to me. The boy wrapped his arms tightly about my neck, burying his head. Since I was of a slight build myself, having an eight-year-old in my arms was awkward. The boy hugged me as if I could make the ugliness he'd experienced go away. All his bravery, all his spirit and spunk were gone. I stroked his back.

"Take the dog," Tarik said, holding my gaze with his and then turning to leave. I wanted to beg Tarik to stay. Not because of fear for myself or for Lib, but for fear something might happen to Tarik. In that moment, a wave of doubt washed over me. I knew that the Book of Mormon said not a single warrior lost his life—but that had been before I had come on the scene. If I hadn't been here, Tarik would have taken his little brother back to camp himself instead of charging into the thick of battle.

But I knew I couldn't stop him. We stood there staring at each other, chaos all around, and I felt as though my heart would shatter into a billion pieces.

And I knew, as clearly as I knew anything, that I loved him.

In the past weeks my feelings for Tarik had grown from dislike to acceptance to caring. And now to love. The feeling was stronger than anything I'd ever experienced. The only thing I could compare it to was the love I felt for my mother and Gracie.

Tarik leaned toward me. I looked up into his eyes, cast in shadows, and wished I could find the words to tell him all this before he entered the battle and the night swallowed him whole.

Despite my holding Lib, Tarik cupped my cheeks in his hands and tilted my face upward. And then he kissed me. As he slowly pulled away, I felt a small ray of hope that everything would be all right.

Tarik patted his little brother's back, then said, "Be safe." And with those words, he turned and ran toward the battle, leaving me standing with Lib in my arms and Ximon by my side.

I watched Tarik disappear into the darkness and tried to swallow the lump in my throat. Even if we made it through this night and this battle, it would not be happily ever after. Could I really leave Tarik and go back to my own time?

"He will be all right," Lib said quietly.

"I know." I squeezed the boy and gave him an encouraging smile. "Right now I've got to get you to your mother."

But I had no idea how I was going to accomplish this task.

‡‡‡

Turning away from Syd and Lib tore at my soul, but I had to leave. My brothers needed me, and Lib was safe with Syd. I knew Syd would do everything possible—even sacrifice her own life—to keep him safe. Her kiss was still fresh on my lips. My feelings for Syd had grown stronger each day. I loved her determination, her temper, and her innocence. And her courage.

Syd had the courage of a pouncing mountain lion, and she would need it before this night was through. She would face death itself. And I knew she would look it in the eyes. I had watched her wait for Nelek to thrust his knife at her. Syd had braced herself for the blow. She had once called me noble, but she was the noble one.

The lamanites were bigger, stronger, and had fought in many battles. Even though they outnumbered our troops, I knew we could win, just as I knew Syd would do everything in her power to take lib safely to Ima.

I raced toward the battlefield, ready to fight and prepared to die for my country, my family, and my God.

⸸⸸⸸

I pushed forward, keeping close to the creek bank. The swamp critters scattered as we made our way. I knew that if we continued on a straight path we'd go into the raging forest fire. If we turned right, we'd run into Cumeni. If we went left, we'd be heading toward the battle.

Despite my strong misgivings, the city was the best of our options. When the Lamanites had first surrendered Cumeni to Helaman, I'd heard rumors that although the city had once been a Nephite stronghold, many of the people were loyal to King Ammoron.

This was puzzling to me. From what I had seen, the people seemed loyal to Helaman. Were the people simply faithful to the victor? Would their loyalties turn Lamanite if they thought Helaman's forces would lose this battle? Would they attempt to kill Lib and me if they recognized that we were on the Nephite side? Traveling through the city was the only possible route. I prayed the people would let us pass without trouble.

We walked for what seemed like hours through swampland. Fearful of snakes and even more afraid of crocodiles, I tried to keep my mind on our goal and pushed forward. I'd carry Lib on my shoulders through the deep areas. As we left the marsh behind, he walked. He never complained. In fact, he was uncharacteristically quiet.

At times Ximon took the lead. The dog was our guide. The night seemed endless. I sent countless prayers silently heavenward as we walked on in the blackness.

Once we reached the dry moat surrounding the city, I strained to see the guards in the towers overlooking the palisades. Through the predawn gray of morning, no guards were visible.

I was surprised by this. I thought Helaman had planned to station some of the warriors on the towers before leaving for battle. Keeping Cumeni under our control had been a major concern.

We cautiously made our way across the land bridge to the city gates. No guards there either. Fear drew its cold finger down my spine. This was not good. I picked up Lib. He wrapped his arms about my neck, his legs about my waist. Taking some comfort from the boy's embrace, I pressed on, not wanting him to know of my uncertainty.

The city appeared to be deserted. The adobe structures seemed empty, ghostlike; they whispered of the life that had vanished. Had everyone fled? Were they fighting?

I decided I didn't really care as long as I was able to sneak through the city and take Lib safely to his mother. Even though the city seemed abandoned, I avoided windows the best I could, using alleyways just to be safe. Trudging through the back streets was like trying to find my way out of a corn maze.

"Where are we?" Lib asked softly against my neck. Ximon stood by my side and looked up as if to say, "Good question."

"We're almost there." I hoped I was right. I continued walking for a while longer, then abruptly stopped as we reached a dead end.

"We are lost." Lib's voice was etched with worry and fear. I set him on his feet.

"No, we're not." I wasn't exactly lying. I knew we were in Cumeni.

Ximon nudged my leg as if to say, "Come on, I'll show you the way." I grabbed his collar and, with my other hand, clutched Lib's hand in mine.

The dog led us directly to the main street. No more playing around with alleys. I felt exposed, but I knew Ximon had not led us astray. If we were ever going to get out of here, we had to use the main route.

I kept us close to the buildings, hoping to stay as much out of sight as we possibly could. Several times, I thought I heard footfalls and whispers. But every time I checked, I saw only adobe walls. Finally the north entrance came into view.

We were home free.

I quickened my pace, feeling fresh energy. However, as we came within a few yards of the entrance, Ximon stopped.

The dog growled, his hackles rising.

A man emerged from the shadows, blocking our path. I pressed Lib to me.

"Let us pass," I said with as much authority as I could. "Chief Captain Helaman is expecting us in his camp."

"Chief Captain Helaman is in battle." Bloodlust echoed in the low, scratchy voice. The man didn't move. Two more men stepped from the shadows. One came fully into the threads of dawn's light, and I saw that he was a Lamanite, his face painted red, hatred in his stare.

They had already retaken the city.

My heart beat heavily in my chest. My stomach flip-flopped. Turning about, I saw we had been followed by at least two others. They had been stalking us. And now they had us cornered. I knew there was no way I could defend myself and protect Lib at the same time. The little boy clung to me, burying his face in my side.

Why hadn't they attacked? I realized as I stared into their glimmering eyes that they enjoyed watching their victims panic—they got a high from the hunt. I squatted down eye-level with Lib. "Listen to me." I took hold of his arms. He stood still, his shoulders slumped. "We have to surrender." The words were bitter on my tongue.

"No!" His little body began to quake. "I cannot go back. You can beat them, I know you can. I have seen you fight." His eyes bored into mine.

"There are five of them and one of me."

"I can help. You taught me to fight—and I have this." Lib pulled out his slingshot. I could hardly believe the Lamanites had not taken it from him—and that he had not used it. "I can fight, and so can Ximon," Lib said.

I nervously glanced at the Lamanites, each armed and ready to fight. Their eyes, framed by the red paint, shone with delight at the targets before them. They began to circle closer.

"If something were to happen to you . . ." I thought of Tarik and Bella; I thought of Gracie and Mom. Mom had never given up, even with the odds that cancer presented.

What would she do in this situation?

I knew the answer: she would fight.

CHAPTER 33
Spilling Blood

The Lamanite stalkers held off their attack as if giving us time to reconcile ourselves to our fate.

I took Lib in my arms and softly said in his ear, "Promise me that when the fighting starts you and Ximon will run and find help." I added the "find help" so he would not feel cowardly about running. I knew he would never have obeyed if I had simply told him to run. Lib looked at me wide-eyed and nodded.

I set him down beside me and stood, taking stock of each of my attackers. Three in front. One held a double-edged sword, one held a club embedded with razor-sharp obsidian, and the other held an axe that looked more like a tomahawk. I didn't turn around to look at the other two; I remembered they carried spears.

My bow and arrows would only be in the way at this close range. I carefully set them down while keeping an eye on the enemy. Positioning my hands at my sides, I stepped one foot back, ready to fight. Every nerve was electrified. My skin prickled. I willed my breathing to slow down. My tongue suddenly became as dry as desert sand. I tried to swallow but couldn't.

The man armed with a sword came at me first. Ximon charged, trying to take him down. I stepped forward and grabbed hold of the Lamanite's weapon. Wrenching his arm backward, I leaped to his side. The dog was all over him, snapping and snarling like a wild beast. Taking the sword from the terrified man, I turned around to see the spear carriers charging. Using a spin move, I parried the spears with the sword and buried the weapon in one man's stomach. He collapsed.

I picked up the fallen Lamanite's spear. The man with the club was almost upon me. I spun around, ready for his attack. He jabbed at me with an outward slash. I deflected his blow by stepping back, then I knocked him down and hit him over the head with the blunt end of the spear. I turned just in time to meet the other spear carrier. I raised the spear back and hit him across the face, then stepped forward and thrust the spear behind me, sinking it into the man's chest.

The attacker with the tomahawk charged, his arms raised. I kicked him in the stomach. He took a few steps back, bending over. Then he charged again, and my dagger pierced his chest.

The Lamanite I'd hit with the blunt end of the spear leaped to his feet only to be smacked in the head with a flying rock. The man staggered, stumbled, and collapsed on top of his slain comrades. I quickly looked about. Lib stood not far away, the empty slingshot in his hands.

The man Ximon was attacking suddenly broke free and took off down the street. The Great Dane charged after him, but quickly returned, not even winded.

I dropped the spear and stared at the pile of bodies in front of me. Tears filled my eyes. I felt dirty inside and out. Their blood was on my hands, clothes, and face. My stomach was queasy. Bile rose in my dry throat. Clutching my side, I ran to a long trough running along the wall and threw up.

My entire body shook. I'd never killed anyone before. I felt as though a black curtain had crashed down on me. I'd never be the same again.

A small hand touched my back. "You had to do it."

I turned to find Lib at my side. He held my bow and leather quiver. I drew him into my arms and hugged him tight, trying hard not to break down and sob. Ximon nudged me, as if he too wanted to console me. I pulled him into the circle.

After a moment I slowly pulled away from Lib and Ximon, still shaking. We needed to get out of there. I slung the quiver and bow over my shoulder and cautiously looked at our surroundings. I stared at the bodies again, then looked away. I quickly retrieved the sword and slid it beneath the belt Tarik had made me. Taking hold of Lib with my free hand, I said, "Let's go find your mother."

⁜

As we entered the camp, we were quickly drawn into a tide of panic. Nursemaids rushed about in makeshift triages. The wounded were everywhere, making me wonder if there was anyone left fighting. But there had to be.

Among the waves of battle-weary people, I found Mariah. Blood smeared her face; bandages and herbs filled her arms. "Have you seen Bella?" I asked.

She looked at me for a second, as if she didn't recognize me at first, and then said, "The medicine tent." Then she hurried on her way.

Before we had reached the pavilion, Bella came charging out. "Lib! My Lib!" She scooped her child into her arms, tears falling freely down her face. My spirits felt a little lighter as I watched the mother and child. Lib desperately clung to Bella as if he'd never let her go. I wondered if I would ever have such a reunion with my own mother.

"How is Ozi?" I asked.

"Still unconscious," she said, a grave look on her face. She let Lib down, but he clung to her waist as if afraid she would disappear.

"Someone must stay with him," Bella said. She looked at me, and I knew the job was mine if I wanted it.

"I can do that," Lib offered. "Syd needs to help Captain Helaman. And besides, Ozi tried to save Jukka. I will sit with him." The little boy looked different to me, older. I knew he would never be the same after the night's events. No more would he dash about with a carefree look of innocence lighting his eyes.

And I knew that I would never be the same either. I stroked Lib's head. He gave me a quick smile, then rushed into the tent to be with his old friend.

"And my other son?" Bella asked. "Where is he?"

"Tarik wanted me to bring Lib to you. He's fighting." I was unable to meet her eyes. Oh, how I wished she knew I was a girl, knew that I loved her son and shared in her fears.

More of the wounded were rushed past us. I anxiously looked at each one, fearful I would see Tarik. He was not among them. Relief and panic settled on me at the same time. And I knew then what I had to do. I needed to find Tarik. "I have to go."

Bella briefly put an arm around my shoulders, giving me a squeeze. "Go with God," she said softly before hurrying off.

Ximon brushed past me, leading the way and making me feel less alone. The battlefield was easy to find. All I had to do was follow the trail of wounded streaming into camp.

Anger pulsed through me as I passed each wounded warrior. As I thought of the Lamanites the warriors were fighting in this fierce battle and the hatred that burned within them, I felt at a loss to understand.

I was surprised to see soldiers marching behind me, coming toward me quickly. These were not the stripling warriors. But they were Nephites. And they were heading toward the battle. Ximon didn't give them a second notice as they passed. Who were these guys?

I quickened my pace to keep up with the soldiers as they passed me. Heading over a rise, I looked down on the battlefield. The tattered and torn banners of the sons of Helaman were strewn across the clearing. A gray haze rose off a ground covered by bodies. Clusters of fires burned throughout the area. Smoke and the scent of blood tinged the air.

The men beside me charged down the hill, yelling as they hurried to the attack, hurried to help the stripling warriors, who had fought so valiantly. A rider on a black mare nearly ran me over. I looked up to see Captain Gid.

So these men running to battle beside me were his troops. I was confused. Gid could not have taken the prisoners to Zarahemla so quickly. Why was he here? My memory of reading this part of the Book of Mormon failed me. But no matter the reason, I was glad he and his men had returned.

I started to run toward the battlefield, too. Slipping and sliding on the mud-slick hillside, I strung an obsidian-tipped arrow to my bowstring and released it. Feverishly shooting one arrow after another, I soon found I had used them all. Charging forward to fight the Lamanites face-to-face, I was surrounded by the deafening cries of dying men, the clang of metal meeting metal, the thud and thump of clubs clashing with shields and spears.

Discarding the bow, I drew the sword from beneath my belt and plunged into the fight.

One scene after another flashed before me; images I never thought I'd see bled into one another. Time stood still as I met each attack. It seemed it would never stop—and then reality rushed forward as a knife sunk deep in my arm as I blocked an attack.

Strangely, I felt numb to the pain. I snap-kicked my attacker, easily taking him down and running my sword through him. Catching my breath, I gazed down at myself. My chest and legs were splattered with the blood of others. The sleeve of my *gi* was torn and wet where my own blood dripped to the ground.

As I stood there, I realized an eerie quiet had settled over the battlefield. I looked around. Everyone, everything had stopped. The battle had drawn its last shuddering breath.

"Syd!" Someone called my name. I turned around and saw Helaman trudging through the battlefield toward me. A small ragtag army of stripling warriors valiantly trailed behind him. Here was Helaman, the mighty chief captain. Despite the overwhelming sorrow I knew he must feel for the loss of life around him, Helaman walked tall.

As he drew closer, I sensed the power of his priesthood calling clinging to him like the scent of rain after a downpour. He, too, was scarred from battle. His clothing was mottled with blood, his helmet was dented, and I could see that he had suffered many wounds. But by the arm of God, Chief Captain Helaman had been preserved.

Ximon, who was coated with blood splatters, left my side to greet the mighty leader. Helaman stroked the dog's head briefly. Then the two came to stand beside me. The warriors who were following the captain stayed back a few feet.

"I fear many of my sons have fallen this day." Helaman's once deep voice had grown raspy. I looked at him, inquiring with my eyes. He seemed to be saying that he was worried some of his sons had been killed in battle. That couldn't be.

A few verses in Alma in the Book of Mormon suddenly came to my mind. I recalled with surprising clarity that in chapter fifty-seven, Helaman and his army were astonished to find that *all* the warriors had survived. But at this very moment, Helaman wasn't sure whether everyone had survived because he hadn't yet found all his warrior sons.

I looked up at Helaman, his anguished face creased with worry as he scanned the bodies around us. His mantle was a heavy one, and I could only imagine the depth of his emotion as he looked at this scene from his perspective. He was the prophet, the captain of the army, and the surrogate father of his warrior sons—all of whom were willing to look death in the eye for him. I wanted to go to him, but out of respect I stayed put.

Helaman glanced at me. "Did you find Lib?"

"Yes. Didn't Tarik tell you?"

He gazed at the ground. Fear rushed over me. I felt dizzy and became more keenly aware of the pain in my arm. Forcing the throbbing ache aside, I asked, "Haven't you seen him?"

Slowly, he nodded and looked at me. The grief in his eyes tore at my heart. Now I stared at the ground. My body trembled. My vision blurred.

"I saw both Abraham and Tarik," Helaman said softly. I blinked away tears and looked up.

He clenched his teeth. His cheek twitched. "They were overcome by the Lamanites."

My mind whirled, trying to take in his words. Fighting to keep my voice steady, I asked, "They were captured?"

Helaman let out a heavy sigh and said, "When last I saw them."

The doubts that had visited me before, that had sat on my shoulder and haunted me, returned. Could Tarik be dead? The Book of Mormon said nothing about young men surviving capture.

I glanced up at Helaman. His copper eyes were red-rimmed as he turned away from me to gaze at the destruction surrounding us. I followed his gaze, scanning the ravaged surroundings. I knew that I could not allow myself to wallow in doubt and pain. There was much to be done here. With Abraham and Tarik captured, Helaman would need my help. So despite the grief in my heart, I followed my captain.

As Helaman and I walked through the desolation and I looked at the dead Nephite soldiers who had served with Gid, I wondered who would tell their families, their loved ones, that they had died valiantly. Would they ever know? As I looked at men whose blank stares would never see their loved ones again, a storm of emotions washed over me. I thought of my own loved ones, my mother and little sister—and

Tarik. My pain ebbed close to the surface as I felt so far away from all of them.

We came to several dead Lamanites. Red painted faces that had filled me with fear during the fight now lay still. They did not seem so foreboding in death. I knew that they too had families who were eager for their return. Why hadn't they been willing to talk instead of fight? Thoughts of my father crowded their faces from my view. I earnestly wished that things could have been different between us.

Helaman had walked a little ways ahead. Although the scene around us was dismal, I felt privileged to be in his presence to witness this moment. I watched as he lovingly and with a heavy heart began searching for his fallen warriors. For some reason, I had been given the honor of helping him, of being his temporary second. I would not fail him.

I took a breath and moved toward my captain. An image of Tarik, his blue eyes sparkling, his mouth curved into a smile, stopped me in my tracks. A lump, sharp as an arrow, stuck in my throat as my grief and nagging doubts threatened to overwhelm me. A voice inside me whispered again, *The battle is over. Tarik did not die during the battle, but since he has been captured . . .*

I shook my head, trying to force the thoughts away.

"Little One." Helaman had walked over to stand next to me.

I gazed up at his grave face. His sad eyes were filled with empathy. I wanted to tell the captain that I was a girl, that my grief was not just for a warrior brother but for a boy I had come to love. But I could not speak. Reason slowly awakened within me. There was work to do. Helaman needed a warrior by his side, not a weeping girl. I swallowed my grief and waited for Helaman to say something.

He laid a hand on my shoulder. "Little One, we shall find him."

AUTHOR BIO

Kathi Oram Peterson was born in the small, sleepy town of Rigby, Idaho. In her childhood, her parents owned a store on Main Street. Whenever they couldn't find her, they'd look in the nearby drugstore behind the book display. There she would be curled up with a book. Though she grew up, married, and had a family of her own, her passion for a good, heart-thumping, action-packed story has never left her. After raising her family of two girls and a boy, she went back to school and earned her English degree at the Univerity of Utah. Upon graduation, she worked for a curriculum publisher writing and editing concept and biography books for children. She now devotes her time to writing inspirational novels. Researching and writing about the stripling warriors and other Book of Mormon heroes has been an honor and privilege. When she's not busy with her family, you will find her in her office either reading or writing a story. You can contact Kathi at her Web site: www.kathiorampeterson.com